CHIEFTAINS

THE BESTSELLING DOCUMENTARY NOVEL OF A WORLD WAR 3 TANK COMMANDER

BOB FORREST-WEBB

This page intentionally left blank.

'Davis seemed to wait forever, until he decided Inkester must have missed again or the shell had failed to explode. Then he saw a brief shower of sparks scatter from the foredeck of the T-72's hull to the left of the driver's hatch, and almost at the same time it exploded outwards like a movie scene in slow motion, He saw the two hatches on the turret fly upwards, followed by the turret itself and the driver's and engine hatches. Soundlessly, to Davis, the hull tore apart, belching a swirling orb of flame. He heard Inkester's awed voice: "My God!"'

Unabridged original 256 pages

Among a myriad of exploits as an adventurer Bob Forrest Webb has crossed the Sahara and back on motor cycle, spent long periods of time in Indian and African jungles, won the British Kayak Championships and has attained Japan Aikido Association 7th Dan black belt status. He has also worked as a journalist on both local and national levels and is the author of THE SNOWBOYS, CAVIAR CRUISE, GO FOR OUT, THE SEALING, and BRANNINGTON'S LEOPARD plus 8 other novels under pseudonyms. An ex-serviceman, he undertook the extensive and detailed research for CHIEFTAINS with the help and co-operation of the Ministry of Defence.

CHIEFTAINS

Bob Forrest Webb

Forrest Webb Productions Ltd

A Futura book, first published in Great Britain
by Futura Publications, a division of
Macdonald & Co (Publishers) Ltd
London and Sydney

This edition published by Forrest Webb Productions
Ltd

TABLE OF CONTENTS

AUTHOR'S NOTE

British army signal communications are both complex and classified! To assist the reader, and maintain security, these have been modified throughout the book but still represent the methods and procedures used, with acceptable inaccuracy.

Technical data concerning weapons, vehicles and equipment is based on information at present available from military sources, and speculation on possible but as yet undeveloped weapons has been avoided.

I have honoured the requests of military informants, in Great Britain and West Germany, to gloss over certain tactical features and have deliberately blurred the precise areas of responsibility of various NATO forces. I have, however, made use of hitherto unpublished facts which I believe to be of importance in the scheme of NATO defence of Western Europe, and which would certainly influence the manner in which a future war might be fought in that theatre.

SUNRAY TO BRAVO TWO. TROOP
MOVEMENT SECTOR MARIGOLD.
FULL RED ALERT...

Chieftains is a frighteningly
authentic novel of the invasion of
Europe by the Russian and Warsaw
Pact armed forces seen through the
eyes of the fighting men on the
ground.

In particular it tells the story of the
crew of Bravo Two, a Chieftain
main battle tank of the British 4th
Armoured Division as they face the
onslaught of the Soviet armour
onto the killing zones of the
German Plain.

'A DRAMATIC AND AUTHENTIC ACCOUNT'
GENERAL SIR JOHN HACKETT

This book is dedicated to the steel of the spontoon within the red diamond. My sincere gratitude to the nameless and to my late father-in-law, a 30-year veteran of the Armoured Corps, Bill Waterson, still remembered at Bovington, and to my wife Wendy.... my favourite 'army brat'.

ONE

There were six empty bottles on the table in front of the three men. The Chieftain crew's driver, DeeJay Hewett, was leaning forward supporting his head with one hand as though in deep thought, but the fingers of the other were drawing large circles in a pool of spilt beer. Inkester, the gunner, rescued his packet of cigarettes as the pool spread, and stared around the canteen. He could see other men of Bravo Troop, drinking and chatting; a few watched a video film on the television, but the tables nearest Hewett, Shadwell and himself were unoccupied, as though the three of them had some kind of contagious disease.

Eric Shadwell, the loader, said wearily: 'Well, you've done it for yourself this time, DeeJay.'

DeeJay Hewett slapped his palm down into the pool of beer, splattering it messily around the table. 'He bloody asked for it, the long-haired git.'

Shadwell grimaced. 'You didn't have to belt him so hard. Anyway, you could 'ave waited until we met him one night up at Angie's Bar...I've seen him drinking there with his mates.'

'Wrap it up, Eric.' Inkester held the damp cigarette packet towards DeeJay. 'I'd 'ave bloody hit him, too, only DeeJay got there first. Look at the fucking mess the bastard made of Bravo Two. Bloody amateurs! They ought to keep

7

amateurs out of tanks...especially bloody Dutch amateurs; the Dutch ought to stick to growing tulips! You want another beer?' Inkester didn't need to wait for a reply, he twisted himself out of his chair and walked over to the bar. He could sense some of the other crews watching him; fine lot of mates they all were! Just because there was a bit of trouble, they didn't want to know. Once it all blew over they'd be fine again, even congratulate DeeJay, buy him drinks; the Dutch weren't popular with British tankies at Bergen-Hohne, but right now no one wanted to be associated with the incident, even remotely.

Inkester carried the bottles back to the table and handed one to each of the two men. They drank for a few minutes in silence and then Hewett sighed, shrugged his shoulders and said: 'Well, I suppose that's the end of my bloody leave.'

'Aren't you getting married next Saturday?' Shadwell asked.

' 'Course he bloody was, you daft twit,' said Inkester. 'It's fucked everything, hasn't it?'

Neither Inkester nor Shadwell had witnessed the fight. It had all happened quickly. They had been returning from the gunnery ranges with the rest of the troop when the Dutch tank had driven straight out of one of the camp entrances and into the side of Bravo Two. The unexpected impact had startled them, jarred them as Bravo Two swerved suddenly and there was a heavy crash and the squeal of tearing metal. By the time they had climbed out of the Chieftain there was an unconscious Dutch conscript lying on the ground and Sergeant Morgan Davis, Bravo Two's commander, was dragging an enraged DeeJay away from the man as a group of Dutch military police ran from the guardroom swinging their batons. The police wanted DeeJay in their cells, but Sergeant Davis knew what that would have meant for the British trooper. He almost threw DeeJay back inside Bravo Two and slammed down the driving hatch, then he argued with the police until Lieutenant Sidworth, the troop leader, arrived.

8

Davis had been angry with DeeJay, but he could understand his feelings. DeeJay Hewett, like himself, was a professional, and he had the same professional's appreciation of the tools of his trade; Bravo Two was DeeJay's tank, at least, that was how DeeJay viewed it. And most of the Dutchmen were conscripts! A tank wasn't the same thing to them, they only worked with them for a short while, not long enough to really appreciate them; their casual attitude to soldiering showed in untidy uniforms and the length of their hair. But Davis knew it was important to remember they were allies, and good fighters; they had shown that in the past. An incident like this would breed bad feelings and the Bergen-Hohne camp wasn't large enough to permit the incident to be ignored. Regrettably, Lieutenant Colonel Studley, the commanding officer of the regiment, would be forced to make an example of Hewett.

'They're still fighting,' said Eric Shadwell.

'Who's fucking fighting now?' Inkester scowled. Shadwell had a habit of picking subjects out of the air and it wasn't always easy to follow his line of thought.

'The Jugs. I heard it on the news.'

'They've been fighting for the past three days...more,' Hewett drained his bottle. 'Yugoslavia's not our problem. Been askin' for it ain't they, just like bloody Poland.'

'Well, the Yanks are helping them,' added Shadwell, defensively.

'Go on, that's bullshit!' Hewett stared across the canteen towards the door, then frowned. 'Oh, Christ!'

'What?' Inkester turned his head and saw Sergeant Davis looking around the room from beside the entrance. Davis's eyes caught his. There was no expression on the sergeant's face to give them an indication of his mood.

'What's he doing here?' asked Shadwell in a stage whisper.

'Fucking looking for us, isn't he?' groaned Hewett. 'And he's not come to give us any bloody gongs I'll tell you that.'

'He's gone to the bar,' hissed Shadwell.

9

'Shut up, Eric. I don't want to know what Davis's doing.' At the moment the fact that Sergeant Davis was Bravo Two's commander meant very little to Hewett. Your commander was a mate so long as you were working together, but when he acted as a representative of authority he placed himself on the other side. Right now, so far as Hewett was concerned, Sergeant Davis was Lieutenant Colonel Studley's man.

'He's coming over,' said Inkester. He straightened himself slightly and ran his fingers through the ginger stubble of his hair.

Sergeant Morgan Davis, a short, dark-haired and sallow-skinned man, stood a whisky bottle on the table and then swung one of the metal stacking chairs between Inkester and Hewett and sat down. He nodded towards the Black Label. 'You'd better all have one.' No one moved. 'Help yourselves,' insisted Davis.

Inkester cracked the seal and poured himself a double into his beer glass. He slid the bottle towards Hewett.

'No thanks.'

'Don't bugger about, DeeJay! Christ knows when you'll see another,' warned Inkester.

'Lay off,' muttered Hewett, but he took the bottle and tilted it over his glass.

'What's going to happen to DeeJay?' Shadwell asked the sergeant.

'With a bit of luck, he'll get away with a hefty fine,' said Morgan Davis. He filled a glass for himself. 'I'm afraid you've had it with your leave, lad.'

'I fucking knew it,' swore DeeJay.

'You shouldn't have lost your temper,' Inkester said, unsympathetically. 'You could have got us all in the shit.'

'You're a fine one to talk.'

'Take it easy...it's got nothing to do with this afternoon. All leave is stopped; everywhere. The patrols are out, bringing in everyone from the town. Personnel already on leave are being recalled.'

10

'What's going on now, Sarge?' asked Shadwell.

'You know almost as much as I do,' answered Davis. 'They began evacuating the families an hour ago.'

'Yeah, some of the blokes are right pissed off. It'll turn out to be another bloody exercise,' said DeeJay. 'Anyhow, I don't see why it should affect my leave; it's special.'

'We'll all be out of here before 20.00 hours, lad. And if I was you, I wouldn't press my luck,' Sergeant Davis warned him. 'The longer you're away from camp, the better. Thumping a Cloggie's bad enough, breaking his jaw was bloody stupid.' He drained his glass. 'Anyway, you three have got ten minutes' start over everyone else. It'll be coming over the PA shortly. Get yourselves sorted out.' He stood, screwed the cap back on to the whisky bottle and tucked it under his arm, like a distorted swagger cane.

'What about Bravo Two?' asked DeeJay. The impact of the Dutch tank had dented the skirt so it dragged on the right track; to Hewett's ears, always tuned to the performance of his vehicle, it had sounded as though the Chieftain was tearing itself to pieces as he had driven back to the sheds.

'Good as ever, lads,' said Davis. 'The sergeant fitter's done us a favour.' He hardened his voice slightly. 'Drink up then, and make a move. I don't want a last minute panic just because Shadwell's forgotten his copy of Wanker's Weekly.'

DAY ONE

In fifty minutes it would be dawn. The night was moonless with the stars obscured by a high layer of thin cloud. Earlier it had drizzled lightly, rain as fine as mist, and now there was the sharp chill of autumn and the metallic scent of damp woodland in the air.

Morgan Davis could feel the cold security of his

Chieftain's armour against his back. Bravo Two rested hull-down below the crest of a ridge of high ground on the Elm Hills, overlooking the plain towards the East German frontier. Tonight the sky was uncharacteristically dark; the black-out of the lights of the town of Helmstedt to the north-east, and those of the numerous small villages, had extinguished the usual warm tinting. A few meters ahead of the sergeant, slightly to his right, small bright glow-worms wavered in the gloom, the fluorescent sights of infantry AR 18 rifles.

There were sounds, unnatural and muffled yet familiar to him; the stifled movement of men in the darkness, whispered conversations, a throat softly cleared, equipment adjusted, the trickle of urine against a tree root; Davis had heard them all before, it seemed like a thousand times.

They had been stationed on the hill for the past five hours, since their night drive down from the 14th/20th King's Hussars depot; the main battle tanks of Charlie Bravo Troop deployed on the left flank of Charlie Squadron, while those of Alpha and Bravo Squadrons were dug in three-quarters of a kilometer to the south, in the fringes of the woods. The battle group's reconnaissance Scimitars, light tanks, fast and manoeuvrable, waited a kilometer and a half away towards the east, on the plain itself.

The moist air was condensing on the leaves and polished limbs of the birches, dripping to the thirsty ground beneath. It had been the first rain for almost a month and, although the earth was still firm, its surface was slippery. It would be difficult for tyred vehicles to move through the woodland for the next few hours; the hard sun-baked soil with its fresh thin coating of mud would be like ice beneath the heavy wheels.

Hewett, the Chieftain's driver, was a lanky Yorkshireman. His nickname DeeJay was an abbreviation of 'double-jointed' and stemmed from his ability to fit his tall frame into the cramped driving section of the tank. He

12

was squatting near Sergeant Morgan Davis's feet, his shoulders wrapped in a waterproof poncho. The gunner, Inkester, was sheltering inside the fighting compartment with Shadwell the loader, who was heating water for mugs of instant coffee.

DeeJay Hewett asked Davis: 'Why don't they ever tell us what we're supposed to be doing?' Avoiding an immediate interview with his commanding officer hadn't reduced his despondency. It was Thursday morning now, and he had a useless civil airline ticket in his locker for a flight out of Hamburg airport at 09.00 hours. His wedding, planned for Saturday in the Leeds Registry Office, was a fading dream. There had been hardly enough time for him to telephone England and ask his brother to postpone everything. He knew all the arrangements had been made, the hall for the reception hired and the catering and drink ordered. There would be more than fifty guests to contact and furnish with explanations. His fiancée and her family didn't always understand the ways of the army, perhaps wouldn't even believe his excuse. DeeJay hadn't been able to estimate the possible length of the military exercise and so couldn't promise a future date.

Davis was going to say: 'We're already *doing* what we're supposed to be doing,' but instead he remained silent. Hewett's complaint was only intended to ensure that his senior understood the trooper's vexation was undiminished. It was a form of blackmail which Sergeant Davis encountered regularly. If there was a vaguely justifiable complaint, some of the men would try to use it as a lever. Hewett would be hoping for some kind of special concession later, relating to his offence, as compensation. Davis knew all the men in Bravo Troop better than his own children; he spent far more time with the men than with his family. The troop had been together for almost two years with no replacements; twelve men in all, including himself and Lieutenant Sidworth. Davis had been married five years, to a German girl he had met in Hamburg. He saw his wife and the twins only at weekends; she refused to live in the regiment's married quarters near Belsen, so he paid a high rent for a small apartment near her parents' home in the Hamburg suburbs. It kept her contented, but the Davis family poorer than he thought necessary. He was thirty-two, the oldest man in the troop by seven years, and one of the longest serving NCOs in C Squadron. His Welsh ancestry showed in his short build, dark eyes and black hair, and he still retained the accent of his childhood spent in the market town of Brecon where his father had been a stone-mason. There were few Welshmen in the regiment, which did most of its recruiting in the north-west of England.

The plain below him was still in darkness, but he could easily visualize its hidden landscape. The ground ahead of his Chieftain's position dropped away quickly through the ordered forest with its plantations of larch, pine and occasional hardwoods, until it reached farmland and the Schöningen Schöppenstedt highway. The fields between the woods and the East German border were hard-worked, interlaced with narrow roads and tracks, their crops of sugar beet almost ready for lifting, the straw for the storage clamps already stacked along the boundaries. Later in the autumn the beet would be delivered to the Schöningen factory for processing.

On the lowest ground was the border itself, the Iron Curtain, one thousand three hundred and ninety-three kilometers of barbed wire, anti-personnel minefields, automatic firing devices, pillboxes and observation towers, where soldiers of the GDR remained unfriendly and aloof.

Davis was brooding over an uncomfortable feeling; more than simply a premonition. Outwardly, this military exercise was little different from many others. There had been the usual theatrically urgent orders and then the deployment to the pre-determined battle stations. The same sort of thing happened frequently, and was designed to keep the army on its toes whilst at the same time acting as a reminder to the Warsaw Pact countries of the readines of the NATO forces.

14

Whenever there was a worsening of East-West relationships, there was a great stirring amongst the opposing armies as each rippled its muscles as a warning to the other. But this time? For months there had been talk of a dangerous change in the balance of power in Europe; the USSR had taken advantage of the recession in the west in the early 1980s to build up their own armies regardless of the cost to their people. Western governments had not responded quickly enough and Russian military superiority had reached the critical level. The scales were heavily balanced in favour of the USSR and, if it failed to act soon, its leaders surely knew there might never be quite so ripe an opportunity.

The strikes and workers' discontent in Poland in 1980 had diminished during the next two years when some of the people's demands had been met by their government and the strikers' enthusiasm cooled by the threats of Russian intervention, but in 1984 the problems had flared again, and then boiled over into Hungary, East Germany and Czechoslovakia. Davis wasn't interested in politics, only their outcome; but the incursion by Soviet forces into Yugoslavia less than a week before had brought an instant reaction from the United States. Part of their Mediterranean fleet was already in the Adriatic, and they were supplying arms and equipment to the Yugoslav army now fighting the invaders in central Serbia. Davis had lived with the threat of war throughout all his fourteen years of military service, but he knew it was closer tonight than it had ever been before.

It was possible that even the evacuation of families was part of some training scheme, but coupled with the manner in which the regiment's tanks had been brought into the border area in darkness under their own power instead of on transports, it was all too close to the real thing for Davis's peace of mind. The map reference of his present position seemed to confirm his thoughts.

A hundred times before, the regiment had been alerted and ordered to some obscure theoretical battle position;

sometimes as far to the west as the Rhine. The alerts were part of the training, exercise scenarios conceived by the intelligence officers who plotted most of the schemes. The fifty-two-ton Chieftains were driven from their ranks in the vehicle parks or sheds, loaded on to transporters to protect the German road surfaces from the ravaging steel tracks, and taken to some piece of ground where they could be off-loaded to roar and crush their way to the fire-points.

This time it had all been different.

Davis had been to this battle position only once before...three years previously, and then not in a tank but as a passenger with his former troop leader in an armoured personnel carrier. Because of lack of vision available to the passengers inside the APC it had been difficult to follow its route, and when it had stopped it was in an overgrown track cut through birch forest. The party had consisted of the squadron leader, troop leaders and their sergeants. The squadron leader had taken them a few hundred meters deeper into the woodland on foot. Davis had been surprised to find carefully constructed fire-points hidden amongst the trees, each excavated to take a tank, hull-down, with just enough of the vehicle above ground to permit the gunner to use his sights and depress the gun its full ten degrees if necessary.

'Satisfied, Lieutenant?' Davis had overheard the major question a troop leader.

The lieutenant stared down across the long easy slope towards the frontier. The ridge commanded a broad open section of the plain between two small hamlets. A stream only visible through binoculars and little more than six meters in width defied the distant border, meandering its way between East and West. Northwards was rich flat farmland, interposed with bands of young pine forests. 'It's a good position, sir.'

'The best we have, gentlemen,' said the squadron leader to the group of men. 'I pray to God we never have to use it.' The officer had spent the next hour discussing the features

16

of the terrain and how they could best be used in the event of a Soviet attack. Davis had heard the map reference mentioned during the return trip to the barracks. His mind had grasped it immediately, filed it away for the future. And the future had become the present. Not once in all the many exercises in which Sergeant Davis had taken part had the hidden fire-points ever been used...until now!

TWO

The Field Headquarters of the 1st Battle Group, British 4th Armoured Division, were two Sultans, modified as command vehicles and situated almost a mile to the west and rear of the regiment's battle positions on the eastern slope of the Grosses Moor. The FV105s, slab-sided and wedge-nosed, had only single 7.62 machine guns for armament and relied on the regiment's armour for protection. They were parked tight beneath the pine trees, the overhanging branches assisting the camouflage netting which draped the hulls. Two Chieftains were at rest nearby, one belonging to Lieutenant Colonel James Studley, the other to Major Fairly, the regimental second in command. A third command Sultan, normally used by the second in command and the operations officer, was sited eight kilometers to the rear with the Headquarters Squadron.

Between the Field Headquarters' Sultans and the regiment's forward armour were a company of mechanized infantry; to the rear, the battle group's two batteries of Abbot 105mm self-propelled guns. On the lower ground of the Elm, where it bordered the plain, six FV-438s fitted with launchers for the Swingfire ATGW missiles were concealed amongst a plantation of immature pines.

The interior of the commander's APC was crowded. Much of its available space was taken up by its two map boards and the radio equipment. Its small penthouse at the rear of the vehicle had been erected and gave a little more working room to the command staff, but even so it was almost impossible to move without jostling someone.

For the hundredth time in the past three hours, Lieutenant Colonel James Studley stared down at the large scale map in front of him, as though its constant detailed perusal might uncover some hidden aspect of the Soviet battle plans. His action was little more than nervous habit; he knew the area as intimately as the Sussex village where his family had lived since his childhood. Knowledge of the terrain was one of the strengths of the NATO armies.

He also knew the positions of the other battle groups of the armoured division. They were all part of the plan, carefully deliberated, debated and practised over all the past years, and soon to be tested. He understood its place in the overall scheme of the defence of Western Europe, although the fullest details remained, for obvious reasons of security, in the hands of the operations staff in Northern Army Group Headquarters.

Flexible defence! He thought it almost Buddhist in principle. Bend like a reed before a gale, against a strong attack give way; but with increasing force turn the enemy in the direction you choose. Lead him unsuspecting to the cunningly prepared traps, the killing zones. And the killing zone for CENTAG was Hannover.

Intelligence indicated that a major enemy thrust was likely to be made at the point where the areas of responsibility of the German and British corps overlapped. Secretly, Studley disagreed. If he were a Russian general, he would base his attack along the highway system from Magdeburg, knowing full well that the NATO powers could not fire a single shot in his direction until the spearhead of his heavy assault armour had crossed the border into their territory – by which time it would have gained too much momentum to be halted.

But no matter where the Russian assault came, the plan was to channel the main thrust south of the Örreler Heide and the densely forested areas to the north of Celle which had been tank training grounds for the German army since the days of the Third Reich Panzers. With even more mountainous terrain on their southern flank the Soviet forces would find themselves trapped in a narrowing funnel terminating at the city of Hannover. The inertia of the attack would be absorbed, diminished until it was lost completely. Assaults on towns and cities digested incalculable amounts of men and machines, which the long and harried lines of Soviet logistics would find difficult to maintain. Valuable time would be gained for NATO reinforcement. Already the Reforger airlift was in progress, bringing more troops and materials to Europe from the USA, Canada, Australia, New Zealand and many other sympathetic nations. Every hour counted, and the next seventy-two would be critical. The longer the Warsaw Pact countries delayed their attack, or the more effectively it could be contained when it began, the better the chances of NATO victory.

Three types of weapons which would surely influence the outcome of the initial battles were enigmatic to Colonel James Studley. He had studied their use, and knew their capability and dangers. They were chemical, biological and nuclear. There had been public outcry in the British Isles against the development of the chemical and biological weapons, but the work had gone ahead in the United States, and amongst the munitions now stockpiled in secret dumps throughout the whole of Europe were shells, bombs and missiles with biological, chemical and nuclear capabilities. In theory, at the moment, they were to serve only a retaliatory purpose should similar weapons be used against allied troops or civilians. But a certain tactical nuclear weapon already deployed by NATO was in a different catagory in Studley's opinion.

Nuclear tactical weapons existed in a number of various forms and strengths, from the diminutive depleted uranium shell, the American XM774, which although it had been designated 'nuclear' by international pressure had been developed for the sole purpose of the effective armour penetration of a single vehicle, to the 400 kt MGM-31A Pershings with their range of over five hundred miles and delivery speeds of Mach 8-plus at burn-out. In between the two were a variety of nuclear missiles, shells and mines, and it was these mines in particular that concerned Studley. He had learnt of them by accident, and the thought he found unpleasant was that they were controlled not by the men on the battlefronts, but by politicians perhaps three thousand miles away from the combat zone. The mines were pre-laid nuclear weapons sunk into strategic positions in West Germany, hidden lines of defence from north to south! Studley did not know their locations. Concealed in special chambers, below the depths where they could be exploded by any accidental method, they were the ugly monsters held in readiness for the protection of Western freedom. He could only guess at the power each of the mines might contain; it would be pointless for them to be small. They must be capable of taking out not just a regiment but perhaps a complete division, unless it were widely deployed, and they would have been laid in sufficient numbers to make one vast tactical nuclear strike effective against a complete enemy army in NATO territory.

The use of the weapons involved the terrible risk of triggering off a full-scale nuclear war against military and civilian targets alike. With much of its army totally destroyed along a complete front, the enemy would be faced with the acceptance of defeat and subsequent negotiation, or a retaliatory strike which would of necessity involve allied civilians and probable further nuclear attack by NATO long-range missiles deep into the enemy's own territory.

The nuclear mines disturbed Studley's thinking. He had been a soldier for many years, trained in the belief that war was the province of experienced fighting men, not of clerks or planners far away in hidden offices, or protected in bunkers or converted aircraft hundreds of kilometers from the front lines. When he had first learned of the mines he

21

had pictured a map of Europe on some distant planner's wall, the sites of the nuclear weapons lighting up as men received the latest information from the battlefields and pressed the appropriate buttons to arm the mines in the areas of the greatest enemy concentrations. At some point, they received a President's orders and turned their firing keys. Without warning to the troops on the battlefront, friend or enemy, the ground erupted with volcanic force and destruction beneath them.

But where, and when?

The West German government claimed to be committed to the policy of not losing even a single foot of land to the East. How far then would they permit an enemy to penetrate before the use of the nuclear mines was considered necessary...and who would make the decision? Was the critical depth of penetration a matter of centimeters, or beyond some planner's line drawn from Hamburg in the north, to Hannover, Kassel, Nürnburg in the south? Perhaps there was no such line! The mines might simply have been seeded at vital strategic points, and would be detonated if it appeared the enemy advance could no longer be resisted by conventional warfare. He was certain of only one thing...the weapons existed!

These unpleasant thoughts were disturbed by the radio operator. 'Division Headquarters, sir.'

He took a headset. 'Hello, this is Sunray, over.'

'This is Nine, Sunray. First chukka imminent. Troop movement sector Marigold. Full Red Alert. Over.'

'Sunray Wilco. Over.'

'Nine. Good luck, Sunray. Out.'

'Good luck!' Studley repeated the HQ benediction automatically, and handed the headset back to the operator. First chukka imminent! Why in God's name did everyone assume all cavalry officers played polo? Chukka was a code word but it still meant that someone, somewhere, had thought it appropriate. Studley didn't approve of the British habit of using sporting analogies in war; war was too serious to be likened to a game even by a figure of speech. 'Philip...' He caught the attention of his adjutant.

The adjutant looked up from the code lists he had been examining. 'Sir.'

'Order the group to stand-by, and tell them I want full radio silence on the UHF nets. Remind the squadron leaders I don't want the men using energy-emitting equipment for the moment.' Soviet locators would undoubtedly be pinpointing any source of energy as possible targets for their artillery.

'Yes, sir.'

'And when you've done that, I'd like the command vehicle moved to the derelict barn at Primrose. Ask the sergeant major to see to the new command platoon positions, and then get someone to do a stag for you...you haven't slept for over twenty hours. Try to get some rest while you have a chance.'

The adjutant nodded. 'Thank you, sir.'

'So it's on, James.' Max Fairly, the second in command had been listening, and Studley found the familiarity of being addressed by his first name unexpectedly reassuring. Max was a close friend, an efficient but easygoing man whom Studley liked, and perhaps more important, trusted. Max was a little more heavily fleshed than when they had first met some years before, but he still kept himself fit with daily games of squash. He was forty-three years old, just a year younger than James Studley, and Studley knew Max, his wife Jane, and their son, well enough to feel he was part of their family – if only in the case of the boy, as a kind of well-liked adopted uncle. Unmarried himself, he had taught Max's son how to shoot and fish, and now the boy had become a grown man; they had spent a leave together only a month previously on one of the best trout beats of the Hampshire Itchen. Memories of the week had saddened Studley during the past hours. He had encouraged Max's son to choose a military career, and he was now a subaltern in a detachment of the Devon and Dorsets, trapped in West

23

Berlin since the city had been sealed by East German forces two days previously.

'It sounds like it, Max. If anything is going to happen today, then it will probably begin in the next few minutes. HQ have reported movement in our sector.'

'I suppose we should thank God for ground radar and electronic sensors. At least we get some warning.' The activity within the command Sultans had increased as the men prepared to move. Fairly lowered his voice and stepped closer to Studley. 'You know, I never expected this to happen...a war.' He made a wry, half-amused smile. 'Playing soldiers for real, Jane would say.' He was watching Studley's face. 'Don't worry, James, I'm not going to hide under the bed with my hands over my ears! I just can't believe what's happening that's all. We talk about civilization, and then somehow allow this to develop.'

Max was thinking about his son, Studley realized. Jane's expression, 'playing soldiers for real', was the one she had used on the first occasion the boy had returned home in uniform. Although she made a joke about it at the time, her face had been strangely pale as though she had glimpsed her son's future. God, how could you defend Berlin? Leaving troops there in wartime was nothing more than human sacrifice on a political altar. They would make a good stand; the lads always did. But in the end it would be remembered as another Arnhem...a place of no retreat and no relief. He couldn't think of any suitable reply to his friend's words, so punched him lightly on the arm. 'Time you left us, Max, old lad.' The second in command should in fact have been at the rear of the battle group's positions, with the third of the command Sultans and the Headquarters Squadron. And James Studley knew his friend's request to be allowed to view the fire-points had been only an excuse for them to spend a couple of hours together. 'Look after things back there.'

Max Fairly nodded, then smiled. 'Trust an Emperor's Chambermaid, James.'

Davis was apprehensive. Although it was claimed men could live for two weeks battened-down inside the hull of their Chieftain tank, breathing pure air through the NBC filter system, in practise he knew it wasn't that simple. Regardless of what they said, none of the tanks were completely air-tight and there was always the danger of seepage; the main gun, when it had been fired and was being reloaded, was just a hollow tube with one end out in the open air and the other inside the tank's fighting compartment. The crews had to expect to fight dressed in their NBC suits, hot, sticky, stinking and unpleasant. Like himself, most of the men would gamble comfort against their lives, and leave off their respirators until the last possible moment.

Thank God, he thought, at least they made damn sure you knew the drill. It was all about surivival in the event of germ or chemical warfare; even following nuclear attack when every dust particle in the area would become radioactive. Inside the tank you lived in the suits because the gas that could be outside was invisible, and there were no gas indicators amongst the tank's instruments; the only warning you might receive would be over the HF, by which time it could already be too late. If possible, you stored the crew's body waste in plastic bags and stuffed them out through the disposal hatch whenever you got the chance, but if the air was really contaminated then no one took off the NBC suits at all. For a time you might try to hang on, but in the end your body's natural functions always beat you.

Tinned compo rations! Three four-men packs to a tank! You heated them in the boiler. If the electrics packed up and it was still safe to get outside, then you could cook over tablets of Hexamine; otherwise, you ate cold. Fortunately, the boiler was usually reliable and also provided hot water for drinks.

If you were wise, he mused, you had a flask of spirits tucked away somewhere out of sight; it was a small enough luxury, even though it was against regulations.

Davis had stayed closed-down once, for a full three day period; Bravo Two's fighting compartment had become a cramped and stinking prison, and clambering out of the Chieftain at the end of the exercise into the fresh air had felt like rebirth. Some of the men in the regiment hadn't been able to take it, the claustrophobic atmosphere and their own filth had become too unbearable. Those who failed the test had been transferred, some to the support vehicles. A few, disappointed, had applied for the civilian re-training schemes and left the army. Sergeant Davis had been pleased by the performance of the men of Bravo Troop. They had moaned, complained, bitched, but they had stuck it out; even better, he knew they would have gone on enduring the discomfort for another ten days if necessary.

Sergeant Davis had Charlie Bravo Two closed-down at the moment. It wasn't necessary, but it was cutting out the chill breeze that was now rippling the trees and shaking the moisture to the ground beneath. There was little warmth inside the tank and he was glad he was wearing a sweater beneath his coveralls and NBC suit. The interior lighting was off and Inkester the gunner was dozing just below Davis's knees, somehow wedged between the hard backrest of his seat and his equipment. Davis had his legs up across the breech of the gun. DeeJay, the driver, was in his forward compartment and in his reclined position was also undoubtedly taking the opportunity to grab a few minutes' rest. Eric Shadwell, the loader, was to Davis's left, propped between the ammunition, the bag-charge bins and the breech mechanism.

Shadwell was awake and restless, his small padded seat in the fighting compartment supported him less than those of his fellow crew members. He stretched himself and pressed his hands into the small of his back. One of his legs had gone to sleep and was now tingling and sensitive as his movement restored the circulation. 'Bloody hell,' he swore softly. To occupy his mind he began mentally counting the ammunition; sleek evil-looking shells. Sixty-four of them in all, most situated in racks beside him. A few lay forward, stored to the left of DeeJay the driver, but they were difficult to reach if the tank was in motion.

Shells. Shadwell knew a lot about them. Bravo Two was carrying only two types at present: High Explosive Squash Head, abbreviated to 'Hesh', and Armoured-Piercing Discarding Sabot, officially 'APDS', but usually called 'Sabots'. He closed his eyes and pictured them striking the armour of an enemy tank. 'Bam...splat...' That was Hesh, exploding, flattening, sending a shock wave through metal that tore off a massive scab on the other side, splintering and ricochetting around inside the enemy's hull. 'Bam...zonk...' The Sabot, a tungsten steel bolt carried by a softer metal shoe which it left on impact, and then drove on through the armour as though it were nothing more than thin balsa wood. 'Bam, splat...bam, zonk...' He made the sounds again, and mimed the reloading of the gun.

The separate explosive charges which propelled the shells helped to make his life easier; no used shellcases came back into his compartment, everything was discharged forward. He could also select the appropriate power of charge, which assisted the shell's trajectory.

The Russians didn't use loaders in their tanks, he remembered. Sod that! The Russians had automatic-loading guns so they only had three men in a tank crew, but their system had a weakness. If the automatic-loading system failed, then their tanks became useless. NATO designers believed hand loading to be more reliable; Shadwell agreed with them. Besides, what the hell would he be doing if Chieftains only had three men to a crew? Bugger being a driver, or a gunner...and there would be fat chance of him making commander for a long while!

What else was there for him to count? Machine gun ammo? Six thousand rounds for the 7.62mm mounted above the cupola! Nice gun, you could aim and fire it from inside the tank. There used to be another...the point-five was used for ranging the main gun...obsolete now the Barr and Stroud laser range-finder was fitted. The range-finder was quicker to use, and more accurate.

He sighed.

It was surprising how big the interior could seem at times, like a bloody cathedral; especially when it was all in darkness. He could just see the dim outline of one of the crew's Sterlings in its clips on the other side of the compartment. It seemed a hundred yards away...too far...the other end of a long tunnel. Even Sergeant Davis's boots looked too small to be real, as though Shadwell was viewing them through the wrong end of a pair of binoculars.

Maybe I'm asleep, thought Shadwell. It's all a bloody dream this caper, I'll wake up in the quarters. No such sodding luck...I'm awake! Maybe everybody's dead? DeeJay's dead...killed by a secret death-ray...dead in his driving seat...his head lolling and his tongue hanging out! Inky's bought it, too...lying there with his eyes bulging in their sockets and his stomach swelling with gases. And Sergeant Davis...sitting there...just sitting...his hands on the cupola control, locked in a death-grip...clutching. Shadwell's thoughts were making him nervous. It was like sitting up alone, late at night, watching a horror movie. Shadows normally unnoticed, suddenly became threatening.

He spoke loudly, his voice echoing slightly. 'It's the same as bloody Suffield.' The remark was less of a genuine observation than a plea for someone to answer him. The fear was growing and he was feeling isolated, and lonely. Suffield was the site of the NATO tank ranges in Canada, where the regiment had spent some weeks earlier in the year. Neither the landscape nor the present circumstances justified the remark. The only link was the time the men had spent on night manoeuvres, firing at targets through the infra-red sights...and it was dark outside Bravo Two now! Dawn was just a thin pale band above the eastern horizon.

Shadwell, as loader, saw very little of the external action when the tank was in battle. He had a periscope of his own,

28

but there was seldom time to use it; often he saw nothing except his racks of shells, the charges and the breech of the gun. If he attempted to use his periscope, everything had already happened by the time he got his eyes re-focused to the longer distance or adjusted to the change of light. It didn't worry him too much. Sometimes he managed to see where the shells he loaded struck their targets, but if not he still found satisfaction in imagining the scene through the voices of the men on the radio or the Tannoy.

No one answered him, so he said bleakly: 'Well, not exactly like Suffield; at least we haven't had all our bloody gear shot to hell by our own infantry.' He was remembering an incident that had happened on their last visit to the Canadian ranges. On the night before a combined armour and infantry exercise there had been a bar-fight between men of the regiment and a number of the infantrymen. The next day when the tanks had been advancing across the ranges, accompanied by the infantry using live rounds in their rifles, the tanks themselves had become targets. All the personal gear carried by the crews in the storage boxes on the outside of the hulls had been shot full of holes.

There was still no reply. Desperately he changed the subject. 'There was supposed to be an old Clint Eastwood shitkicker in the barrack's cinema tonight. I was going with the corporal's daughter.'

Shadwell was a few months short of his twenty-first birthday, lightly built and thin featured. His home was a small council house semi on a Manchester estate. The youngest of a large family living in crowded conditions, his first night in army quarters had been an almost agoraphobic experience. He was a man whose friendships gave him as much anxiety as pleasure. 'Are you asleep, Sarge?'

Morgan Davis said, 'Yes.' He could almost hear Shadwell sigh with relief at the sound of a human voice. 'What's on your mind, son?'

'For Christ's sake,' groaned Inkester the gunner, from below Morgan Davis's legs, 'why don't you take an

29

overdose, Eric!'

Shadwell ignored him. 'You think we're going to have to fight, Sarge.' It was a statement, not a question.

Morgan Davis decided to be honest. 'Yes, I think so.'

'What's it going to be like?'

'Magic,' interrupted Inkester. 'We take a few of them out, then retire to a new position before their artillery can range in on us, then we brew up a few more. When the odds are reduced, we push them right back to the Urals. It'll be magic.'

'Be quiet and go back to sleep, Inkester.' ordered Davis. He spoke towards Shadwell in the darkness. 'No one knows what it's going to be like. It's a new kind of war. All *we* have to do is to obey orders, and keep our heads down.'

'My dad was in the last war,' said Shadwell, in an attempt to prolong the conversation. 'RASC. He got one home leave from Egypt in three years. Three bloody years, Sarge.' It seemed like a lifetime to the young loader.

'This war won't last more than a few days.'

'Just so long as I get a crack at a T-80,' said Inkester. 'Just one T-80 in my sight, broadside on...I dream of them, Sarge. A whole long row of them silhouetted on a skyline, moving along like ducks in a shooting gallery. Pop...pop...pop...there they go. Magic!'

The radio crackled. Sergeant Davis adjusted his headset, pulling it down tighter over his beret. 'All stations Charlie Bravo, this is Charlie Bravo Nine.' The troop leader's voice was penetrating. 'Stand to, and prepare for action. Load Hesh, and keep to your own arcs. Out.'

Davis acknowledged, and then switched on the Chieftain's Tannoy. 'Okay, lads, stand to. Shadwell, load Hesh.' He didn't give them time to question him. 'It sounds like we've got a war...'

Inkester's voice was pitched high with surprise: 'Christ!'

'Now take it easy...all of you. Inkester, no itchy fingers, wait for your orders. If someone's going to start something, it's not going to be Bravo Two.'

'Loaded,' bellowed Shadwell, his voice cutting through the still air.

'You daft pillock,' complained Inkester, loudly. 'You bloody near deafened me! We all watched you load a minute ago.'

'Shut up,' said Davis. 'Keep your eyes open, and stay alert. Hewett, everything okay your end?'

DeeJay revved the engine slightly and checked his gauges. 'It all looks good, Sarge.'

'Keep it that way.' Davis dimmed out the compartment lights and leant his head back against the rest. He reached out and touched the steel of the turret with his fingertips. It was cold, damp with the condensation of the crew's breath. He could feel the throb of the engine. Bravo Two! She was a good tank, reliable, responsive to the treatment she received from her crew. He remembered being told how it had been when the cavalry regiments lost their horses before the start of World War Two — men had wept as their mounts had been led away to be replaced by armoured vehicles. If the situation were reversed, Davis thought, he would have identical feelings...you got to know a vehicle, trust it, understand its likes and dislikes. He had never owned a horse, but three-quarters of a million pounds worth of Chieftain took some beating. The womb-like darkness and security of Bravo Two's fighting compartment was comforting.

THREE

Any doubts which were in the mind of Captain Mick Fellows of the Royal Tank Regiment concerned not the rapidly developing situation, but the sanity of being placed in his present position by a foreign commanding officer. He felt sure the scheme in which he and his small unit of Rarden-armed Scimitars were involved, on detachment to the Armoured Infantry Division of the 1st German Corps, must have been devised by a lunatic with no concern whatsoever for the lives of his men.

Officially, Captain Fellows' troop was known as a 'stay-behind-unit'. There were others, mostly infantry. Their job was to remain in concealment until the first echelons of an enemy attack had passed, and then to harrass and disrupt the logistics columns or communications wherever possible. That was fair enough, sensible tactics, but the German commander had, in Fellows' opinion, allowed his enthusiasm for guerrilla warfare to obscure the impracticability of the plans he had developed for a unit whose normal duties were reconnaissance.

Mick Fellows was waiting with his Scimitar troop in a concrete bunker within a kilometer of the East German border, in dense pine woods between the villages of Bahrdorf and Rickensdorf to the south-east of Wolfsburg. His German commander's belief was that any major Soviet assault in his sector would have as its centre-line the autobahn which ran from Helmstedt to Hannover, and he had deployed his troops for that eventuality.

The bunker was carefully concealed. The Scimitars it contained were not those Fellows' troop normally used for training; these four had lain in readiness in the bunker since the slow build-up towards hostilities two and a half years previously. No tank or vehicle tracks, which might reveal their presence to enemy aircraft or surveillance satellites, led to their position.

The red glow of the lighting within the Scimitars' bunkers removed all the opposing colour, blending the overalls of the men and the camouflaging of the tanks into the rose shadows. The air was warm, oil-scented. Earlier in the day the exhausts of the vehicles had been coupled to the ventilation system and each engine tested; now there was little to do but wait. At the far end of the bunker were a platoon of the 22nd SAS, their faces daubed with camouflage cream. They appeared casual, relaxed, some of them dozing or playing cards. There was no way in which Fellows could have identified their officer or the NCOs by their dress or weaponry.

His Scimitar commanders, all lieutenants, were studying the map on a low table near the bunker's radio equipment. He joined them. He could sense the keen edge of nervous anticipation in the tense manner of their conversation; it was no different from the pre-patrol anxiety they had all experienced in Northern Ireland. Tonight none of them knew exactly what to expect. Even Fellows himself had no experience of battle, other than that simulated in exercises; but he knew that no matter how startling the explosions of dummy mines and shells close to the aluminium hull of the Scimitars, they would bear little resemblance to the real thing. Fellows had awakened from a nightmare when he had attempted to sleep earlier in the evening. In his dream his Scimitar had faced a ring of Soviet T-80s, a hundred of them encircling him, the muzzles of their 122mm guns following him as he sought desperately to escape. His own gunner was picking target after target with the Scimitar's Rarden, firing the light 30mm cannon in short bursts. The

33

shells were splattering ineffectively against the massive T-80 hulls, and Fellows' driver seemed unable to manoeuvre to find the weaknesses on their sides. Helplessly, he watched as one moved towards him, as though to indicate it desired single combat; a Goliath against a David. Fellows had experienced the terror of imaginary death, watching the dark muzzle of its gun selecting a target on the Scimitar's vulnerable aluminium body. He had seen the belch of white fire...and awakened sweating. He understood the feelings of his men.

'Winning the war?' He tried to sound lighthearted and casual, but realized his attempt to reproduce the kind of conversational voice he might have used in the mess probably had the opposite effect. He had spoken to Sache-Worrel, a baby-faced twenty-one year old less than a year out of Sandhurst. Sache-Worrel was barely five feet eight in height, and looked as though he should still be at school. Fellows doubted if the second lieutenant needed to shave more than once a week.

He suspected the man was blushing. Sache-Worrel always blushed whether the words addressed to him were a compliment or a reprimand. 'No, sir.'

A first lieutenant, a little older and much more confident, joined the conversation protectively. 'We were discussing Hannover, sir. It's bound to be a key Soviet Red.'

'Probably. The areas of densest population always have it rough in wartime. They'll come in for heavy bombing in the industrial regions. I don't think I'd like to be a civilian in any of the German cities, and Hannover is a major link in the rail and road systems. But it's not our problem...' He jabbed a finger at the chart. 'This is our patch; and now, this sector...'

'His grandparents live in Hannover, sir,' interrupted the first lieutenant.

'I'd forgotten,' admitted Fellows. That was careless, he thought. He should have remembered Sache-Worrel's mother was German. His father had met her while serving

34

in the British Army. He too had been a professional soldier; an officer in the infantry. 'Don't worry, we'll hold them long before Hannover.' He tried to sound convincing.

'At the River Fuse,' the first lieutenant spoke firmly, as if he felt it necessary to confirm Fellows' words for his friend's benefit.

Fellows didn't bother to reply. He glanced at his watch, it was 03.40 hours exactly. It would be dawn in forty-five minutes. He wondered what was happening behind the frontier. Intelligence would have a pretty good idea back at headquarters, but Fellows' squadron was committed to total radio silence.

FOUR

The most northerly-situated tank of the Fifth United States
Force was commanded by Master Sergeant Will Browning.
He was one of the few men in November Squadron with
battle experience. He was one of the even fewer men in the
entire United States Army in Europe who had survived a
direct hit on a previous tank by a communist shell fired
from a Russian-built T-54. He had been in action below
Mutter's Ridge, north of Dong Ha in Vietnam.

Browning tried to think about the incident as little as
possible. His survival was miraculous...a mistake had been
made...he should have died with his crew. Almost
superstitiously, it seemed better not to remind a God that he
had overlooked a heavenly candidate who was now living
on stolen time.

The 100mm high explosive shell had struck between the
centre of Browning's M48's track and the bustle of its
turret. The US tank's gunner had been following a VC
target moving away to the right.

The M48's cast-steel turret was torn clean from the tank
and hurled fifteen meters away. Somehow it carried Will
Browning with it, still in one piece. A fraction of a second
later the tank's ammunition exploded, tearing the already
wrecked hull and the bodies of the crew into fragments.
Browning was protected from greater injuries by the casing
of the turret. He had suffered multiple fractures, burst
eardrums and shrapnel wounds in his thighs and buttocks.
Had he been a conscript the wounds would have ended his

service, but as a regular cavalryman he was pronounced fit for further service eight months later.

It had not rained in the mountains of the Hohe Rhön east of Fulda, and the night had been clear and sharp with a touch of frost in the air above the high ground. To the front of the cavalry position the River Ulster followed the line of the East German border, before dissecting it two kilometers to the north. Backing them, three kilometers to the rear of the hill, was the highway linking Tann with Fulda where the Black Horse 11th Cavalry had been stationed.

Like most of those guarding the eastern frontier at this time, Master Sergeant Will Browning had been thinking about his own future. There was every possibility of war, and he knew that unlike most occasions in the past it would not begin with the signing of a declaration. Pearl Harbour had taught the USA a hard lesson, and with modern weapons a determined enemy would be foolish to give formal notice of its intentions by more than minutes. The preparations he had watched during the past hours no longer resembled those of an exercise. Three minefields had been laid in the fields beside the river; meadows which normally contained grazing cattle were now empty. Helicopters had flown across the woodland on the far slopes, seeding the forest tracks and glades with anti-personnel mines. When he had left Fulda, he had seen a party of German combat engineers placing demolition charges in the bridge. It was a simple and precise task, for every bridge of possible strategic importance built in West Germany since the Second World War had been constructed with future demolition in mind: special chambers to hold explosives were sited at critical points of their structures.

War? Maybe. Another war, another tank! Browning thought about Utah, his Abrams; she was a hell of a lot bigger and tougher than his old M48, safer too. They claimed her Limey armour was almost shell-proof. Goddamn Limeys...they could invent something good like this, and then not be able to afford it themselves! Browning hadn't met many British soldiers, but knew their reputation as tough fighters and drinkers; someone in the Pentagon even cared enough about the latter to print a warning in a pamphlet issued to all American personnel serving in Europe. Limey soldiers were supposed to be a bad influence on John Does! When he had read it, Browning had laughed; it was only a year since the American Armed Forces had solved one of their own problems, the taking of drugs by almost fifty per cent of their men. The solution had been simple – remove the crime and you improved the statistics. They had legalized the smoking of marijuana in the US. Overnight, the illegal use of drugs by servicemen was cut by three-quarters!

Armour. Browning stared up at the Abrams silhouetted against the night sky like a desert rock, indestructible, angular, solid, sleeping. Awake, Utah was a fearsome powerhouse. The regiment had only recently been equipped with the Abrams, the Chrysler XM1s, heavier and faster than their old tanks, and capable of a useful fifty kilometers an hour from an engine producing six hundred horse power more than that in the M60A1s. The Abrams' profile was low, sleek and functional, the weaponry familiar: a 105mm gun, a Bushmaster co-axial cannon, a 12.7mm machine gun mounted on the commander's cupola, and a lighter 7.62mm machine gun on the loader's hatch. The fire-power was impressive.

Browning wondered how they would fare against the Soviet armour. If the East Germans were involved in the assault they would probably use T62 and T72 tanks...perhaps a few T10s. It was unlikely that they would yet have the new T-80, for US intelligence claimed these were in limited production and available only to the Soviet armoured regiments in small numbers. But intelligence was often incorrect.

Browning realized he was allowing himself to grow apprehensive. He knew what war was like, he knew the feel of it, the stink, and he knew this was going to be different from all the others; the ultimate horizon perhaps, for mankind.

Less than four kilometers away were the enemy, waiting, as he waited, for the signal that would hurl them forward into action. It was believed they were part of the Soviet 8th Guards...what a title, Browning thought, for aggressors! They were somewhere in front of him, hidden in the forest beyond the first ridge of hills. Sometimes when the wind had blown from the east, he had heard the engines of their tanks, the distant squeals of labouring tracks, the roar of exhausts.

Browning had been in Germany for a little over a year. He enjoyed the posting, though it would have been better if the dollar exchange rate had been more favourable. Before that his appointments had been at Fort Sam Houston, Fort McClellan, and finally Fort Dix. Down Barracks in Fulda was a pleasant break from the routine of Stateside army life. 'Smile, the border community cares', advised the notice at the barracks entrance; some of the men seemed to interpret it as an order and intensified their gloom deliberately. Browning spent far more of his free time out in the German countryside than most others in the camp.

'Coffee?' It was Del Acklin, the commander of Idaho, the neighbouring Abrams. He was a hundred meters from his vehicle and, in view of their orders, was taking a risk leaving it. He held an aluminium mess tin towards Browning.

The warmth of the metal was pleasant, and the smell of the coffee sweet in the cold air. 'Thanks.' He sipped it, the hot liquid was laced with Austrian Stroh rum.

Acklin said: 'I'm scared, Will.' He kept his voice low so Browning's gunner, above them in the turret, wouldn't hear the remark.

'We're all scared.'

'I keep thinking about my kids.'

'Well, that's good.' Browning could hear the nervousness in Acklin's speech, almost feel the tension of the man's body. He and Browning drank together a couple of times a

39

week and were fairly close buddies, but Browning wasn't
feeling like conversation now. 'You'd better get back to your
tank before the lieutenant decides to take a walk around.'

'It's going to happen, isn't it?'

'What?'

'The war is going to happen.'

'Maybe not a real war, just a limited action to straighten
out a few of the kinks in the frontier. Perhaps it won't even
happen at all. We've got pretty close before...this could be
the same.'

'You don't think I'm chicken, do you?'

'Nope.' He handed back the mess tin. 'Thanks.'

Del Acklin half turned away, then hesitated. 'I just, er,
thought it wouldn't be good for my kids to grow up without
their father.'

'Then don't let it happen.'

'No, sure.' He walked away a few paces until he was
barely visible in the gloom of the woodland. 'Good luck,
Will.'

Browning ducked his head to light another cigarette in
the shelter of his overalls. How long had it been since the
last battle...since Dong Ha? 1968! Seventeen years! He
had been nineteen years in the cavalry! Good God, he was
an old man...thirty-eight! Maybe that wasn't too old,
though. Too old for what? He hadn't got any special plans!
He didn't want to quit the service to open a shop, or become
a salesman, or find a job as a clerk in some government
bureau; he liked things as they were...nicely regulated...no
hassle. Retirement? He didn't think about it too often. A
small house somewhere, in a small town...a stoop to relax
on...wasn't that what all vets wanted? A place to fade away
in.

Shit! He was getting maudlin. Browning had never
married; it seemed like making trouble for yourself, perhaps
he would sometime...settle down. Settle down! Jesus, you
were in the army or out of it! Being army was being settled;
what the hell more did you need?

40

Women. Browning grunted, dropped the butt of the cigarette and ground it out with his heel. He had few illusions about his looks; some guys were handsome, he wasn't. Some guys found women everywhere, he didn't. His face hadn't been much to write home about before Vietnam; it was worse afterwards. A long wound from the centre of his forehead, running across the bridge of his nose and down his cheek, made him look like the loser of a knife fight. Because he was balding a little at the front of his head, he kept his hair cropped short. And he wasn't some tall lean clothes-horse who could make every suit he wore look straight out of Fifth Avenue; he had the build of a middleweight, broad shoulders, heavy chest and narrow hips. Out of uniform, he looked like an all-in wrestler. It frightened women...well, most of them...he couldn't even smile straight with the wound, it had severed a couple of cheek muscles. A grin from Browning could make some women think he was sizing them up for a chain-saw murder! Most didn't take the risk to find out what he was like underneath.

'The captain's flapping his jaw on the air.' Podini, the Abrams' gunner, was leaning out of the turret above him.

'So what does the nice guy say?' The squadrons' leader wasn't Browning's favourite officer. As a graduate of West Point Military Academy, he had a habit of treating his NCOs like first-year plebs.

'He thinks he's Terry and the Pirates,' said Podini. 'Says gung-ho and all that kind of crap.' Podini cleared his throat and spat into the darkness. 'Remember the Alamo!'

'He said that?'

Podini chuckled. 'Well, not exactly. But he sure meant to.'

'He's hoping it's going on tape back at HQ, so's maybe he'll get a field promotion and a Distinguished Service Cross...it's his fuckin' bullshit. He should have stayed with the Iron Brigade. I got my own plans.'

'Like what?'

41

'Like staying alive. If the captain wants to play Buck Rogers, he can do it on his lonesome. I don't aim to buy the farm for someone else's benefit.'

Browning shivered, pulled his collar closer to his neck and wiped a drop of moisture from his nose with the back of his gloved hand. He stamped his feet a few times, wondered why the hell he was standing out in the chill air, and clambered back up into the turret. He could smell the scent of sweat and fuel oil drifting up from the fighting compartment and decided to keep his head and shoulders outside for a few more minutes. He leant against the metalwork, it was ice-cold; below him the hull of Utah was white-dusted with hoar frost. To the north and west the stars were still bright in a dark sky.

There was soft music, just audible outside the tank. It came from the driving compartment where Mike Adams was relaxing, listening to a tape recorder. Adams' driving compartment was as customized as the US army would permit...which was only a little. Given a free hand, he would have filled it with gadgets, stereo, additional lighting, a coffee machine, mirrors. As it was, he managed to get away with an imitation leopard-skin seat cover, and his Japanese tape recorder. An official request to be allowed to fit a cigar-lighter had been met with a horrified refusal from the captain. Not only was smoking forbidden inside a tank because of fuel fumes but, in any case, Adams was informed, a cigar-lighter was aesthetically out of place in an American fighting vehicle. Adams had retaliated by bribing a German waiter to post 'No Smoking' notices at various strategic places throughout the officers' mess; they had spent an uncomfortable week smoking outside on its terraces before they found it had nothing to do with their colonel. A New Yorker, from Winfield Junction, twenty-four year old Mike Adams looked on the XM1 tank, Utah, as the kind of supercharged super-rod he had always wanted as a kid.

Utah had lost her name. So far, no one other than Will Browning was aware of this. She had lost not only her name, but also the white stars on the front of her hull and turret sides, the ordinance numbers, and her red and white shields containing the rampant black horse insignia of the 11th Cavalry. Despite the fact that all of these items were revered by the captain, Master Sergeant Will Browning had painted them out with a can of matt camouflage green earlier that night. His action had been the result of something which had occurred to him in Vietnam. He had decided that distinctive markings gave a convenient aiming point to VC infantrymen with a missile launcher. As the international tension had escalated over the past days, the thought had reappeared in his mind. In war you had to expect to be a target, but there was no need to make it easy for the marksman. And if Will Browning could find any way of lessening the chances of having to survive two direct hits in one lifetime, he was going to make use of it...however small a protection it might give him, and to hell with the captain!

There was an observation helicopter somewhere towards the north, and Browning was attempting to pick it out against the sky. He could hear the steady thrashing of its rotors. It sounded like one of the West German Heeresflieger BO 105s, heavier than the US Bell. The BO 105, on patrol along the frontier, would probably be armed with anti-tank missiles.

Browning suddenly saw what he first thought was a shooting star; a bright trail of light above the distant woods. With a tightening of his stomach muscles he realized the meteorite was travelling the wrong way, from earth skywards! The trail of light was joined by others, soundless from this distance.

The throb of the helicopter's rotors, now faint, was joined momentarily by a shrieking sound, followed almost instantaneously by a vivid white and orange explosion which balled out into the night as an expanding incandescent cloud, lighting the forest and open grassland

43

beneath, and blinding Will Browning for a few seconds.

He felt tugging at his legs, and heard the anxious voice of Podini, Utah's gunner. 'What the hell was that?'

Before he could answer, the thunderous roar of the explosion reached the tank. He let his legs collapse, dropping into the interior and pulling the hatch closed above him. He could feel the heavy hull of the Abrams vibrating.

'What...' began Podini, again.

'Get your eyes to the night sights, and keep them there.' He was shouting. Hal Ginsborough the loader was somewhere in the darkness. 'Gins, load APF and stand-by.'

There was a clank of metal as Ginsborough obeyed. 'Loaded.'

Podini called desperately, 'You want me to fire? I don't see a target, I don't see a target!'

'For Christ's sake don't fire...just prepare for action.'

The hull of the tank was vibrating again, and the thunder in the distance was continuous. There was a crackling in Browning's headphones. A voice, urgent. 'November Squadron, this is Godfather, affirm radio contact. Over.' There was interference on the wavelength – which Browning knew was jamming by some communications unit across the border. If it became too efficient then the short-range communication could be maintained by HF which was more difficult to block out, and the squadron had a wide choice of alternative wavelengths. There was a pause as the troop leaders made their answering calls, then the squadron captain again. 'Hullo November we have Daisy May...' Jesus! What a code name for full hostilities, thought Browning. 'November...prepare for incoming...'

Communication was lost in a tumult of sound that swelled around the Abrams; the mingled screams and howls of rockets, the whistling roar of howitzer shells. Browning peered, startled, through his periscope lenses. The sky was criss-crossed now by hundreds of white trails of fire. The woods beyond the frontier were alight with countless explosions. Mistakenly, for a moment he thought the barrage was solely that of the NATO artillery to the rear, but then the ground heaved and rippled. A blue-orange flash erupted a few meters to the left of the tank, hurling earth, tree branches and shrapnel skywards.

Metal splinters shrieked from the Abrams' hull.

FIVE

The first shells to touch NATO-defended soil were those of a battery of 152mm D-20s fired from eleven kilometers behind the East German frontier, the battery commander anticipating his orders by several seconds. His twenty guns began a steady rate of fire of four rounds a minute each. They were joined by several RM-70 missile batteries stationed beyond the second ridge of hills and closer to the border, their rockets launched in 'ripple' sequence from the forty muzzles on each vehicle. The intense barrage erupted along almost the entire east-west borders, from northern Germany to southern Austria, the town of Lübeck coming under an artillery blitzkrieg from the Soviet heavy 180mm S-23s with their rocket-assisted shells.

The NATO forces' response was immediate. The previous days had not been wasted. Satellites, air reconnaissance, the intelligence units working in the East German territory, ground radar and the pre-laid electronic sensors, had provided a vast quantity of information on the positioning of Warsaw Pact troops and equipment. The pilots of the NATO air forces had been briefed and rebriefed many times during the past hours in anticipation of imminent conflict, the artillery brigades closest to the border already knew of any concentrations of armour or mechanized infantry.

Although earlier defence plans had ruled that no NATO troops, vehicles, aircraft or projectiles should in any circumstances cross the West/East demarcation line, the enormous build-up of enemy war materials in the border areas, indicating the determination of a Soviet invasion once it commenced, had forced the NATO military commanders to hastily revise their orders.

The first aircraft into enemy airspace were a USAF squadron of uprated F-111s, each with a full pay-load of 31,000lbs of explosives. Coming in from the air base at Zweibrücken to the west, snaking a way through the mountainous country, and crossing the borders only a little higher than the maximum trajectory of the shells of the heavy artillery, they launched a fierce attack on the headquarters of a Soviet mechanized rifle brigade at Wernigerode. Swinging north to bring themselves back across allied territory, two were destroyed by SA-3 Goa surface-to-air-missiles stationed close inside the East German border; the wreckage of the aircraft spiralled down unnoticed in the heavy concentrations of artillery fire across the dense woodland of the plain.

The West German Heeresflieger were in action within minutes of the landing of the first shells and rockets. Nine of their ATGW-armed Wiesels attacked a forward concentration of Russian assault armour to the east of Dannenberg.

The strength of the Soviet artillery barrage had taken a number of senior NATO officers by surprise. Many had come to believe that the effectiveness of artillery prior to ground attack was merely psychological and the Warsaw Pact countries were unlikely to waste time and ammunition by such tactics. They had thought the first signs of hostility would be the forward movement of enemy armour. The depth and power of the artillery fire caused some momentary concern until the pattern of the barrage became more obvious. The Soviet artillery, both gun and missile, were concentrating on the blanketing of known NATO positions, fortunately mostly unoccupied by the defending forces. Barracks and garrisons within range of the Soviet weapons were destroyed within the first few minutes of the barrage. Sites which had been used in training exercises over the past ten years were all covered, as were many of the more obvious defensive situations facing the frontier. Casualties in the forward combat units of the NATO armies were minimal, though there were many amongst the unevacuated maintenance and civilian staffs of the garrisons, and in villages of the border areas.

A short break in the artillery barrage in the Helmstedt region east of Braunschweig heralded the entry of the Soviet air forces into the initial stages of the attack. A squadron of Mikoyan/Gurevich MiG-28s, the latest versions of the Flogger, swept across the borders at little more than tree-top height. They were picked up by NATO radar and, as they reached the plain to the east of Hannover, came under fire from three missile batteries deployed for defence of the city. At the same time, a formation of Antanov AN-22s, some of the largest aircraft in the world, made an attempt to deliver a diversionary paratroop attack west of Braunschweig. All eight aircraft were destroyed by a patrol of RAF-piloted Rockwell XFV-12s, vectored on to the troop carriers by the computer-linked radar. The Soviet aircraft, with low maximum speeds, were defenceless against the air-to-air missiles of the XFV-12s, powering in from the north in excess of a thousand miles an hour. Over eight hundred Soviet paratroopers were killed while still inside the aircraft. None reached the ground alive.

In several areas in the northernmost sectors of CENTAG, the first troops of the Soviet invasion forces were landed successfully on NATO soil from Hind-H helicopters and quickly formed into assault groups, aided by transport carried in by Mi-10s and Mi-14s of the 16th Frontal Aviation Army. The deepest penetration, and the largest number of men landed, was in the Fulva valley south-east of Melsungen, where heavy fighting resulted from almost immediate encounters with a NATO armoured reconnaissance unit of the Federal Republic Heer, mounted in their Spahpanzer 2 Luchs with 20mm Rh202 cannons and MG3 machine guns.

SIX

Sergeant Morgan Davis in Bravo Two heard his troop leader's voice on the radio for only a few seconds before the first of the countless explosions that followed. Lieutenant Sidworth had sounded breathless, excited: 'Hullo Bravo, this is Nine, deploy to battle positions...' Christ, thought Davis, we're already deployed, what...Sidworth corrected his orders. 'Hullo Bravo, this is Nine, deploy to battle situation, cancel...' The remainder of his words were lost in an eruption of sound that made Sergeant Davis flinch involuntarily, then duck lower in the fighting compartment. He swung his legs from the breech of the gun down to the floor, feeling his boot catch Gunner Inkester on the side of his head. Inkester swore, loudly. The Chieftain bucked as the ground beneath it moved. The sounds Davis had encountered on the exercise ranges were nothing to those that now surrounded the Chieftain. He heard someone cursing in the HF, shouted conversation, then silence in the earphones. The Chieftain was pitched forward on its suspension by an explosion somewhere close to the rear of the tank. Another on the right made the hull ring and Davis's ears throb with the shock.

He pushed himself upright in the turret and gazed through the episcope. The sky was bright with fire and the searing trails of rockets, the ground pocked by explosions that briefly illuminated drifting clouds of smoke. There were flames leaping above the trees somewhere two hundred meters to the right, along the troop's position. It looked like a diesel-fuel fire, perhaps one of the Chieftains brewing-up. Davis hoped the crew had had time to bale out.

He didn't want to use the HF so switched back to the tank's Tannoy system. 'Inkester!' The metallic voice was loud in the compartment. He felt movement against his legs. 'Keep your eyes to the sights, lad. DeeJay, you okay down there?'

He heard DeeJay Hewett's voice, distantly. 'Fucking stroll-on!'

'Check your equipment.' The HF interrupted him, and outside the barrage had diminished briefly. He heard Lieutenant Sidworth the Bravo troop leader checking the tanks.

'Hullo Charlie Bravo all stations, this is Nine, come in, over.'

Davis answered. 'Charlie Bravo Two roger, out.'

Sidworth called again. 'Hullo Charlie Bravo Three, this is Nine, come in, over.'

There was no reply for a few seconds and then Corporal Sealey of Charlie Bravo Four interrupted on the wavelength. 'Nine, this is Charlie Bravo Four. Three is brewed, sir. We saw it. Direct hit. Over.'

God, there were troop casualties already! A few moments of war, and men, friends, began to die! It was unreal, terrifying, but Davis admired the cool way Sealey had made his report; the man had only recently been promoted, and David had helped with a recommendation.

'Hullo Charlie Bravo Four, this is Nine. Any survivors?'

'No survivors, Nine. Instant flare-out.'

'Nine, roger. Out.'

No survivors. Instant flare-out. Four names to go on the first day's casualty list. Four dead, but how many affected? There would be wives, parents, children! One bloody armour-piercing shell in the first half hour of a war! Although Davis had been trained for many years to expect death in battle, it was hard to accept it when it happened. It suddenly made him aware of the illusion of protection the tank's puny armour gave to its crew. Men measured the strength of steel against their own flesh, it was a cruel deception!

The barrage returned suddenly, and for a moment Davis wondered if Soviet sensors had reacted to the troop's HF transmissions. The dawn sky had lightened and he could view the open landscape below him. With horror he saw shell explosions, like an advancing tidal wave on a beach sweeping up the lower slopes of the hill, tearing aside trees and shrubs, building a terrifying wall of flame, smoke and hurtling debris. Before he could even react the explosions were upon them, around them. He ducked his head between his arms as the Chieftain was smashed sideways, tilted fifteen degrees to the left. The metal of the hull felt alive, shuddering, vibrating...and then there was an eerie silence. Davis could hear the rasping of his own breath. Something warm trickled down his chin. He wiped at it with his hand. It was saliva.

DeeJay called through the intercom: 'Are we hit?'

Davis tried to see through the lenses of the episcope, but some of the glass blocks were crazed, restricting his arc of visibility. He swore to himself. The lenses were a weakness which had been known for a number of years; somewhere a bloody desk-bound civil servant who was never going to have to rely on them for his life had probably jammed the funds needed to have the unit redesigned and replaced.

'What's going on, Sarge?' Inkester was peering up at him, his eyes wide in the dim light.

'Nothing. Keep your eyes front, lad,' Davis answered bluntly. He refused to acknowledge the fear he had experienced at the thought of fighting partially blinded.

The explosions were now distant; the roar of shells and the howls of missiles had ceased. Davis unhitched his headphones and pulled on his respirator before cautiously opening his hatch. It was possible there was gas outside. He moved quickly, pushing himself from the cupola. The air was thick with smoke. He thought he could smell cordite and burning diesel, but knew it was only imagination; the mask filtered out all scent. He jumped hurriedly to the ground and found himself sliding down the side of a deep crater beneath the left track. He shouted with pain as something stabbed through his gloves into the palm of his hand. The shell crater was lined with red-hot pieces of sharp metal, and the ground was steaming around him. He scrambled out. A large calibre shell had exploded less than two meters from the side of the Chieftain, and the vehicle's weight had caused the excavated ground to collapse. A little closer and they would have been irretrievably bogged-down...closer still, dead! Sergeant Davis's mouth felt dry. In the lower section of woods he heard the unmistakable sound of Swingfire anti-tank missiles. Whatever their targets, they had to be within the Swingfire's 4000 meter range...close. He could imagine the chunky missiles, shedding their casing as they left the launchers, wire-guided by their operators through separation sights towards enemy tanks or vehicles. It would be tanks...assault tanks first, then the armoured personnel carriers, the Soviet infantry combat vehicles.

He clambered back into the Chieftain. The smoke was already thinning above the scrub and visibility was now beyond a hundred meters and increasing rapidly. He hooked the earphones over his cowl. 'DeeJay, back out slowly...carefully.'

'Hullo Charlie Bravo Two, this is Nine. Hold your position, over.' Lieutenant Sidworth was keeping a close ear to the conversations of his troop.

'Charlie Bravo Nine, this is Bravo Two. Sorry the ground beneath us is unsafe. We have to move, out.'

'Charlie Bravo Two, roger, out.'

Davis felt the Chieftain shudder as it settled more, drifting gently sideways as DeeJay gunned the engine. He called 'Steady...' through the HF, then switched on the Tannoy again. 'DeeJay, you've a bloody great hole right under your left track. Take her back dead straight.' The

52

Chieftain shuddered as DeeJay rammed her into reverse, and then eased his boot down on the accelerator. It wasn't easy to move a Chieftain smoothly, but DeeJay had always claimed he could make Bravo Two feel like a Mercedes 250 SL if he wanted. He eased the tank delicately backwards. The stern slipped again, rocked and dipped. DeeJay pushed his foot down hard and the engine surged responsively. The left track skidded, then gripped. With a heave Bravo Two straightened then leapt back three meters, levelling as it did so.

'Steady,' shouted Davis. DeeJay let the revs drop and reversed the Chieftain another five meters before manoeuvring it parallel to its former position. 'Bring the bow up a fraction...more...okay, kill it. You satisfied, Inkester?' he asked the gunner.

'Yes, Sar'n.'

Eric Shadwell, the loader, called, 'There's something wrong with the Clansman, I've lost the troop net.'

'Jesus, why now?' swore Davis, then remembered he was still speaking through the Tannoy. He switched it off. 'Then get it re-netted...and move, laddie.' The last thing he wanted to happen now was to lose communication with the rest of the troop. Everything seemed to be happening too quickly, and he knew how dangerously mistakes could compound.

Shadwell was twisting at the controls of the radio set, then yelled: 'It's okay...I think it's okay.'

Davis spoke into it: 'Charlie Bravo Nine, this is Charlie Bravo Two, Manoeuvre completed successfully. Over.' He ducked into the turret and slammed close the hatch.

Sidworth's acknowledgement was laconic. 'Roger Charlie Bravo Two...' Then there was a break and Sidworth said, 'Here we go, Bravo. Watch for the command tank...wait as long as you can...out.'

The last black fog columns of the HE explosions were drifting clear of the plain and joining to form a rising grey curtain when dark smoke grenades began bursting.

53

Davis saw the enemy armour. He had expected perhaps a single squadron, edging cautiously into the fields of the plain in the direction Sidworth had indicated. But far below him were row upon row of Soviet tanks, sixty or seventy, already crossing the misty corridor of ploughed ground that with its barbed wire had constituted the frontier. As his fear magnified them, for a moment they appeared as invincible monsters far greater in size, far more heavily armed than anything he had ever imagined. Where was the minefield? Could nothing stop them? What were the NATO gunners doing? Why weren't they firing? A minefield was only any good when covered by artillery. Davis controlled his growing sense of panic. Fear could take away a man's reason, make him commit fatal errors. He had a lot to live for...Hedda, the twins,...their future...his own. His hands were trembling, so he gripped the turret controls more tightly. Work to the book, he told himself. Take it easy and stay calm. Don't forget the lessons, the hundreds of hours of practice. Trust Bravo Two, she's a good tank. He took several deep slow breaths, then forced himself to concentrate on the terrifying landscape ahead.

The smoke screen was becoming denser but he could still see the advancing Russian tanks. They had already suffered heavy casualties. Several were burning in the ploughed strip of land that was freshly pitted with craters. In the woods beyond, more smoke, obviously from oil and fuel fires, was wreathing above the trees. He tried to identify the enemy vehicles. Some, at the head of the attack formation, were the new T-80s fitted with mine-clearing ploughs, but he recognized T-72s and the earlier T-62s. It looked as if the Soviet division was using every available piece of armour it could find to add weight to their thrust.

Part of the battle group's Swingfire battery was concealed in a shallow gulley skirting a thin plantation of larches. From his position well above them on the ridge of high ground, Davis could see their vehicles, and even a few of the men. They were less than three thousand meters from the first wave of Soviet tanks, and had either survived the storm of the barrage, or been moved quickly into position under cover of the smoke. He watched two of their missiles leave the launchers almost simultaneously. He was unable to follow their course, but one of the leading T-80s disappeared in an inverted cone of fire, and a second later there was explosion at ground level beside a T-72, which slewed sideways as it shed a track.

There were two Soviet Hind-F gunships swinging across the border woodland, and Davis heard himself shout an impossible warning to the crews of the Swingfires. The two aircraft came in at little more than a hundred feet, ominous dark vultures hovering above the ATGWs. One of the vehicle's gunners must have seen them for there was a burst of fire from the GPMG on his cupola, and the helicopter on the right jinked, then steadied. There was flame beneath its stubby wings and momentarily Davis thought it had been hit, then the flame left the gunship as a pair of rockets traced downwards. They struck the slab side of one of the FV 438s simultaneously, bracketing the maintenance hatch. Davis saw the vehicle explode into fragments, its wreckage hurled high into the air by the force of the detonation. A second pair of 'Spirals' had left the other Hind, and one of the two remaining FV-438s received a direct hit to the rear of the cupola. The third, its tracks racing, was hurtling in reverse through the thin woods almost as though it were out of control, the pines flattening beneath it, smashing out of its path. It jerked to a stop, and as it did so one of its Swingfire missiles left the launcher, ricochetted from the ground a hundred meters along its path, and then exploded above the woods. Davis could feel the terror of the men within the vehicle. Its tracks churned again, failing initially to get traction, then it spun briefly as the driver desperately sought a route through the trees that would lead him to deeper cover. The first of the gunships hovered above and behind the vehicle, its pilot taking time to give his gunner a clear shot. It seemed to Davis that the gunship was toying with

55

the FV-438, a hawk-suspended above its prey. He saw white trails from its missiles, then the smoke of their explosions hid the destruction of the remaining Swingfire vehicle. But the Hind-F had remained stationary too long and at too low an altitude. One of the battle group's reconnaissance Scimitars on the lower slopes of the woods had watched the destruction of the FV-438s, its gunner following the movements of the second helicopter through the sights of the Scimitar's Rarden 30mm cannon; the temptation when the gunship remained stationary at point-blank range, and within the elevation of his cannon, was irresistible. A four-round burst of armour piercing special explosive Hispano shells tore through the fusilage. Three failed to explode against the light materials of the aircraft's body, but the fourth struck the port turboshaft, blowing away the upper part of the engines and the complete rotor assembly. Davis swore jubilantly as the aircraft plunged nose first into the ground and instantly caught fire. There could be no survivors in the inferno of blazing fuel and detonating ammunition. He felt a sharp pain in his mouth, and tasted blood. In the excitement of the past minutes he had bitten through the inner part of his lower lip. Davis's war was only forty-six minutes old.

SEVEN

At the 1st Battle Group Field Headquarters, Lieutenant Colonel James Studley was attempting to ingnore casualties in terms of human death, and view them instead as incidents requiring only tactical assessment. It was not easy. The British Chieftains being destroyed were *his* tanks, and no matter how hard he tried it was impossible to forget they contained the bodies of *his* men. Out there in the smoke were young troopers he had lived with, trained from civilian to soldier, congratulated, promoted, reprimanded. He had learnt early to hate the enemy.

One complete squadron of his Chieftains was already out of action, the vehicles destroyed, and the crews either dead or wounded. It had happened in the first few minutes of hostilities. The squadron's positions had been struck by a massive rocket attack that had immediately wiped out about half of Alpha Squadron's tanks. The fire on the Chieftains had been so accurate that Studley was convinced their location had been radioed back to the Soviet artillery by infiltrated or sleeper artillery observers, who must have been inside NATO territory well before the outbreak of war.

He had ordered the remaining tanks of Alpha Squadron to withdraw towards Königslutter, but before they could do so, further artillery fire and a strike by a formation of helicopter gunships had obliterated them.

The other two squadrons of the battle group had both suffered casualties in the artillery barrage. C troop of Charlie Squadron had lost all their vehicles although there

57

were several crew survivals; all wounded, who had already been evacuated to the casualty collecting post at Burgdorf with the survivors of Alpha. B and C Troops of Bravo Squadron had both lost one Chieftain apiece, with no crews surviving. The leader's tank of Bravo Squadron had received a hit near the turret ring from an armoured piercing shell which had failed to penetrate, but dislodged the turret, crippling the vehicle and breaking the leader's right arm.

Studley, although he was finding it difficult to analyze the situation beyond his own frontage, had a clearer picture in the Elm Sector than most. Division HQ were keeping their battle group commanders reasonably well informed, and from his present field headquarters in the derelict barn, Studley could see far across the lower ground of the moor and northwards to the positions of the 2nd Battle Group between Helmstedt and the Hassenwinkel. South-west, but hidden by the ridge of high ground of the moor, was the 3rd Battle Group on the outskirts of the town of Wolfenbüttel.

The wind had veered to the south-east, and the cloud was beginning to break. The sky, in the direction of the coming weather, was bright. Later in the day there would be autumn warmth in the sun. Studley had been praying for rain; a torrential downfall to flood the rivers and turn the ploughed fields into quagmires, swamps beneath the tracks of the invading armour. Now, drawing on a lifetime's experience as a trout fisherman, he could sense the rising barometer and knew the weather would favour the enemy for the next twenty-four hours.

The heaviest Soviet attacks, on the positions defended by the battle groups of the 4th Armoured Division had, as Studley expected, come from the direction of Magdeburg behind the East German frontier. Here there was the autobahn and railway, which had undoubtedly been used in the reinforcement of the Soviet army in the past few hours. They would continue to make use of it until it was destroyed. The first heavy thrust of Soviet assault armour, following their artillery bombardment of the NATO forward positions, had carried them across the NATO border minefields. Under cover of further intense artillery fire and using dense smoke, despite their shattering casualties the Soviet army had forced the withdrawal of the 2nd Battle Group, pressing it quickly north-east as their spearhead attempted to widen the breach between the 2nd and Studley's group south of the main Soviet attack.

There were secondary thrusts in both the north and south of the 4th Armoured Division sector, one cutting north-west directly at Wolfenbüttel, the other towards Wolfsburg. The 3rd British Armoured Division to the south was under heavy pressure between the Oderwald and Goslar where the front had already buckled to a depth of eight kilometers; its battle groups were facing attacks from two directions as a result of successful landings of Soviet airborne troops and light armour.

Studley was now watching the advancing Soviet tanks through his binoculars. It was difficult, for their artillery was laying smoke ahead of them and the screen was effective. Occasionally the blanket of smoke swirled and within, for a few seconds, he would glimpse the dark hulk of some vehicle.

The battle group's two batteries of Abbots had been involved in almost continual activity, their guns were already hot. Each carried forty rounds of ammunition for the 105mms, but would soon need replenishment. It had been nearly impossible for the observers to detect clear targets for them, but they were doing a useful job of work with local harrassing fire. To minimize the risk of accurate pinpointing of their positions, and subsequent retaliatory bombardments, Studley was keeping them on the move; a few quick shots and then away. Their movement on his situation map was beginning to look like a spider's web.

Somewhere deep inside the layer of smoke, the Soviet armour had reached the second line of minefields. Added now to the thunder of their artillery support were the satisfying dull thumps of the mines, and where they exploded the mist turned crimson and churned black with fuel smoke.

Studley had been attempting, with no luck so far, to obtain the use of a command helicopter. It had been promised but had not arrived. He wanted to get above the position, if only briefly, to obtain a clearer idea of the enemy's intentions. The information he was getting over the rear net from Division was frequently too broad to be of great use to him. It seemed to him his battle group was facing the spearhead of a main Soviet thrust, but this could be a feint to lead him to commit his men when perhaps the real attack was yet to come, elsewhere.

The air activity had increased over the battle zone, though much of it was at a high level above the broken cloud. There had been a brief attack by three East German Sukhoi Su-15s, who had come in from high altitude in the east, lost in the glare of the rising sun, in a Mach-2 30-degree dive. AA-8 missiles had been fired into a position evacuated minutes before by the Abbots. The battle group had suffered no casualties in the attack that lasted only seconds, and the Su-15s had not returned.

His adjutant drew his attention away from the battlefield. 'Charlie Squadron are engaging, sir.'

'Good. Order them to retire as soon as it gets too hot.'

'Yes, sir.' The adjutant thought it unnecessary to tell his CO the identical message, with the coded reference, for Charlie's new positions had already been sent out on the net.

EIGHT

Inkester shouted: 'Where is it? I've lost it!'

'Calm down...there, two o'clock, on the edge of the smoke.' Sergeant Morgan Davis saw the T-72 as a dark silhouette through the 'times-ten' magnification of his sight. The Soviet tank was three-quarters-on to Bravo Two, bucking as it crossed the furrowed land three thousand meters away, swerving occasionally to avoid the wider craters in its path.

'I've got it.'

'Take your time.'

'Sod...the bastard's gone.'

'Steady...there.' Davis was using the coupled sight giving him an identical view to that of Inkester the gunner. The sights were settled on the hull of the T-72 as Inkester traversed the gun. The tank heaved upwards with the shock as the gunner hit the firing button and the propulsion charge detonated in the breech. With the engine on tick-over the roar of the gun was impressive within the confines of the fighting compartment. An automatic flashguard within the sight protected the eyes of the gunner and commander from the glare of the barrel flame, but smoke from the muzzle blurred their vision for a few seconds.

'Load Sabot,' ordered Davis.

There was a heavy clank of metal from the vertically sliding breech-block as Shadwell reloaded, and a mist of cordite smoke swirled inside the hull; most of the fumes were exhausted outside the tank, but some always drifted back. Shadwell shouted: 'Loaded.' He made certain he was well clear of the gun before he did so. Gunners could get a shot off fast if they had a target and to be caught-out standing behind the gun was a sure way to die as the recoil hurled it backwards. It was only one of several ways a loader could come to grief; more commonly they managed to get themselves caught in the traverse, getting a leg or foot trapped behind the charge bins as the gunner or commander swung the turret.

'Shit!' Inkester swore, not at Shadwell but because the burst of the Chieftain's 120mm shell was ahead and to the right of the Soviet T-72. As he brought the sight onto it again, he suddenly realized with horror that he was staring right down the black muzzle of the T-72's gun. Through his sight's magnification the T-72 seemed little more than two hundred meters away. There was a burst of flame from the barrel of its 125mm, and Inkester instinctively ducked instead of firing.

'Inkester! What the hell?' shouted Davis. There was an explosion on the slope forty meters to the rear of the Chieftain. Davis didn't see it, but he felt the ground shake and the violent thud of the pressure wave against Bravo Two's hull. The shell must have passed within centimeters of his turret...his head. He felt sick.

Inkester's sight picked up the T-72 again, and again the Chieftain's gun roared. This time vision was better as Bravo Two settled back on her suspension. The T-72 had begun to jink once the driver had realized he was under fire.

Davis seemed to wait forever, until he decided Inkester must have missed again or the shell had failed to explode. Then he saw a brief shower of sparks scatter from the foredeck of the T-72's hull to the left of the driver's hatch, and almost at the same time it exploded outwards like a movie scene in slow motion. He saw the two hatches on the turret fly upwards, followed by the turret itself and the driver's and engine hatches. Soundlessly, to Davis, the hull tore apart, belching a swirling orb of flame. He heard

62

Inkester's awed voice: 'My God!'

Davis stared through the lens. '50 traverse right...one o'clock. Infantry combat vehicle...a BMP. Pick it up, Inky.' He felt the turret swing and dropped his eyes back to the sight. 'Good...good.' Inkester was silent, concentrating now, just as he would be at Lulworth or Suffield. The range was less than for the T-72 — thirteen hundred meters.

The Chieftain lurched. This time Inkester had fired quickly, but more calmly. The shell struck the BMP just under the thick sloping armour of its bow, and exploded on impact. The vehicle stopped as though it had run into an impenetrable wall. A second later Davis saw the eight infantrymen it had contained, and two of its crew who were apparently unwounded, leap from the vehicle and dive for the shelter of a nearby shell crater. He could see them clearly. Instinctively, he found them in the sight of the 7.62mm machine gun. The Chieftain's turret was moving again as Inkester sought another target. Davis corrected his aim, adjusting the movement of his cupola to oppose that of the turret. He pressed the firing button and heard the satisfying response from the gun; the bullets tore the lip from the crater in a burst of dust and earth. It was difficult to keep the fire accurate. One of the Soviet infantrymen scrambled from the shell hole and ran to Davis's right. He didn't bother to try to follow the man. The bodies he could now see in the crater were motionless.

Inkester had the main sight on another tank, a T-80 which had appeared at the edge of the smoke. Davis anticipated the explosion of the gun, but before Inkester could fire the tank swerved and began belching flame through ventilators and hatches.

'Blowpipe missile,' shouted Davis. He could see movement on the lower ground to his left. 'Some of our infantry. Why the hell don't they keep us informed?' There were shell bursts in the trees near the infantry position, and the smoke laid by the enemy artillery was much closer. The noise of the battle had become as great as that of the initial artillery barrage. Davis could hear the crump of mortar shells and feel the ground shivering beneath the Chieftain. It was like standing in a railway tunnel as a ten-coach inter-city roared by.

He was about to try to help the infantry with prophylactic fire along the hedges beyond their position, when Inkester shouted again: 'Traversing right...three o'clock.' Davis saw movement at the edge of the barrage. Dark hulls in the smoke...the sudden flashes of white flame. Inkester began bringing the turret around.

The bank of earth three meters ahead of Bravo Two was hurled aside. The concussion knocked Davis backwards, his head smashing against the equipment behind him. He heard a second explosion and was thrust forward out of his seat. Someone was screaming...the interior of the Chieftain was pitch-black, the atmosphere thick with the stench of fuel and swirling dust. 'We're going to brew up,' thought Davis. 'Any second now we'll go.' Bravo Two was quivering as though it were alive. He tried to struggle upright, but could find no purchase for his feet. Shadwell was yelling beside him. There was a burst of light above, then a terrifying crash. The Chieftain's hull echoed...there was excruciating pain in Davis's ears. Bravo Two rocked as though it were resting on a water-bed, then something seemed to hammer down on the turret with terrible force, twisting the tank sideways, forcing it deep into the earth as though struck by a gigantic fist ....

Magpie, the stay-behind-unit of the Royal Tank Regiment, had not suffered from the intense Soviet barrage that preceded their armoured assault. Few of the missiles and shells had landed in the strip of ground that included their underground bunkers, though they had felt the thump of explosions transmitted through the heavy clay to the concrete chambers in which they and their light Scimitar tanks were sealed. The position was shell and bomb proof, and even the heavily camouflaged entrance which was its weakest point was protected by an overhanging shelf of concrete looking, with its natural weathering and subtle design, like nothing more than an outcrop of limestone.

There was a sense of isolation making the men even more nervous. They were now totally cut off from the NATO armies; a small island, encompassed by an ocean. The war had swept past them, friends must have already died, but as yet they had seen none of the action.

Captain Mick Fellows hoped he had transmitted none of his own doubts to their minds. It was bad enough that he himself should be having misgivings about the entire project. And waiting through the long hours until darkness came again, and with it his final instructions from HQ, was making him even edgier.

What the hell was he doing here anyway? Volunteer? They'd said that; made him feel proud about it too, for a while. They had used an insidious form of pressure: 'Need the best man, Mick...someone reliable, cool-headed...any ideas? Important task. It'll do your career a bit of good!'

'Captain Fellows, sir.' It was Lieutenant Sandy Roxforth, one of his Scimitar commanders, at the observation platform. 'There's some movement outside.'

There were two periscopes built into the roof of the bunker, their view covering a full three hundred and sixty degrees around the position. Roxforth had been using the one which covered the area towards the north-east in the direction of the East German border town of Oebisfelde a few kilometers away. Beyond the first chequerboard of fields was the 248 highway following the line of the border. Fellows lowered his head to the periscope and adjusted the focus to suit his eyes. The field of vision was blurred at the edges where grass and small shrubs close to the position interfered with the clarity of the lenses. A pall of smoke drifted in the easterly wind, from the direction of the woods beyond Bahrdorf. The village itself must have come under heavy shelling. Even at this distance, its familiar outline had

65

changed. The bell tower of the church was missing, and many of the buildings looked ragged. The devastated farmland no longer had the prosperous and orderly appearance of the previous day, the surface of the fields heavily scarred by shell, bomb and missile craters, the formerly neat boundaries destroyed and tangled. A grain silo some six hundred meters from the bunker was blazing, and through the periscope's magnifying lenses Fellows could distinguish the carcasses of a herd of Fresian dairy cows nearby.

Even as he examined the changed landscape there was a flurry of explosions around the village. It was like watching the silent movie of another war. The barrage intensified as though some artillery observer had called for an Uncle Target and all the guns of the division were joining in. Perhaps a Russian commander had been foolish enough to allow his armour to be drawn into the collection of buildings.

Much closer and to his right where he traversed the periscope, he could distinguish the movement of enemy vehicles and he was attempting to identify them when the ground they were crossing disingegrated in one single eruption of fire and smoke. The giant explosion separated into individual shell-bursts. It seemed that nothing could survive in the holocaust that Fellows recognized as a defensive barrage from NATO aritllery positions to the west, but the dark armoured vehicles were pressing forward out of the smoke, joined by others on their left flank. Their charge was no longer ordered, the shelling had destroyed any semblance of formation. They were T-72s and T-64s, the latter easily distinguishable by the remote-controlled 12.7mm AAMG sited above the main gun. Close behind the battle tanks were a number of BMPs, tracked infantry carriers.

The artillery were now ranging on individual targets. He saw one tank swerve to avoid a deep crater, only to collide with another which had moved too close. He could almost

66

feel the grinding of metal against metal, but the vehicles separated with a barely noticeable lowering of their speed.

They must have crossed the minefields south of Oebisfelde, and Fellows wondered about the casualties this must have cost them. The mines had been laid densely, and the invaders would have been under artillery attack as well. The tanks he was watching now, and the infantry combat vehicles, were the survivors.

'You want a closer look, sir?' It was Hinton, commander of the platoon of 22nd SAS. A lieutenant, there were no badges of rank on his smock. 'Use the other 'scope.'

Fellows walked with him in silence to the eastern end of the bunker, stepping through the groups of camouflage-streaked men who sat or lay on the concrete floor, many asleep. Hinton nodded towards the second periscope. Fellows put his eyes to the binocular lenses. He pulled his head back in surprise, then stared out again. Not fifteen meters away was the stationary hull of a 122mm self-propelled gun; on the slab side of its turret was a white circle, encompassing a red star.

He looked at Hinton and raised his eyebrows.

'We counted eleven of them,' said Hinton. 'They've positioned themselves in a line running towards the south-east.'

There were normally only eighteen SPGs to a Soviet tank division, thought Fellows. As they would have had to cross the minefields while under artillery fire, the eleven Hinton had seen were probably the only ones to have made it. And they were on the left flank of what appeared to be a Soviet division's main thrust. 'Are they all the same type?'

'I don't think so. There were others, with a flatter profile and a grill on the hull just forward of the turret.'

'M-1976s. Self-propelled howitzers. There's a lot of West German armour facing Oebisfelde, so these SPGs must be part of an encircling movement. The Soviet recce units have probably passed us further to the south.' It was tempting to use the VHF and get the information back to HQ; one

67

quick air strike would remove the danger to the defending armour, who were probably already within the closing jaws of a pair of giant pincers. But they had been ordered to maintain complete radio silence; the men and vehicles encapsuled within the bunker already had their job to do. Regardless of anything which might happen out in the battlefields, they were to sit tight until contacted by HQ, on the evening of the first day of battle.

Hinton seemed to read his thoughts. 'If they're still here tonight, sir, we can do something about them. My lads will enjoy a bit of excitement close to home.'

Fellows raised his eyebrows, but remained silent. Hinton's cockiness was what he expected from the SAS. He didn't like them. They'd caught the press and public imagination, and came in for a lot of publicity which they claimed they didn't want. In Fellows' opinion, there were plenty of units in the army as capable, a fact which had been proved in Ireland.

Many times, Lt Colonel James Studley had been in his regiment's mess, and heard descriptions of Second World War tank battles from officers who were retired or nearing the end of their service. He had listened, interested in the early part of his career when their memories had been fresher and their stories new to his ears, and then politely but with increasing boredom over the next few years. With time and alcohol he had heard the same stories repeated again and again until eventually he was able to switch off part of his mind yet still make the appropriate noises of amazement, horror or amusement, at the correct intervals. He had heard some of the troopers refer to old sweats as 'when we's', from their habit of beginning a story with: 'When we were at...' or 'when we were in...' One day, somebody would probably give him the same label; now he hoped so, it would be proof he had survived.

He had never before seen a landscape such as he viewed

from the command post. Primeval was the word he found to describe it best – if it could be described at all! A panorama incapable of sustaining human life, violent, ragged, volcanic, it contained no beauty, no peacefulness. Layered by heavy nauseous fumes, it erupted fire, spewed rock, earth and steel, convulsed and shuddered in a cacophony of deafening sound.

At first he had been able to distinguish the battle group's own guns, the throaty roar of the Chieftain's 120mms, the M109s. They had soon become lost amidst the howls and shrieks of the rockets, the clamorous thunder of artillery, the whines, moans and demonic screams of a hundred kinds of projectiles and their explosions.

The barn which concealed the command Sultans had been hit twice. First unintentionally, by a cannon shell fired by one of the many aircraft over the battlefront, and in the second instance by a heavy mortar bomb, which Studley believed might have been a Soviet M-160. The trajectory of the bomb, one of several to have landed in the area, had been checked-out on the three-dimensional surveillance radar and revealed the firing position to be located six kilometers to the east. The fire-point had been neutralized by artillery, but that was no comfort to the two infantrymen of the command platoon who had been killed.

Colonel Studley was feeling pleased with his command staff; everything seemed to be operating smoothly and efficiently. Young Douglas Whitley, the signals officer, had set a good example to the men when the mortar bomb had exploded, remaining cool and checking the equipment for possible damage even before the dust had settled. Philip Donelly, the adjutant, had almost ignored the incident, and continued his plotting of the group's movements on the situation map with a Chinograph.

'By the way, the French are in.' One of the Divisional HQ staff had told Studley on the divisional network a few minutes previously. The radio communication had gone through the security scramblers.

'Thank God! When?'

'One minute after it all started. They mobilized reserves two days ago and are moving up their armour behind the Americans. It'll ease things.'

'One hell of a lot,' agreed Studley.

'What's your situation?'

'We're holding at Mooonraker, but we'll retire shortly. There's a lot of Red armour in this sector.'

'There are four Soviet divisions between Helmstedt and Wittingen. The Russian 16th Division's main thrust appears to be towards Braunschweig. We believe this is their present Red. Helmstedt has been overrun by the Soviet 9th Division, and we think they will try to link-up with the 16th Division as they progress. We have reports of a Soviet recce battalion at Boitzenhagen, and a considerable drop of air assault troops at Wahrenholz. We also have a report of the use of chemical weapons on the front south of Lübeck...it's confused and unconfirmed. Do as well for you to bear it in mind.'

'Thank you.'

The adjutant had been listening to the conversation on one of the spare headsets. 'Perhaps we should move back behind the river Ise, sir.'

'Too early yet. If we pull back so far we'll make life too easy for them.'

'We won't be able to hold them much longer, sir, nine more of the tanks are out of action. That leaves us with thirty-two, plus your own command Chieftain. There have been a lot of casualties amongst the infantry and the forward positions have just reported contact with Soviet patrols.'

Studley grimaced then said: 'I'm going to look around. Let me know immediately if anything unexpected develops. We'll move as soon as I get back.' He wondered if it was conscience drawing him out of the command post; the thought of his men fighting for their lives on the lower slopes of the moor while he remained in a relatively safe position.

Perhaps it would help their morale if they saw him alongside them for a while. Guiltily, he knew he was just seeking an excuse. He wanted to take part in some of the action, himself.

He walked outside. There was the sound of rifle and machine gun fire towards the east, and the sharp crack of hand-grenades. It was distorted by the heavier gunfire, but with its inference of close combat sounded more urgent and deadly.

An NBC-suited figure snapped to attention beside the Chieftain. 'Sergeant Pudsey, are all the crew ready?' Studley asked him.

'Yes, sir. They're as twitchy as greyhounds in their traps. Want to be with their mates.' Sergeant Pudsey was standing parade-ground straight. He acted as the colonel's loader, and had the reputation of being one of the fastest in the regiment.

'Let's go then, Sergeant.' Studley began climbing into the tank.

'Yes, sir.' There was pleasure in Pudsey's voice at the command. He swung himself easily up on to the front of the hull and yelled at the driver's hatch, 'Drum her up, Horsefield.'

Studley waited until Pudsey had climbed inside and settled himself into his seat, and then followed. 'We'll give the infantry a hand, eh Sergeant,' he shouted as Horsefield the driver stirred the Chieftain's twelve-cylinder engine to life.

He slipped the headset over his beret, ignoring the helmet strapped to one of the seat supports. The helmet was too uncomfortable to be worn for long, and it was bad enough fighting in an NBC-suit. He switched on the tank's intercom. 'Load HE, Sergeant...Horsefield, take it easy when we get near the infantry positions. They know we're coming down but it will pay to be cautious.' He didn't want some trigger-happy soldier to mistake the Chieftain for a T-80 and loose off a Milan missile in the heat of the moment.

71

'We'll use the long gulley at two o'clock. The infantry are about two thousand meters down the hill, and I don't want to charge straight over their positions.' He had checked the situation map before leaving the command post; Charlie Squadron and the infantry were close together. He would visit both and then work his way back around the lower side of the hill.

They had driven several hundred meters when he saw one of the battle group's APCs overturned at the side of the gulley, with several corpses amongst the wreckage. It's loss had been reported and Studley knew of the casualties, but it was still a gut shock to see the twisted metal and torn bodies that turned an impersonal radio message into brutal reality. He felt the hair on his neck bristle as though a chill breeze had caught him.

Horsefield avoided the debris of the APC and brought the Chieftain into the open ground of a fire-break. Two more APCs rested in the shelter of the bordering trees, their crews kneeling or squatting beside them, waiting until the infantry needed them again. There were craters in the narrow clearing, still hazed with smoke.

Studley halted the tank and signalled over a drawn-looking lance corporal who had been squatting beside the front of one of the APCs, his Sterling Mk4 tucked ready beneath his arm. The man smartened himself and saluted, recognizing the colonel.

'Much trouble, Corporal?'

'Mortars, sir. They got the APC on the hill, and we lost one of our own men, sir. We haven't seen a bloody Russian yet, sir.'

'I don't doubt you'll see them soon enough.' Studley was having to shout to make himself heard above the sound of the fighting lower in the wood. The heavier gunfire was now to the left, but there were mortar and grenade explosions no more than four hundred meters away.

'Are we holding them, sir?'

'Leading them, Corporal. Leading them.' Studley made

72

himself sound cheerful. 'That's the way we're playing this game.'

There was no reaction on the lance corporal's face to Studley's words. He doesn't believe mé, Studley thought to himself. They had code-named the battle plan 'Hamlin' after the town where a mythical piper had once led away a plague of rats to the sound of his flute. Hold and withdraw, hold and withdraw; forcing the enemy to use maximum effort at all times, and turning the head of the thrust cunningly so that the enemy was drawn along a route already decided by the NATO forces. The final traps were the killing zones, minefields covered by all the fire-power the NATO ground and air forces could muster. He ordered the Chieftain on, then watched for a moment as the lance corporal saluted briefly and turned to hurry back to the cover of the APC.

The Chieftain had entered the fire-zone, the shredded trees, the mist of battle, the sounds of death. Studley saw his first Soviet infantrymen two hundred meters ahead; scurrying, half-crouched, to the cover of a low wall. He decided they must be part of an artillery observation team, known to operate well up with the assault troops. He gave their position to Riley, the gunner, and then watched with satisfaction as the HE shell destroyed a five meter section of the wall and tumbled bodies out into the open.

Riley said quickly, 'Traversing right one o'clock, sir.' He swung the turret and brought the Chieftain's gun to bear on a personnel carrier that was one of several thundering diagonally across a broad flat field that had contained root crops less than two weeks previously.

Studley switched the radio to the group net. 'Hullo Charlie this is Sunray Rover One.' He heard Captain Valda Willis, Charlie Squadron's leader, acknowledge. 'Charlie Nine, this is Sunray Rover One, expect Wolves twenty degrees right your position. BMPs, over.'

'Roger Sunray Rover One, we see them. We are engaging, over.'

'Roger Charlie Nine, out.' Damn, thought Studley. He

shouldn't have interfered. Obviously Charlie Squadron hadn't been sitting there with their eyes closed; they would be all alert, keyed-up, waiting for targets. Now, they would probably think he had been keeping an eye on them, looking for an opportunity to criticize their performance.

'Sir...' Corporal Riley's voice drew his attention. The gunner was thinking that if he didn't get a shot in quickly, then the BMPs would be annihilated within the next few moments by the squadron's guns.

To the gunner's relief, Studley said: 'Take it out, Riley.'

The Chieftain kicked, and Studley watched the front of the leading BMP disintegrate, half of one of its tracks scything eight meters into the air. The vehicle burst into flames, then blew to pieces as the ammunition of its 73mm gun exploded. The Soviet attack, he thought, was a foolish waste of manpower and vehicles; to use unsupported mechanized infantry against deployed armour was suicidal.

Riley was seeking another target, but already a further three of the BMPs had been hit. A fourth the corporal was ranging on was demolished before he could fire.

Some of the infantrymen had survived the destruction of the vehicles, but the battle group's machine guns and rifles concealed in the woods were picking them off.

Studley was moving to join Bravo Squadron when there was uncharacteristic shouting on the group net by the Command RTO. It was incomprehensible gibberish. Studley heard the man yell wildly and the sounds of violent static before the net went dead. He tried to regain contact without success. There were a number of possibilities to account for the failure, but he knew simple breakdown could be discounted. It was more likely the command post was under fire. He called Bravo Squadron who were positioned closest to the command post, and ordered them back to the higher ground. They reported they were already under severe attack from Soviet self-propelled guns out of range of their own 120mms, and sounded pleased to be moved from the area.

Six hundred meters to the rear of the regiment's forward

battle positions, Studley's Chieftain was attacked. It was unexpected, only a little way from the clearing where the infantry APCs had been stationed. Fortunately, Studley had the tank's hatches closed-down, but he didn't see the Soviet infantryman hurl his grenade which bounced off the deck of the tank and exploded close to the right track. The grenade was the light RGD-5 whose frag liner failed to penetrate the Chieftain's armour. Studley's driver swerved the tank instinctively. As he did so there was a heavy concussion to the rear of the vehicle and more metal sprayed the hull.

The woods appeared to be alive with green-clad infantrymen and there was little room for the Chieftain to manoeuvre. The driver hesitated as another grenade exploded against the thick armour below the main gun. Studley shouted: 'Keep going...and fast.' He felt the Chieftain accelerate. Trees snapped beneath its weight as it crashed forward through the undergrowth. A group of men scattered thirty meters away and Studley followed them with a long burst of fire from the machine gun. He saw an infantryman run diagonally towards him from the left, the man's path curving through a patch of open ground as he ran to meet the Chieftain. His arm was already raised, and Studley caught a glimpse of a long-handled anti-tank grenade trailing its drogue towards the tank as the man threw himself flat. The grenade only fell short by a meter, exploding in the soft earth as the Chieftain reached the clearing where the APCs had been stationed; all that remained were their wrecked and smoking hulks, the crews dead, nearby.

'Don't stop...' There was no need for Studley's order, Horsefield was already pushing the Chieftain towards its maximum speed. It lurched and bounced across the open ground, crashing through a dense copse of young trees as the ground dipped towards the command position.

'Hullo Bravo Nine, this is Sunray Rover One...' Studley was being thrown around in his seat by the violent movement.

'Hullo Sunray Rover One this is Bravo Nine.'

'Where are you?'

'Four hundred meters south of Primrose...and still under attack, over.'

'Infantry?' questioned Studley.

'Armour. Two T-64s...wrong, three T-64s in position near derelict barn.'

'Barn?'

'It's on fire. There seem to be vehicles burning, too. The T-64s are downwind, in smoke.'

God, so that was why the RTO had sounded hysterical. The command post had been attacked, and by the sound of it, destroyed. Studley's immediate emotion was anger. 'Disengage, Bravo Nine. Russian infantry in woods to your left. Get through them. Go to Firefly. Verify.' There was no response. 'Hullo Bravo Nine...Hullo Bravo Nine...verify, over.' Studley was dismayed to find he was directing his anger at his own men, and felt ashamed. He spoke again, more calmly. 'Hullo Bravo Nine...verify please, over...'

There was a lengthy pause, then a voice. 'Shit!' Another short break and then he recognized the voice of one of his junior lieutenants. 'Hullo Sunray, this is Colin...damn sorry, sir. We've lost Nine...lost contact...a lot of Soviet armour...Sunray. Go to Firefly, wilco...' There was a pause. 'It's getting warm here, Sunray...sorry, sir, over.'

'Roger Bravo...out.' The lieutenant was too polite...terrible radio technique thought Studley. Still young for leadership of a squadron, he had sounded overwhelmed, temporarily confused. Keep your damned head, lad, Studley willed. There was no time for him to contemplate the destruction of the command post and the loss of the staff.

He called through to the Headquarters command Sultan. 'Hullo Ops, this is Sunray Rover One, have you been eavesdropping? Over.'

'Hullo Sunray Rover, this is Ops. Yes, we understand the situation.'

'Give me Amphora.' This was Max Fairly's code name. It was a small personal joke, a reference to the 2nd IC's slightly pear-shaped figure.

'Hullo Sunray Rover One. Reference Amphora; regret no can do. Amphora is MBK.'

Missing believed killed? Max? Perhaps he had misheard the Operations Officer. 'Say again. Over.'

'Hullo Sunray Rover One. Reference Amphora; regret Amphora is MBK. We have had a report on the incident from Kilo Nine.'

'Ops, take over. Send all to Firefly. I'll join you soonest.' He switched to the intercom. 'Horsefield...move us out.' He tried the group net a few moments later, but the Soviet jamming had taken over the wavelengths. It was more efficient than had been estimated, and was making communication difficult...at the moment impossible as the high-pitched whine cut deep into his head. He switched it off. Poor old Max...Max! Damn them! And how complete was the encirclement of the battle group? Total? If so, could the circle be broken? Studley realized he should have pulled back when his adjutant had suggested it earlier. Studley had erred in his decision that the group should hold its position longer. Everything had looked fine...no reason to suppose a breakthrough would happen so quickly. God, he had cocked it up, his first battle! He had made a mistake; a costly one.

The thought of the adjutant drew Studley's mind back to the overrun command vehicle. 'Horsefield...go right...more right...I want a look at the command APC's. And keep your eyes peeled...'

Corporal Riley interrupted him: 'Sir...traversing three o'clock.' Broadside on, not thirty meters away, was the green hull of a Soviet fire-support tank, the insignia of its parachute battalion clearly showing on its skirt. At point-blank range, it was impossible for Riley to rotate the turret fast enough to counter the forward movement of the tank. 'Halt the bloody tank, Horse,' Riley yelled fiercely. Horsefield dug both his feet hard on the brake pedal.

The turret stopped traversing. The fire-support tank was

not more than sixty meters away, standing amongst the trees. Studley could see men moving near its rocket launcher, silhouetted against the skyline. It seemed a lifetime before Riley fired and the Chieftain echoed the instantaneous explosion of its shell against the hull of the Russian vehicle. Studley saw one body arc high into the air before the smoke obscured the wrecked tank.

Horsefield had no intention of remaining stationary longer than necessary, and began moving the Chieftain forward at a brisk pace. The smoke cloud from the wrecked vehicle was drifting across their path, a useful screen. Visibility was now less than forty meters; the smoke thickening. Studley could feel heavy concussions but couldn't hear the sounds of the explosions which accompanied them. The ground ahead was clearer, and he thought they must have reached the outskirts of the wood, only a hundred meters from the command position. A vehicle was burning, spurting red flames in the smoke. There were bodies hunched around it; he couldn't identify them, but thought the helmets were Russian. There was another wrecked vehicle, this time a British APC, and beyond it a burned-out Chieftain, its hull ripped open and its turret and gun missing. The ground was churned and cratered...more bodies. Horsefield swerved, found it impossible to avoid the corpses, and drove over them...he recognized their combat smocks as NATO-issue and hoped there were no wounded amongst the motionless figures he was crushing beneath the tracks.

There were dark shapes in the smoke not twenty meters away, closer, men moving. Studley identified a T-72, the nearer of the vehicles. 'Reverse, Horsefield.' The figures scattered as the Chieftain loomed out of the smoke behind them. The turret of the T-72 began moving. Horsefield crashed the gearbox into reverse so fiercely the tracks skidded. For a few moments the fifty-two tons of the Chieftain kept her slithering forward, then the tracks gripped. The muzzle of the Chieftain's 122mm gun was no more than four meters from the rear of the T-72 when Riley fired. The close proximity of the detonation twisted the Chieftain sideways and a billowing spray of burning fuel swept over its hull. Horsefield was trying to regain control when a second explosion tilted the Chieftain on to her side. It dropped back with a bone-jarring crash then settled. Horsefield began accelerating again. He couldn't see where they were going, and was hoping the colonel was watching to the rear. He locked the right track and hammered the Chieftain into forward gear, to swing her round. The Soviet RPG-7V anti-tank rocket, fired by an infantryman forty meters away, hit the Chieftain on the flat slab of armour directly beneath Horsefield's feet. The hollow-charge high explosive round punched its way through the metal as it exploded, killing Horsefield instantly, wrecking the driving compartment, and spraying the interior with fine shrapnel; a heavy scab of metal ricochetted from the floor and buried itself in Sergeant Pudsey's chest as a searing white flame leapt around the breech of the gun, the charge bins and the stacked ammunition. Studley's head felt as though it had burst. He could smell explosive, burning fuel. The air was unbreathable. He was choking.

He attempted to force open the turret, the hatch lever was jammed, but gave way slowly. Everything was confused, unreal. He was unable to focus his eyes, and when he tried to shout to the crew his lungs contained no air; his chest muscles and diaphragm were cramping in painful spasms. He grabbed at the edge of the turret and fell forward, sliding down the hull and landing on his stomach beside the track. He was immediately sick. He knew the Chieftain's ammunition might explode and tried to drag himself further away, flopping like a seal across the ground as his arms gave way beneath his weight. It was all night-marish...swimming in fine dry sand...the sour taste of bile in his mouth...throbbing pain...

He lay still.

He was thrown on to his back with a jerk that almost

dislocated his neck. The brightness of the sky was blinding. There was a man's face above him; mist slightly clearing. He felt his NBC clothing pulled apart, roughly...hands searching his coverall pockets. The helmet? American? Russian! Cut high above the man's ears, grotesquely sinister. He was dragged on his back, his head jolting against the earth before he was hauled into a sitting position against a tree. He recognized an AKM rifle aimed at his chest, then vomited again. More hands searched him. He tried to say: 'Let me die in peace, in my own time,' but the only sounds he could make were deep rasping groans between his retchings. He collapsed on to his side.

They let him lie for a few more minutes, until the surging waves of nausea had passed, then pulled him back against the tree. He faced the smoking wreckage of the Chieftain, fifty meters away. Beyond it, a mass of twisted metal was all that remained of the Soviet T-72.

His breathing was easier now, and the throbbing in his head had lessened. He felt mentally numb, each individual thought leaden. One of the men who had been supporting him was kneeling beside him winding an olive-green field dressing around the lower part of his left leg. I'm wounded...wounded and they're dressing it...that means I'm alive...and they aren't going to kill me...not yet anyway...maybe they'll kill me later...I'm a prisoner...God, I'm a prisoner.

There was no sign of any others of the crew. He stared at the wreckage...how had he escaped? The others were still inside...dead! His stomach heaved again, but he managed to hold it.

He turned his head and spat his mouth clean. There was the iron taste of blood at the back of his throat. One of the soldiers shook a cigarette from a packet, lit it, and pushed it gently between Studley's lips. He had seldom used tobacco, but rested his head back against the trunk of the tree and drew in the pungent oriental smoke.

What now, he wondered? Dear God, what now?

'Charlie Bravo Two, this is Nine...' The voice was persistent in Morgan Davis's ears – Lieutenant Sidworth acting as mother hen to his diminishing brood. 'Charlie Bravo Two, this is Nine, over.'

'Bravo Nine, this is Charlie Bravo Two, over.' Davis's voice was shaky. The screaming to his left was continuous, and the Chieftain's engine was revving so high the whole tank was vibrating.

'What the hell's happened Charlie Bravo Two? I've been trying to contact you for the past four minutes, over.'

'I think we've been hit.'

'What's the damage?'

'I don't know yet, Nine...'

'Then damn well find out. We're pulling back to Firefly. Make it quick...understand? Out.'

Davis shouted down into the fighting compartment but the sound of his voice was lost in the noise. He switched to the Tannoy. 'Hewett...what's going on down there?'

'Fuckin' linkage is jammed.' DeeJay's voice warbled, competing against the roaring motor.

'Get it bloody well unjammed. Inkester!' The Chieftain was full of swirling dust. Davis reached down and found the gunner's shoulder. 'Inkester?' The shoulder moved. 'Are you okay?' Inkester nodded, his head just visible in the dim light. The roar of the engine dropped suddenly and its sound reduced to a steady throb.

'It's clear, Sarge...it might jam again, but it feels okay.' The engine sound increased again and died as DeeJay tried the pedal.

'Shadwell? What the hell's the matter?' The screaming had diminished as the sound of the engine had lessened; almost as though Shadwell, hunched on his loader's seat, had suddenly become aware of the shriek of his own voice. Morgan Davis leant over and shook him. 'Shadwell...' The man moved and Davis could see his face, blood-spattered. 'Oh, Christ!' He twisted himself out of his seat and wriggled into the fighting compartment. 'Where are you hurt, lad?'

Shadwell held up his left hand, he was gripping it tightly at the wrist. Davis reached out as Shadwell groaned again. Three of his fingers were missing. 'Breech, Sarge. Fucking breech got me.'

The dust was settling, slowly. Blood was dripping from Shadwell's hand. Davis wrenched open the medical box and grabbed a dressing. 'Inkester, get across here. Fix Shad while I try to get us out of here...'

'There's a live shell on the floor, Sarge...' Shadwell's voice was shaky. 'By my left foot.'

Davis groped downwards and felt the smooth cold shape of the projectile. He lifted it carefully, slightly off-balance as he reached behind the breech. He knew it was a miracle it hadn't exploded, and the thought dried the saliva in his mouth. He would have liked to dump it outside, but it was quicker to get it into the gun. He moved to slide it into place in the breech, then hesitated. Shadwell's fingers hung on the mechanism, one with a heavy silver ring still in place below a misshapen joint. Davis clenched his teeth, balanced the shell with one hand against the breech, and snatched at the fingers. They felt like knobbly sausages. He stuffed them into the pocket of his suit and then slid the shell into place. 'Where's the charge?'

'Still in the bin.'

Davis completed the loading of the gun, prayed that the barrel was still clear, and worked his way back to his seat. Inkester squirmed past him. The only undamaged vision blocks of the episcope were obscured by something resting against them on the outside of the turret, and Davis found it impossible to open the hatch. It seemed as if the Chieftain might be buried. 'Hewett, try to get us out.' The Chieftain's engine surged and the vehicle swayed. Davis could hear the links of the track squealing. 'Try rocking us...and gently, lad, there's something lying on us...trees maybe.' He tuned to the troop network. 'Charlie Bravo Nine this is Charlie Bravo Two, over.'

'Charlie Bravo Two, this is Nine. Over.'

82

'Loader's wounded. We're bogged down...can't see what's holding us...I don't know the full extent of damage. Over.'

'We're coming to you Charlie Bravo Two...we'll be with you in about three minutes. Keep trying to free yourself, but don't make matters worse.'

'Thank you, Nine. Out.' God Almighty, thought Davis, what a mess! The enemy was only a couple of hundred meters away, the loader was out of action and the Chieftain stuck. It wasn't how he had visualized war. It was chaotic, disorganized and dirty...bloody dangerous.

'Eric's okay.' It was Inkester nudging at his legs.

'Yes, I'm okay, Sarge.' Shadwell's voice was apologetic. 'I fucking messed things up, didn't I?' He paused. 'I'm sorry I yelled.'

'I didn't hear you,' lied Davis. Bravo Two was heaving as DeeJay tried to reverse, her engine throbbing, the hull picking up the resonance of the exhaust, making it sound as though she was moaning in frustration.

'Charlie Bravo Two, Nine here...we see you...you're wedged against a heap of rock and half-buried under a big oak. It looks as though the rock slid from the hill behind you. You'll have to go forward over the ridge. I think we can nudge the tree clear of your hull. Bravo Four will give cover as you move. Make it quick. There are seven T-80s moving this way across the lower fields.'

'Wilco Nine.' Davis used the Tannoy again. 'Hewett, keep going forward, get a move on, lad. Inkester check the gun.'

'Charlie Bravo Two this is Nine...traverse your turret right a full hundred and eighty degrees. Try to go forward at the same time...'

Bravo Two lifted herself slowly over the low ridge like a gross elephant pushing itself from a mud wallow. The lens in front of Davis's eyes partially cleared and there was more light in the fighting compartment.

'Charlie Bravo Two...can you see us now?'

'Yes, Nine.' The olive hull of Charlie Bravo Four was thirty meters to Davis's left; to the rear was Sidworth's Chieftain. 'Charlie Bravo Four this is Nine...cover us all...Bravo Two, move left to the woods behind the ridge...we'll be behind you. Get into a fire position about six hundred meters west. Bravo Four, when we get there you leapfrog us.' Sidworth was shouting his orders, his words clipped by anxiety, but remembering the need in tank movement always to keep one foot on the ground.'

Davis heard Charlie Bravo Four acknowledge as he ordered Hewett to swing the Chieftain along the slope. There was still a lot of smoke on the plain and shell explosions in a small copse below and to the Chieftain's right. A pair of Lynx helicopters were taking turns to dodge above the low cover, firing their missiles at targets which the smoke concealed from Davis. He couldn't see the other tanks of Charlie Squadron. They had to be somewhere, it was inconceivable they should all have been knocked out. Perhaps they had already retired beyond the hill on to the lower slopes of the moor.

'Charlie Bravo Two this is Nine...enemy infantry right...two o'clock.'

'Roger, Nine.' Davis saw the minute figures three hundred meters away. Their carrier was somewhere, hidden by the smoke. He brought round his cupola and pressed the firing button of the machine gun. Nothing happened. He tried again; the weapon was dead. He looked towards Sidworth's tank, the lieutenant was using his GPMG, the muzzle flickering orange flame. Davis felt frustrated; the infantry had scattered to cover and he could no longer see them.

'Charlie Bravo Two...get yourself into position and wait...Charlie Bravo Four, this is Nine...come and join us now, over.'

'Charlie Bravo Four, wilco Nine.'

Sergeant Davis didn't see the single Polish SU20 which swept down towards the troop, its pilot making a second circuit of the combat zone where he had been picking off the Lynx helicopters who were slowing the advance of the right flank of the Soviet division's armour. The Sukhoi was the only surviving aircraft of a squadron which had been brought down from Warsaw twenty-four hours before. The pilot had been reluctant to operate against the NATO forces, until he witnessed the loss of his friends in the first minutes of battle.

He had two Kerry missiles left in his pylons. As he dived from the north-west, the battlefront was a broad band of smoke across the plains. He could see the explosions of shells and rockets, and the spearhead of the Russian attack in the direction of the distant town of Braunschweig that was just visible on his horizon. On his first circuit his 30mm cannon shells had destroyed one of the Lynx helicopters; it had exploded violently and he had only just missed the disintegrating wreckage as it fell. He had seen the movement of the NATO tanks against the hill, and the chance of a shot at a new type of target was attractive. He cut his speed to sub-sonic and narrowed his turn, keeping the hill in his view as he did so. At first as he returned he could not see the Chieftains, then he spotted two close together and a third some distance to the east, moving through the scrub at the edge of the woods. He had little time for decision, and chose the tank on the left of the pair, cutting his speed further and holding the aircraft level. The target grew in his sights.

Several smoke shells had exploded on the lower ground ahead of Sergeant Davis's tank, the dense dark smoke swirling across the fields. Somewhere inside would be the Soviet armour in their familiar patterns of eight tanks, supported by the infantry carriers. Just ahead of the screen, in the lower woods, the artillery barrage had increased again.

'Charlie Bravo Four passing you now Nine...sixty meters to your rear. We'll go ahead another hundred meters and cover you.'

'Roger Charlie Bravo Four...you still with us Charlie

Bravo Two? Give Charlie Bravo Four a minute and...' In Lieutenant Sidworth's mid-sentence his Chieftain blew to fragments. Davis had been able to see it from the corner of his eye as he watched down the slope. One moment it was there, and the next the concussion of the explosion rocked Charlie Bravo Two, and the troop leader's tank had become a mass of flying metal and flame.

The Sukhoi swung upwards. The pilot glanced behind and felt satisfaction at the sight of the orange ball of fire where his rockets had struck. He opened his throttle and pushed the SU20 into a spiralling climb, levelling out at 29,000 feet and turning east towards his airfield. He had flown three sorties since dawn, and hoped he would be allowed to rest for a few hours.

Davis was now in command of the troop; at least, in command of what was left of it...two Chieftains. 'DeeJay, don't go berserk, I want to see what's going on. Keep the speed down.' On the troop net: 'Charlie Bravo Two. The boss has bought it. We'll move back to Firefly and rejoin Charlie. And remember your training; keep a good overlap. Less than half gun range on each move...a foot on the ground, Sealey. Off you go, we'll hold here until you're in position. Out.' Christ, thought Davis, talk about unauthorized procedure! He could hardly have been more casual, but Sealey hadn't commanded a tank for long and there were the lives of two crews at stake. 'Hold it here, DeeJay.' There was a convenient fold in the ground which would hide the deep hull but still leave the gun turret clear.

Jamming was still total on Charlie Squadron net, isolating the two survivors of Bravo Troop. Davis had been in this kind of situation before, leading the troop when Lieutenant Sidworth's tank had been put out of action; only then it had been during the Defender 83 exercise, and the lieutenant had spent the next few hours drinking tea with fellow casualties, and discussing the remainder of the operation. And now Sidworth was dead!

Sod it, Davis suddenly thought. We're not supposed to be

86

running, we're here to fight a bloody war. It's our job. 'Charlie Bravo Four, this is Bravo Two. Hold it where you are.' Sealey's tank was already three hundred meters behind them. Davis got his shoulders beneath the hatch and pushed upwards. For a moment he hesitated, remembering the danger of gas and considering fitting his respirator. Mentally he shrugged; if there had been gas around, then he would be dead by now. Bravo Two was pretty much of a sieve, he had been able to see daylight through the side of the hatch for the past hour, but she'd done a good job of keeping them all alive. He rammed open the hatch; it moved squeakily, one of the hinges twisted out of line. He stood and looked out. The air, though heavily tainted with gunsmoke, smelt fresh after the interior of the tank. He called down inside: 'Shadwell, do you think you can manage some fast loading with one hand?'

'I can try, Sarge. I'm not feeling too good, though.'

'How many rounds do we have left?'

'Twenty-three.'

Davis didn't remember using so many; it was easy to lose count. He would have estimated they had used only a dozen shells. 'You won't have to load that number,' he told Shadwell. 'Charlie Bravo Four this is Charlie Bravo Two. We're moving down the hill until we meet the road. Do you see it?'

'Affirmative, Sarge.'

'There's a cutting to the left of the small wood at four o'clock...got it?'

'Cutting to left of small wood. Right of the line of trees?'

'That's it. We'll get down there. When we're in position, you follow.'

'That's towards the bloody Russians.' Corporal Sealey didn't sound enthusiastic.

'DeeJay, head down the hill.' Davis felt a strange sense of exhilaration as the Chieftain swung itself around, the same feeling he had experienced the first time he had climbed inside one of the huge vehicles and heard the powerful roar of its engine. Familiarity had dulled his appreciation, now it had returned. He could see why his machine gun had failed to operate, the barrel was twisted down against the cupola, its casing shattered. The main gun appeared undamaged, but there were shrapnel scars on the hull and turret, some several centimeters deep. Half the camouflage paint had been burnt off; Bravo Two looked like a candidate for the breaker's yard. Whoever had decided to do away with the .5 calibre ranging machine gun was a bloody fool, decided Davis. It was a useful spare weapon. Now all he had apart from the main gun, which wasn't much use against infantry, were the Sterlings. Still, it was good to be out in the open again after hours closed-down. It might be dangerous, but it felt better, and his field of vision was greatly improved. The smoke was thickening again now they had moved down closer to the fields, but visibility was almost three hundred meters. DeeJay bucked a shallow ditch and then they were on the narrow roadway, barely as wide as the length of the tank. Opposite was a steep bank, just over a meter high. The gunner wouldn't be able to depress the gun fully, but that wouldn't be necessary. It wasn't too bad as a firing position Davis decided. There was reasonable protection for the hull, and not too much of it showing above the bank. With luck, the rising ground behind would help conceal them, though they would be vulnerable to air attack. He watched Bravo Four begin to move down to join them.

Almost three thousand meters above on the slopes of the hill, out of radio contact with both his squadron and the battle group headquarters, Charlie Squadron Leader Captain Valda Willis was watching the two Chieftains through his binoculars. He had just identified them as Two and Four of his squadron's B Troop. Willis, and another survivor of the squadron, had only a few minutes previously managed to force their way through the encircling Russian armour. It had been a close thing, with only a narrow corridor remaining clear. Willis had seen the two Bravo Troop Chieftains on the slopes, before they had turned off down the hill. Their manoeuvre had been unexpected. They were being driven straight towards the enemy as though going in for an attack! It was impossible for him to contact them by radio, his two aerials had been blown away by an HE shell explosion on his turret. The two Charlie Bravo Chieftains he was watching were now facing north-east, the bulk of the moor to the left of them. The Russian armour had occupied most of the woods on the eastern slopes of the moor and was encircling the lower ground to the south. He was surprised that any of Bravo Troop had survived; their position had been heavily shelled and then overrun.

He saw a line of Russian T-64s clearing the smoke. 'What's the range?'

'Three thousand five hundred, sir.' The gunner was following one of the lead tanks.

Sergeant Davis saw the leading T-64 just as Captain Willis' shell struck it below its main gun. He thought that Bravo Four must have fired as the tank was now in position some eighty meters to his left. But as he glanced towards it now, he could see no gunsmoke.

He was searching the ground for other British tanks when Inkester fired without warning. Davis had no time to duck into the fighting compartment. The blast almost deafened him. He dropped inside and jerked the hatch closed. 'You okay, Shadwell?'

'Yes.'

Davis noticed the loader struggling, and wished he was better positioned to help the man. It seemed an age before the breech slammed closed and Shadwell shouted; 'Loaded.' Inkester fired immediately. 'Two, Sarge. Two...one after another. How's that for bloody shooting?'

'Shut up. Bravo Four, you okay?' Davis's head was still ringing from the sound of the gun.

'Affirmative, Sarge.'

'Fuckin' hurry up, Shad.' Inkester was shouting, working the turret around to the left. The Chieftain bucked again.

'Okay Bravo Four, get moving, fast.' Sealey didn't need

89

encouragement. He was imagining a dozen guns ranging on the spot where his tank rested. His driver spun the tank on the road, and felt relief as the tracks bit into the tarmac surface.

Get going you bastard, get going! Davis knew he had to give Sealey enough time to get well down the road and into another firing position. But he was finding it almost impossible to resist the temptation to follow him. There was movement on his horizon, a turret top below a ridge of ground.

'Bravo Two this is Four. In position.'

Inkester had been monitoring the net, and shouted at DeeJay. Bravo Two wallowed for a second and then spun, showering sparks from her tracks.

The road took the Chieftain diagonally away from the advancing Russian armour, its smooth surface giving them the edge in speed, while the bank at the roadside was good cover. An enemy gunner would have to be damned efficient to get a sure sight on their fast-moving turret, thought Davis. Pray to God there weren't any helicopters! He pushed up the hatch again. The road curved to the right and he could see Bravo Four. 'Okay Bravo Four, we're going on past you.'

Sealey shouted back in the radio, 'You're fucking mad. I'm not waiting here.'

Davis changed the tone of his voice. 'Bravo Four, this is Bravo Two. You make a move before I radio, Sealey you bastard, and I'll put a Sabot right through your bloody hull. Out.' There was no comment from the shocked corporal.

A thousand meters farther down the road Davis stopped the tank and swung the turret ninety degrees to the right before calling Bravo Four. A couple of minutes later Sealey's Chieftain thundered past them at almost thirty miles an hour, shaking the ground as it went.

'Bravo Four, this is Bravo Two. I'm holding here for a while. Get yourself well back, but keep us in range.'

'Wilco, Bravo Two.' Sealey sounded subdued.

There wouldn't be long to wait, decided Davis. The battle smoke was drifting parallel with the road, and the visibility in the fields was better than six hundred meters. 'Traverse right, Inkester. Hold it...there...BMP, alongside the hedge.'

'I see it...come on love, come on now...' Inkester was talking to the gun as he fired. He yelled: 'Hit...hit, Sarge.'

Davis missed the destruction of the troop carrier, but heard Inkester's shout of satisfaction. 'Shut up, Inkester...Bravo Four this is Bravo Two, we're moving again.' Davis was trying to find the road on his map. It curved north, taking them directly across the line of the Soviet advance! They would have to leave it and move across the fields towards the west. He stuffed the map between his legs and pressed his eyes to the sight. It was aligned on a T-64. He flicked on the times ten magnification just as Inkester's shell struck; it was impressive, watching it happen only a few meters away. 'Move, DeeJay. Get her rolling...Bravo Four as soon as we reach you, move off...we'll head west off the road and get out of here...'

'Wilco, Sarge...' Corporal Sealey acknowledged gratefully.

'BMPs...BMPs...' Inkester's voice rose. The computer locked to its target, adjusting the gun as the tank moved. Inkester fired.

'Go left now, DeeJay...keep with us Bravo Four... Inkester, BMP three o'clock...don't lose it...Bravo Four, stay close...we're heading west of the small wood ahead.' The gun roared once more. 'Okay, Inkester, leave 'em.'

A shell exploded a few meters ahead of Bravo Two just as DeeJay rammed her through a hedge and into the open field. He began jinking, maintaining the speed but driving in a series of opposing curves as he braked first one track and then the other. There were more explosions, one close enough for its pressure wave to slam violently against the hull. A few meters more and they would be behind cover. Don't let it happen...please don't let it happen to us...Davis was praying. It took an eternity to cover the few hundred meters, but the shelling eased and finally stopped. DeeJay straightened the course and rammed his foot down hard. He had been in action long enough, and now all he wanted was to get away as fast as he could. 'Steady...for Christ's sake, DeeJay!' Bravo Two was pitching dangerously, hammering her bow on the ground as her suspension was strained near breaking point. 'Easy, lad...easy.' Bravo Four was in line with them now, a hundred meters to their left.

The panic which had gripped DeeJay gradually slackened. He managed to get himself and Bravo Two under control. For a few moments, the terror which he had kept contained during the fighting had overwhelmed him.

He could hear Davis's voice, calm, unemotional. 'Fine, DeeJay...keep it like that...nice and steady. Left a little...left...good...well done, lad.' The knots in DeeJay's stomach muscles relaxed and he began listening to Bravo Two. Her tracks were slapping badly, needed adjustment...her engine was beginning to sound rough; he hadn't helped it by driving like a lunatic. She didn't deserve that kind of treatment. Her steering was getting difficult as well, he was having to use a lot more strength on the left lever. Everything needed servicing, and badly. Christ, the sergeant fitter would go bananas when he examined her. There was a strange rattle, a deep knock that reverberated through the driving compartment...an engine mounting? Bloody hell, that would be all they needed. He began to nurse her, encourage her.

Davis too was beginning to relax as the distance between Bravo Two and the advancing enemy increased. I've survived again, he told himself; survived for Hedda and the boys...so we can be together...God, when? Afterwards! Hedda? It would be good when he saw her again...Christ, it would be good! He tried to send his thoughts to her...I'll be back soon, love...just you take care of the kids, I'll look after myself...don't you worry...I'm okay...doing fine.

'Ahead...tank...' Inkester yelled the words just as Davis caught a glimpse of a partially camouflaged hull, close to the wood on their right. Inkester was swinging the turret trying to get the tank in his sights.

'No...it's one of ours...a Challenger,' warned Davis. 'Bravo Four...Challengers to our right.' The ground dipped unexpectedly in front of Bravo Two. DeeJay braked fiercely and swung left. There were a line of Challengers in the hollow, hull down, waiting. 'DeeJay, slow...okay, lad...stop her. Bravo Four come alongside us.' Davis opened the hatch and clambered out, trying to decide which of the tanks was likely to contain an officer. He recognized the skull and crossed bones insignia of the 17th/21st Lancers. A figure waved to them from a tank further down the line. He jumped down to the ground and was surprised his legs held him; they felt shaky, numb. He ran to the vehicle and climbed on to her hull. 'Sergeant Davis, sir. Bravo Troop, Charlie Squadron...Battle Group Cowdray One. We've got ourselves lost, sir. No radio contact.'

The officer's rank wasn't visible on his clothing, but Davis sensed he was a captain, possibly a major. 'You should be a mile further south, Sergeant. Your group is pulling back towards Warberg. You'll be reforming there. You can leave the Russians to us for a while. Get there as quickly as you can.'

'Yes, sir. Thank you, sir.' Davis jumped from the Challenger's hull. The officer's voice stopped him.

'Sergeant...what was your name again?'

'Davis, sir. Morgan Davis.'

'You men have done a good job, Sergeant Davis. Head due south. You'll hit the Esbeck to Warberg road.'

'Thank you, sir.' He saluted, then ran back to Bravo Two. There were four helicopters coming low across the fields, Lynxs, heading towards the advancing Soviet armour. The sound of artillery was quickening; a flight of rockets howled away from a battery hidden in the woods. The war was catching up with him again. It was late afternoon, on the first day.

NINE

There was sufficient aggressive determination in the voice of November Squadron's Captain Harling of the US Black Horse Cavalry, to convince Master Sergeant Will Browning that the man was a homicidal megalomaniac and that he'd conceived some sadistic plan that would lead to the extermination of his whole squadron.

The captain's exaggerated Texan enthusiasm bordered on hysteria as he made a wild speech over the squadron net about pride, the need to sacrifice and the old-fashioned spunk of true-grit American fighting men when faced with some difficult, if not impossible, task. Harling intended it to make the men of his squadron forget they might be about to die — it had the opposite effect. Those who had not remade their wills in the past few days now regretted the omission; more than a couple of the nervous were reduced to mental wrecks of no fighting use whatsoever, and they needed long and real encouragement from their individual commanders to combat Harling's damage to their morale.

It had come only a short while after the end of a series of attacks on their positions, which November Squadron had successfully repulsed. The nerves of the survivors were already ragged; the earlier artillery bombardment had been fierce. The lull, when it came, had been welcome. Then the captain's lengthy bullshit pep-talk.

He had ended: 'I can't tell you not to think about KIA...but I tell you, men, when they do a body count out there, there are going to be one hell of a lot more Popskis than Johnstons.' That was great, mused Browning, one of the November drivers was a Mike Popski! 'We're going right back in. We held the head of their assault army, *and* beat 'em. Now we're going after them, into their flank.' Harling had suddenly remembered security and switched to code after a fit of coughing. 'H minus 1237 Shark Fin. You get...' The squadron network picked up a steady howling interference that drowned out Harling's voice. Browning didn't hurry to retune to a different wavelength. Shark Fin...counterattack...so that was what all the bull was about. H...that was the datum time, so H minus 1237 meant it would all begin to happen in around ten minutes.

'How come we held the head, and we're about to attack their flank?' began Podini, incredulously. 'The guy's a nut!'

The troop radio net interrupted him. 'Utah, Idaho, Oregon?' The troop lieutenant's voice, easy and relaxed. 'What you got left?' Will Browning heard the ammunition count and added his own. 'Thirty-nine rounds; mixed. Smoke unused. Machine gun ammo okay, out.'

'H minus 1233 we move, okay. They've got a bridgehead over the Ulster a kilometer north of Gunthers. Avoid the hundred meter strip near the river, it's heavily mined. There are some T-80s ahead of us, but according to information the captain's got, they're thin on the ground, and we believe they don't have much infantry support now. The rest of November will be on our right. We'll keep to the open ground to the west. Out.'

Six minutes? There were only five left now! Browning was trying to collect his memories of the past hours; the barrage spreading south until it had engulfed them and finally passed on. There had been no casualties then in the squadron, although the infantry and one of the artillery batteries had suffered. The squadron had moved forward a thousand meters to battle positions on lower ground, and fought the enemy massed on the shallow slopes on the far side of the river Ulster. It had been long-distance warfare at first, maximum range, indistinct targets hidden behind smoke as the Soviet assault force attempted to gain a foothold on the western bank. The river defences had been hard pressed, yet they had held...but not, it now seemed, everywhere. Browning had seen the temporary military bridges blown in the first few minutes of the initial attack, demolished by the charges of the US Division's Combat Engineers. There had been several attempts by the Soviet troops using BTR-50 amphibious troop carriers to cross the river, but these had all been foiled by the artillery on the western hill overlooking the valley, and steady mortaring and small-arms fire had wasted the enemy infantry. A renewed artillery barrage by Soviet long-range field artillery had again failed to displace the US Division, and full daylight provided the Army Air Corps' gunships and Thunderbolt Threes with a wealth of targets. The US Command's plans that their ground forces should always be able to fight under a canopy of air superiority was paying off in the sector. There had been no time so far, in the battle, when Browning and the men of November had found the sky clear of American aircraft of one type or another. It had been comforting.

Napalm had ignited much of the forest on the eastern side of the border territory, and the strengthening breeze from the south-east was sweeping the fires northwards across the Soviet supply routes, and forcing them continuously to move their close artillery support. The immediate effect had been to take the pressure off the northernmost flank of the American Armoured Division.

Mike Adams was gunning the motor like some twitchy racing driver at the start of a Grand Prix. Browning was about to tell him to cool it when he heard the lieutenant again. 'Okay Indians, let's roll.'

India Troop came out of the woodland in line abreast and for a few seconds Browning felt naked, then the other tanks of November squadron were with them, and Browning was happier. Christ, he thought, war's changed...even as I remember it! You no longer saw lines of weary infantrymen trudging their way up to the front and into battle. Now they travelled right to the battlefield in their armoured personnel carriers...they arrived fresh and unsullied. At least, that was the principle. The infantry were with them now, only a couple of hundred meters behind the leading tanks, well-protected in their XM723s, sufficiently weaponed to be capable of fighting their way forward with the main armour, each of the personnel carriers equipped with TOW missile launchers and 25mm cannon; inside, twelve infantrymen and the crew.

The appearance of the small village of Gunthers startled Browning. He had driven through it less than thirty hours before. It had been tidy, neat and spotless; the houses with their steeply pitched roofs smartly painted, their verandahs and windows decked with carefully tended boxes of bright scarlet geraniums and ferns. The men had been hurrying about their business with the usual Teutonic dedication, as though their ignoring the increasing tension so close to their homes would encourage it to go away. The women had been at the shops, the children in school. Browning had slowed his vehicle to watch a group of boys, supervised by a tracksuited teacher, playing soccer. Browning didn't understand the rules too well, but it was increasing in popularity back home in the States, and it looked active enough to be interesting. Now, it was all an area of terrible desolation and smoke-blackened wreckage. Not a single building was left standing above its first level. They were a thousand meters to the east of it.

Hal Ginsborough said quietly, 'Will you take a look at that! God almighty!'

'Mother-fuckers...' It was Podini.

'Shut up,' snapped Browning. Who needed comments to emphasize the civilian horror? He couldn't see a living soul in the wreckage, though doubtless there'd be some. Somebody always survived, no matter how bad it looked; he'd seen it happen many times in Nam, but it was always hard to believe. Maybe some of the villagers would have left before the battle began, but he doubted if all would have quit their homes. Some did...but many didn't. They sat in the cellars and waited, praying desperately that the war would pass them by. He knew what the wreckage of the buildings would smell like; it would be worse in a few days. Someone, perhaps him, would eventually have to help dig out the bodies, hoping all the time they might find someone alive, some kid perhaps, protected by a beam of timber, a collapsed wall. The smell...the stink, and the flies. There would be rats...Jesus, why was it so many of *them* seemed to escape destruction? Lean, starving dogs; worse, cats that could sometimes look obscenely well-fed, licking themselves clean amongst the tumbled and bloodstained rubble! There were fires in the wreckage, and a heavy layer of smoke drifted above the remains of the village like a shroud.

The lieutenant's voice was on the troop net again: 'Best speed, Indians, but maintain your formation. Good luck, guys.'

Best speed! 'Step on it, Mike,' he ordered, and felt the Abrams surge forward, bucking over the uneven ground, as the roar of the engines increased. Sound was always relative to discomfort in a tank, he thought wryly. The only good thing was you didn't hear most of the noises of battle. It was still there, though; not far in front of him now. Five thousand meters...closer. Much closer!

He saw the explosion of a shell two hundred meters ahead. It looked like an error, or an optimistic ranging attempt by some distant gun crew. Mike Adams had seen it too, and he steered the Abrams in a series of sharp but uneven zigzags that shook Browning's head from side to side as the direction continuously changed; a few hundred meters of driving like this and he would begin to feel travel sick.

It was barely possible to distinguish the riverbank several hundred meters to their right. Like everywhere else the ground seemed to be on fire, the grass and trees smoking, hazy; wreckage, twisted and spewing black fumes. Far ahead were the remains of a small wood on a low hill, and a few scattered and blasted farm buildings at the foot of the rising ground.

The barrage began to increase in intensity. Where the hell was the American smoke, Browning wondered? It was madness charging straight into enemy guns; the only protection they were getting was from the smoke of the Soviet shell explosions. The horizon was blurred, but the advancing American tanks must be obvious targets to the enemy gunners. Browning couldn't pinpoint their positions, but had the ghastly feeling he was being driven into the heart of a maelstrom of artillery fire.

Two heavy calibre shells bracketed the tank, forcing Adams to correct the steering. Hell seemed to open its doors ahead of them; shell-bursts as dense as forest trees were columns of fire leaping up from the ground. Was the squadron getting air support? Browning thought he caught a glimpse of a line of gunships above him. If it were imagination, it helped a little; he had lost sight of the other tanks. He was experiencing a growing sense of indecisiveness and terror. Should he order Adams to slow down...increase his speed? Should he tell him to swing the Abrams out of line, try to get away to the side where the barrage might be lighter? Get the hell out of here...that was important...chances of survival were nil...it was only a matter of time...seconds...and they'd be hit...this was crazy...madness...

The lieutenant was shouting on the troop net, static punctuating his words. 'Indians engaging...Indians engaging...'

Adams swerved the XM1 again as the burning hulk of a Russian T-80 loomed through the smoke. Someone, something, had hit it...visibility was little more than forty meters. The corpses of a Soviet mortar team were strewn across the path of the Abrams, their bodies blackened and twisted by napalm, still smouldering. The XM1's tracks

99

churned them into the filthy earth.

Infantry. They would be around somewhere, hidden, waiting, as deadly as howitzers with their anti-tank rocket launchers. Was the barrage easing? Browning sprayed the area ahead with his machine gun...keep the bastards' heads down. Ginsborough was doing the same...and experiencing identical fears. Browning knew Podini would be seeking targets for the main gun, but there seemed to be none. There was a Soviet BTR-60 personnel carrier to the Abrams' right, but its wheels had been blown off and its tyres were burning. He saw movement beside the hulk and swung the .5 towards it, firing before he aimed, a line of heavy bullets ripping a deep seam across the ground. He concentrated a long burst on the rear of the carrier and saw green-suited figures stagger and fall. Ginsborough's 7.62 was chattering...short regular bursts that seemed to be timed to the pulse in Browning's temples.

Adams was yelling in the intercom: 'Jesus...oh Jesus...Jesus Christ...Jesus Christ!' He wound the Abrams through a field of craters, the wreckage of vehicles and men, its speed little more than jogging pace. The smoke was thinning, visibility increasing.

There was a heavy blow on the side of the XM1's turret which sent a violent shockwave through the fighting compartment and rang the metal of the hull as though it were a vast bell.

'Shit!' Ginsborough was swearing. In the gloom of the interior the side of the turret was glowing dull red where an armour-piercing shell had failed to penetrate as it glanced off the thick steel. The ground was rising more sharply, smashed woodland lay ahead, stumps of distorted trees, pitted earth, gaunt roots. A thin hedge ran diagonally across the landscape to the left, partly destroyed, the bushes torn and scattered. Browning saw another group of Soviet infantry eighty meters in front of the Abrams. There were the sounds of light machine gun rounds against the hull, pattering like hail on a barn roof and no more effective. He

100

brought the Abrams' Bushmaster Cannon on to the target by remote control, but before he could depress the firing button the Abrams' M68 gun roared and the infantrymen were lost in the burst of the 105mm shell only fifty meters ahead.

Browning was angry. 'Save your ammo, Podini...leave the infantry to me.'

'What infantry?' Podini sounded exasperated.

The Abrams had reached the rubble of a low wall where the main gun's shell had exploded. The tracks were grinding harshly, the hull bucking. A couple of meters to the right of the bodies of the Soviet infantrymen were the twisted remains of an ASU-57, its light alloy armour ripped and torn by the blast, its gun barrel buckled. 'Sorry, Podini...nice work.'

'Yeah, thanks!' Podini's sarcasm was lost on Browning.

ASU-57, an airborne assault gun, mobile and light. So that was how the bastards had got across the river! A quick airlift of men and light armour to establish the bridgehead and give the heavy tanks cover while they forded. God almighty, the thing had almost wiped them out. A few degrees' difference in the angle of impact and the Russian shell would have penetrated, and the Abrams and its crew been wasted. Only Podini's quick shot had prevented the Russian crew getting a second chance!

There'd be others...Jesus, where?

The Abrams was slithering, tracks churning. Much of the surface earth of the woods had been stripped from the stratas of damp limestone, greasy with shattered roots, branches and fallen leaves.

'Left, Podini, eleven o'clock on the ridge, for Christ's sake.'

'Got it...I see it...' The Abrams' turret was swinging. Fractionally above the brow of the hill, Browning could distinguish the domed turret of a T-62, badly camouflaged, its gun moving against the skyline. Its commander had chosen a poor position but it had been protected until now

101

by the battlesmoke. 'Yeah...yeah...yeah' Podini fired and the T-62 burst into flames. '*Yaheee...*'

Adams was having difficulty moving the XM1. She could climb an obstacle a meter high but facing him was a steep limestone shelf, its edges soft and crumbling. The Abrams was bucking like a mule, lurching as the driver reversed her and repeatedly charged the greasy slope. Browning tried the troop net. 'November India this is Utah...India this is Utah...come in India Leader...' he paused, waiting. There was no response. He repeated the request for contact but there was only silence. The XM1 was jerking, swaying, as Mike Adams kept butting the limestone like a demented steer. 'Cut it out, Mike...hold her where she is.' The tank settled and the engine roar decreased. Browning tried the troop network again.

There was a howl of electronic interference from a Soviet jamming station, and a voice, distorted, barely distinguishable. 'Utah...India...where the hell...' The pitch of the oscillations rose. 'Utah...read...Utah we don't...' Interference drowned the network completely. Browning tried the alternative wavelengths but the Soviet jamming covered the entire range. The artillery had stopped and he could see no movement on the hillside. He opened the hatch slowly and stared around. There were no accompanying American APCs in sight...nothing moved within the mist of the battlefield, nor in the woods above.

He dropped back into the fighting compartment. 'Get us the hell out of here, Mike.'

The Abrams rammed the shelf of rock again with a jolt that nearly dislocated Browning's spine. 'Backwards, you asshole; go out backwards!'

There was a scream of metal sheering metal, and the Abrams swung broadside to the limestone and stopped abruptly.

'Track.' Podini's and Ginsborough's voices shouted the word in unison.

'You creep, Adams...you stupid no good black son of a

102

bitch...' It was Podini.

'Knock it off! Mike, try and ease her forward, see if you can get the track free.' Browning knew it was probably hopeless, but it was worth a try. The Abrams shuddered as the right-hand track brought her back a little. The left stayed jammed. 'Hold everything.' He levered himself out on to the deck and jumped down. The left track was half-off the driving wheel at the rear. He put his hand on the links and swore. They were too hot to touch. He could see the upper run of the track, as taut as a steel bowstring between the front bogey and the drive-wheel.

Adams was leaning out of the driving hatch, his dark face streaked with sweat. His eyes asked the question.

'Utah's not going anywhere,' Browning told him. 'The track's off the drive.'

Ginsborough's head was above the deck. 'The networks are all jammed. How did they jam HF? Oh God!'

'Keep trying. We want a recovery vehicle.' There was gunfire some distance away, but the immediate area was quiet, the silence adding tension to the situation. The landscape was so shell-sculpted it had an artificial lunar quality. Wisps of smoke drifted through the broken woods or hung in the craters. The air stank of diesel fumes, burning rubber and explosive...alien.

It was the same feeling Will Browning had experienced as a child, closing his eyes and counting to a hundred before searching for his friends; discovering they had run away in the woods and left him alone. The impression was strong now, undeniable.

He was trying to think, to reason. Losing radio contact was one thing, but losing your entire squadron another. When they had all entered the smoke and the artillery barrage, Idaho, Oregon and the lieutenant's tank, Nevada, were all stationed to Utah's right. And beyond the troop had been the remainder of the squadron; behind them,

Browning assumed, the mechanized infantry support. He had listened to the shouted conversations, the orders and comments on the troop and squadron radio networks as they had advanced. He had heard them right through until...until when? Until the noise of battle grew too loud, the jamming had begun, when everything was confusing and demanding his total attention, and all sound had become white and unintelligible. Had he heard them only in his mind?

'What the hell are we going to do?' Podini yelled from the fighting compartment. Podini always sounded as though he were on the verge of panic, but never quite got there. Browning accepted it as a characteristic of Podini's Latin background; the gunner made up for it in plenty of other ways.

'You want to start walking back, alone? No? Then dry up!' The smoke of the battlefield had thinned to the kind of watery mist that the master sergeant liked to associate with New England valleys on fall days, but this mist stank of war. In scattered places on the landscape fires burnt, spiralling dense and evil thunderheads in the warm afternoon air. Occasionally in the fires there would be small firecracker explosions, but the sounds of battle no longer surrounded them. The noises were still there, but for the time being they belonged to someone else.

Undulations in the ground made it difficult for Browning to see far beyond the first three hundred meters. He climbed back on to the tank and swung himself down into the turret. 'Get your head out of the way Mike. Podini, bring the gun around.' He switched the lenses to full magnification as the electric motors began humming and the turret moved. 'Slow, I want a real easy scan.' The lenses were concentrating the smoke mist and exaggerating the mirage effect of the sun's heat on the damp ground. The landscape was hazy, shimmering. 'Stop...hold it.'

There was wreckage.

'Russian T-60,' said Podini, dryly. He moved the turret a

couple of degrees to bring the wrecked vehicle to the centre of the lens, then checked the range with the laser. 'Two thousand six hundred meters.'

'Okay, go on some more.'

The turret revolved slowly, then stopped. 'XM1...an Abrams.' There had been no change in the tone of Podini's voice; it was flat, mechanical. 'Two thousand nine hundred meters.'

'Confirmed.' The hull of the squadron's Abrams was torn open at the side, exposing the still-smoking fighting compartment.

'It's Idaho.' There was more emotion with Podini's recognition of the vehicle.

'How the hell can you know that?'

'It's Idaho...Acklin's wagon...you think I'm dumb?' Podini's voice level was rising.

'Okay, okay. Take it round again.'

In the next two minutes they identified nine more of the squadron's XM1s. There were other wrecks, too far away for either of them to be certain they belonged to friends or enemy. And no living thing moved on the battleground.

'He always has to be first,' Podini complained loudly and bitterly. 'Adams has to be first every time. Adams, why the hell you want to be first, always up-front? Why aren't you last sometime, like ordinary people?'

'Fuck off, Pino. I only drive to order.'

Browning knew that the squadron's counterattack had failed, destroyed by the power of the Russian barrage from across the river in East German territory, and from Soviet positions ahead of the US armour. What little smoke there had been was no protection against the BM21 rockets fired from behind the border where they had obviously been deployed in battalion groups capable of landing more than seven hundred missiles on a square kilometer of ground in twenty seconds. Coupled with conventional artillery fire, it had blanketed the area occupied by the XM1s and their support. Shell and rocket craters were so close together in places on the battlefield that they overlapped. Sometime, while Browning's XM1 had been grinding its way through the inferno, jinking the shell explosions with its crew deafened by the howls and shrieks of the missiles, the radio useless with interference and jamming, there must have been an order for the survivors to withdraw. He hadn't heard it.

'I guess we're up to our eyeballs in shit,' commented Hal Ginsborough.

Adams called up from the driving position, 'Well, at least we ain't dead!'

'But you tried, man, you sure tried,' taunted Podini.

The Podini versus Adams duelling didn't bother Browning; it was part of the two men's friendship. It worried outsiders who didn't understand that it was an essential feature of their communication process. Only a few days previously, Adams had rescued Podini from a bar fight that developed when a black artillery corporal had tried, uninvited, to defend Adams' dignity.

'I'm going outside to have a look around,' Browning told his crew. It seemed to him Utah was situated in the calm eye of a tornado, and at any minute it would be swirled back into the violence. The peace was surely artificial. There should be Soviet patrols pacifying the area, their battlefield police taking charge of prisoners, engineers recovering tanks and vehicles for the workshops. He could only think the Soviet bridgehead had been far stronger than the intelligence information had led Divisional Command to believe, and that when the main thrust of Soviet armour across the river had remained undeflected by the abortive counterattack to its flank, then it had continued to follow their commander's original orders and attack route. Soviet tactics tended to be inflexible. He tried to guess at their objective; the city of Fulda and the multiple highway linkage were almost due west, and possibly their first Red. 'Mike, Hal, both of you stay inside here. Keep out of sight. Pino, get your sidearm and come with me.'

Browning didn't enjoy being outside his tank in combat zones. There was security in thick steel, even if the infantry referred to tanks as 'Ronsons' and swore they would rather fight as smaller and less inflammable targets out in the open. Now, as he began climbing the hill through the stumps of the torn woodland, he felt vulnerable and defenceless; the Remington automatic pistols which he and Podini carried were poor substitutes for Utah's powerful weapons.

Much of the low hill had been scalped by artillery fire, but there was some protection close beneath the limestone outcrops. Near the top he paused and looked back across the battlefield. The ridge of forested hills which had been the squadron's earlier position were eight kilometers to the south and were still hidden by smoke drifting above the ruins of Gunthers. It seemed impossible Utah could have survived the barrage which had destroyed many tanks. He counted thirty wrecked vehicles, and realized there would be more south of the village. It was no longer simply a question of repairing the XM1 to get her back to the regiment, but a matter of survival for the crew and himself...he couldn't see how they would make it.

He moved cautiously, avoiding the skyline and working his way past the blazing remains of the Soviet T-62 until he found better cover in a gorse thicket on the ridge.

Podini was staying so close that when Browning hesitated the gunner crawled into him. He signalled for him to wait while he slid himself on his belly for the last meter.

He caught his breath as he pushed aside the gorse. A regiment of Soviet armour had reformed on the farmland below him less than two thousand meters away. Thirty or forty tanks, T-80s and T-60s. Beyond, a battery of self-propelled guns; nearby, three rows of armoured personnel carriers. The tanks were moving, swinging away westward, the roar of their engines drowning out the sounds of battle. The river, six hundred meters to the right, had been bridged by a pair of GSP ferries, and field engineers were already constructing a second bridge fifty meters downstream, protected by two Quad self-propelled anti-aircraft vehicles and an SAM battery, lightly camouflaged near the riverbank. There was no doubt the Soviet commanders had anticipated their rapid advance, for there was already a queue of vehicles waiting to cross; heavy cargo carriers, pillow tanks loaded with fuel, artillery tractors and their guns.

How far had they advanced in the hour or two since the first dawn battle had started? Browning studied his watch, wondering for a moment if it had been damaged. It showed 16.30 hours. Noon had passed unnoticed...eleven hours since it had all begun! His mind was momentarily confused. They called it battle amnesia didn't they? The real and the unreal blended together, time compacted and lost, incidents jumbled. It was the reason pilots were debriefed the instant they landed; minutes later, as their minds relaxed after long, intense concentration, the memories were no longer accurate.

Ten hours; almost eleven. The Soviet spearhead could already be twenty kilometers into NATO territory, now they had penetrated the defences...perhaps even further. He remembered Captain Harling's words: 'We're about to counterattack their flank.' Flank! Had the captain lied? Was it an attempt by the squadron to break out of their encircled position...an attempt which had failed? The amount of materials the Russians were accumulating east of the river seemed to indicate they felt the bridgehead was secure, and for the first time that day Browning could see no NATO aircraft in the skies above.

Podini was waiting nervously, his Remington so tightly gripped in his hand the knuckles were white, his body pressed hard beneath the gorse.

'What did you see?'

'Half the Commie army. The best part of a full tank regiment, artillery and logistics. The whole darned lot down there in the fields...bridges, combat engineers.'

They returned to the Abrams by a more direct route

down the cratered slope. The plain towards Gunthers where the carcasses of the squadron lay had the air of a bone-yard about it, reminding Browning of photographs he had seen of drought-sticken African deserts scattered with the dry skeletons of dead animals. For once Podini was silent, keeping his thoughts to himself as they scrambled down the hillside.

Adams and Ginsborough must have been watching through the lenses, for as the two men returned they climbed from the hull and waited for Browning to speak, their faces begging him to say something encouraging. Browning dropped his Remington back into its holster, squatted beside the Abrams and rested against the crippled track. The men stood looking down at him anxiously. He spoke slowly. 'Just over that hill is the end of the war for us. All we have to do is to walk slowly around there, with our hands up. No more shelling or bombing...no more rockets or napalm.' They remained silent. 'One thing I ought to tell you. The Russians took a lot of Germans prisoner in the '39-'45 war; the last ones they released didn't get home until '57. Some never made it at all...they used them as labourers in the Arctic Circle; maybe some of them are still alive, still up there. They'd be about sixty-five years old, could be even seventy.'

Adams said, 'We've got your point.'

'Maybe we could walk out, travel at night, try to reach the lines,' suggested Ginsborough.

'Could be,' agreed Browning. 'We might still have to try. Only the way I see it, we have a problem. The Russians could be advancing faster than we can walk. They do thirty kilometers a day in their vehicles, we do ten every night on foot. The end of a week, and we're further behind the lines than when we started.'

'They'll be stopped somewhere, maybe at the Fulda river,' said Podini, hopefully.

'I guess we ought to get Utah mobile.' Adams ran his hand along the taut links of the track. 'All I want is a gas cutter to get this sonovabitch back on the road. I ain't built for walking, and my idea of a vacation isn't ten years down some old salt mine.'

'It occurred to me when I was coming down the hill that there'd be everything we need in Gunthers. There'd be a garage there; I've seen one. The stuff we need could be in the wreckage.' Browning was deliberately avoiding giving the men orders. This was a difficult situation and it was going to get worse. It was essential he had a hundred per cent backing from the crew, and that would be more certain if they developed his ideas themselves.

Podini nodded. 'Maybe we could do it after dark.'

'Hole up until then,' added Ginsborough.

'They might send out patrols...pick us up.' Adams looked up at the hull of the XM1. 'Baby ain't easy to miss.'

'I think we've got a chance.' Browning pushed himself to his feet. 'The Russians' main concern is the front line. They'll use everything they've got up there, and do their tidying afterwards. I think we can make Utah look worse than she is...enough to fool a helicopter. Let's get to work. Gins, dismantle your machine gun and get yourself up on the ridge. Keep your head down, it's busy over there. Pino, you and Mike go and get a few bodies...'

'Bodies!' Podini looked stunned.

'Bodies the man said,' shrugged Adams. 'You made 'em, what you complaining about? I guess they're for decoration!'

Browning leant some of the broken tree branches against the hull of Utah, then lowered her gun until the barrel was fully depressed – it made her look forlorn. He opened all the hatches. There was a twisted sheet of metal a few meters away, part of the shield of some wrecked field-gun. He wedged it against the right track. There was already an abandoned look to the XM1.

Podini was examining the bodies of the men he had killed sixty meters to the right of the Abrams. They lay amongst the wreckage of their equipment, their bodies torn and

110

mangled. It was the first time he had seen the effect of a shell burst on a human target at close quarters; it was horrifying. He wanted to throw up, but kept swallowing the acid bile that rose in his throat. Bodies, Browning had said. Jesus, there didn't seem to be one that was anywhere near complete! He'd seen his grandmother when she had died, but she had looked as though she were sleeping...a little yellow maybe, parchment-skinned, but only sleeping. These men, the bits of them, were wide-eyed, if they had any faces left at all; their mouths grinned through bloody smashed teeth and their bodies were grotesque, shattered, dismembered.

There was one partly covered by the loose stone of the wall. Podini could see both arms, its chest, head. He bent over it, biting his lip.

'Mike...Jesus Christ! Mike, over here.'

Adams was beside him, quickly. 'What the hell?'

'This guy ain't dead. I saw his eyes move. Feel his pulse will you...'

Adams knelt beside the man and stared at him for a few moments, then put the hard outside edge of his hand against the man's neck. He leant forward and pressed down with all his body weight.

'What are you doing, for God's sake?'

'Taking his pulse,' said Adams, coolly. The man's eyes flickered, then opened. Suddenly there was no more movement; muscles relaxed. 'I don't feel none. I'd say he was dead.'

'Mother of God, you killed him!'

'Me, or you, Pino? Take a good look at him. Look down there.' Adams rolled aside a large stone that was lying across the man's abdomen. Intestines were trailed across the rubble. A sharp splinter of white bone from the crushed pelvis stuck up through the bloody mess of cloth and flesh. 'There ain't no MASH here...wouldn't do him no good, anyway. I did him a favour. Now help me lift him.'

There were three bodies draped across the hull of the XM1, one obscenely dangling from the main hatch. Without close examination, their nationalities were unrecognizable. A fire of dry branches and the rubber-tyred wheel of a wrecked gun curled black smoke across her. It would smoulder for a long time, well into darkness. Utah looked no different from the other wrecks on the battlefield.

Browning, Podini and Ginsborough lay beneath the heavy trunk of a fallen chestnut, its branches a cave around them fifty meters to the left of the tank. Adams was hidden in the gorse on the ridge, with the machine gun.

That's what we could be looking like, thought Browning, staring at the XM1 and its bloody corpses. It could be us there. It could be us in any of the hulks out there in the fields, twisted, broken. God almighty! There had been guys back home who thought he was crazy when he had joined the army; maybe he had been...maybe he still was.

Thirty-eight years old, and the only thing he could do well was kill. Some of the men he had been at school with were executives in companies now...owned their businesses, were married, with kids at college, mowed lawns in the evenings, watched television. Family? All he had was a sister somewhere, wedded to an insurance salesman. Last he heard of her was that she had gone to live in Detroit. He'd lost her address, and she hadn't written again. He couldn't remember her married name.

Podini. For Christ's sake, he would never lose a member of his family. There seemed to be dozens of them, scattered across the States from Jersey City to Los Angeles. 'You hear on the radio, Pino, some guy in Memphis killed eight cops in a raid on a gas station?' 'Memphis...gee, I got an aunt there.' Podini always had aunts, and uncles, sisters, brothers, cousins...family.

And what about Adams? Six kids! Pretty wife too. She was sixteen when they got married. Half Sioux, half black; the best of both. Was going to be a dancer, ended up a baby factory. Got a good lively sense of humour...you needed one with six kids in eight years, in military accommodation. They were back home in Fort Dix, waiting for Mike Adams to finish his tour of duty. He'd have been with them in another eight weeks. Eight weeks. Shit...eight weeks was no time.

Hal Ginsborough, twenty-one years old. A loader in every sense of the word. All he was interested in were girls, booze and craps; which meant he never had any money.

Three weeks ago...two...even one, there hadn't been a war. There hadn't been a war yesterday. Browning hadn't wanted one...perhaps no one in the whole world wanted a war, but here it was.

One week ago in Kohlhaus, the Edelweiss Bar. Gins drunk and Podini paying. Mike Adams back in camp writing a letter home; he did that three nights a week, at least. Fritz behind the bar, a German American accent. 'There will be no war.' Germanic finality. 'We have fought two wars this century, that is two too many. Here we know what war is like.' Christ, hadn't they heard that the Yanks fought, too? And in Korea, and Vietnam. 'This is Communist bluff. All talk...big wind. Have more drink, enjoy yourselves. No war...this time there will be no war. In two weeks my wife and I go to Spain...close bar for one month. Take vacation and sit in sun and forget politics. Eat paella. Drink wine. Dance a little. There can be no war, Sergeant.' Fritz was wrong.

'Ulli, what time d'you finish? Like to come for supper some place?'

Her place...afterwards. Ulli Waldeck, age somewhere around twenty-nine. Waitress in the Edelweiss. Divorced. Black curly hair, reasonable looker, a little on the plump side.

'You like to stay, Will?'

'Yes, sure.' Her arms around his neck, her lips soft.

Bed. Energetic, warm, damp and then comforting afterwards.

'Why you never married, Will?'

113

'Who knows? Never got around to it.'

'Sergeant Acklin's married.'

Del Acklin. He was out there now, in the wreckage of Idaho. Maybe he was still alive, lying there in the twisted steel and smoke, trapped, wounded. And he'd told him this morning maybe it wouldn't happen. No, Del Acklin was dead...Browning could sense it. Like Jones, Stromberg, Woolett, Hughes, Valori, Erikson, Scarsdale...Browning could name twenty more. Vietnam! Just names, rifles dug into mounds with helmets on the butts. Identity discs wedged between teeth...plastic sacks. All they'd found of Stromberg was a kneecap, and that could have belonged to someone else. They'd put it in a bag and sent it home in a coffin, just like a real body. Whoever carried the coffin to the grave must have thought Stromberg had starved to death; he weighed less than a kilo.

Harvey Kossof had been killed in the tank sheds, rolled along the wall by the hull of an XM1 only five weeks ago. Kossof had never even seen the war! He was just signalling a tank into the service bay and didn't leave himself enough room. He'd screamed until they gave him a heavy shot of morphine, and then died. Now he was a name, just like all the others. They promised you a stone in Arlington; the only bit of land most of the guys ever managed to own.

Podini was snoring, his thin face buried in the crook of one arm, his helmet cradled protectively like a kid's teddy bear in the other. Podini had a fiancée; Italian, very respectable. Her father ran a pizza bar in Jersey City, decorated with Chianti and Frascati bottles, so Podini said. He would marry her when he was Stateside again; a hundred guests, all in tuxedos or dark wedding suits. Then he'd quit the army, start work in his father-in-law's pizza bar, and get fat. If Browning ever dropped in there, Podini would beam a welcome. 'Hi, well I'm damned, Will, Jeez, great to see you. Heh, Momma, see who's here...you remember Will! Best table, Will...it's on the house, vino, anything. How are you? You look great! Remember how it

114

was; you, me, Mike and Gins. Jeez, those were the days! How about that?'

The days? It was one of those days, today. They'd all forget how bad it had been...one day.

TEN

'This is London. Seventeen hundred hours Greenwich Mean Time. BBC World Service. Here is the news, read by Hugh Dermot.' The newscaster's voice was grave. *'A state of war now exists between Great Britain and the Soviet Union.'*

'Switch that fucking tranny off, Corporal.' The staff sergeant's temper was barely under control. Not a minute previously he had been requested to organize coffee for the C-in-C and his staff; as it wasn't his job and he was already busy, he was feeling as though he had been demoted to a mess orderly.

'It's the BBC, Staff...first news we've managed to get.' The corporal was speaking over the newscaster and the men standing nearby leant closer to catch Dermot's voice.

'...Soviet troops, backed by mechanized infantry from the Warsaw Pact countries and with heavy air support, simultaneously invaded the territorial sovereignty of West Germany, Turkey and Austria at dawn today.'

The staff sergeant wanted to hear it himself. 'Okay, two minutes then.' There was a gangly private standing beside a filing cabinet, he made the mistake of catching the staff sergeant's eyes. 'You, Roberts, go and get a can of coffee from the cooks. And about two dozen cups...get 'em up to the boss, fast...get a move on, lad.'

Someone said: 'Shhh...' and the staff sergeant glowered, angrily.

'...our ultimatum, delivered to the Soviet Foreign Minister by the British Ambassador in Moscow, gave the Soviet government until noon to indicate it would order the

immediate cessation of hostilities, failing which Her Majesty's Government, in conjunction with its NATO allies, would consider a state of war to exist between the invading members of the Soviet bloc, and the Western Alliance.

'This assurance was not forthcoming. Consequently, the United Kingdom, the United States of America, Canada and our European allies are now at war.

'First reports of the Soviet attack were received in London shortly before 04.00 hours this morning. Soviet artillery launched a heavy barrage along an entire front from Lübeck in the north, to the Austrian border; shortly afterwards, armour of the Russian Second Guards Tank Army invaded West German territory to the east of the city of Lübeck, and Soviet airborne troops were landed in the Fulva valley.

'Soldiers of the 1st British Corps of the NATO Northern Army Group have been in action since the onset of hostilities in the British zone of responsibility to the east of Hannover.'

'Too fucking true, mate,' agreed the corporal sitting beside his transistor.

'Shut up, Nash,' growled the staff sergeant.

'...NATO Defence Headquarters, now evacuated from Brussels to minimize the risk of attack on the Belgium capital, reported in a communique issued a few minutes ago that forces of Belgium, Britain, Germany, the Netherlands and United States are all involved in the fighting, and that there are at present eight major defensive actions along the entire front.

'The communique said that the Soviet advance had been slowed down, and although no casualty figures were available those of the Soviet Union were very high.

'Soviet fighter aircraft and medium range bombers, bearing the insignias of the Frontovaya and Dal'naya Aviatsiya have made repeated raids on the north German towns of Lübeck, Hamburg, Hannover and Braunschweig. Heavy casualties are reported among the civilian populations.

117

'At 06.00 hours this morning, ministers of the North Atlantic Council, NATO's governing body, were called into immediate session. We will have more news of that later in the broadcast.

'In New York, the United Nations Security Council emergency debate on the crisis was resumed. Earlier today, the Soviet and Chinese delegations staged a brief walk-out when the Japanese delegates denounced the invasion of Western Europe as "wanton treachery by insatiable expansionists!" '

'Sodding Chinese! Last bloody Chairman was supposed to be a mate of *ours*...they're like the bleeding Vicar of Bray.' The staff sergeant had a pinch of dark tobacco in the palm of his hand and began rolling a match-thin cigarette.

'...here, at home, the Prime Minister, Mr James Newlin, called the invasion an "act of unparalleled insanity and barbarity, more dangerous to the future of all mankind than any the world has ever previously experienced". He called on all world leaders to support the determined fight to maintain the freedom of the West, and congratulated the President of the French Republic, Monsier Charles Dupré, on his government's decision to join those of the NATO alliance in the defence of West Germany. Five divisions of the French First Army, including three mechanized divisions, are expected to move eastwards in support of the American forces.

'In Turkey, Soviet forces crossed the frontiers at Batumi, Yerevan and Nachichevan, while a Soviet naval assault force has made landings on the Turkish Black Sea coast between Sinop and Samsun. Concentrations of Bulgarian troops have been reported on the Turko Bulgarian frontier at Malko, three hundred and twenty kilometers from Istanbul.

'In Yugoslavia, despite strong resistance, Soviet authorities this morning announced the capture of Novi Sad and Belgrade. Throughout the early hours of today Belgrade Radio played continuous recordings of the

118

Yugoslav national anthem. This was silenced a little after 09.00 hours...'

'That'll do, Corporal. Turn it off now.' The staff sergeant's slim cigarette was already a butt between his lips. He picked it out carefully, and dropped it into a near empty mug on the table. 'All right you lot, don't hang around...get back to your work...this is an official war we've got...earn your bloody money...'

The headquarters of the Commander-in-Chief of the Allied Forces in Northern Europe was situated, temporarily, a few kilometers east of Münster. Commander-in-Chief, General Sir Alexander Dormer, had moved his staff two days previously eastwards from Rheindahlen to its present battle headquarters. He had slept for less than three hours in the past twenty-four, but a Benzedrine tablet had cleared fatigue from his mind. There would be time for rest when the situation in NORTHAG became more settled.

Dormer was feeling satisfied with the intelligence reports he was receiving. The Russian forces were continuing their advance, which had been expected. But the advance had been neither as fast, nor had the initial penetration been as deep, as had been forecast. Their losses in the first kilometers had been astronomical, despite their advantages in military strength, their armour outnumbering that of the NATO forces by almost three to one.

Three to one. Sheer weight, Dormer knew, could win a war no matter how dogged the adversary. There had been sufficient warnings given over the past few years, and yet many of the NATO governments had ignored them, seeking political popularity while endangering the future military security of their countries. Britain had been no exception; in 1980, the British military budget had been cut by two hundred million pounds.

There had been an attempt, far too late, to redress the military balance, but many engineering companies which

119

could have been used on military projects had gone to the wall during the recession, and new ones to replace them had not been fully developed. Defence projects had been allowed to decay too far to be hurriedly salvaged. Much of the NATO weaponry was out-dated and long-serviced, but what there was of it was being well used. To his present satisfaction, the 1st British Corps were giving a good account of themselves, as were the men of the German and Belgian forces. In the north the Netherland Corps, reinforced by the German Federal Republic's territorial army, had slowed the Soviet forces east of Hamburg.

It had been no surprise to Dormer when the French entered the war immediately it had begun. He had worked closely with their High Command many times and never doubted their intentions, despite their government's apparent determination to remain non-commital. The French armour was already being brought into reserve, behind the American army in CENTAG.

The Atlantic air-bridge, 'Reforger', was not only holding but was growing rapidly. The massive Lockheed CXs which had been built in increasing numbers over the past five years, and the old Galaxies, were now proving their worth. With near maximum payloads of 220,000lbs -- as much as two M-60 tanks, or three helicopters -- they were refuelling in the air while en route from the USA to the airbases in Europe. Most aircraft of the European and American civil airlines had been immediately brought into service as troop and supply carriers. Dormer was feeling increasingly confident that if the Soviet advance could be contained for a further forty-eight hours they might be willing to negotiate a peace. At this stage, when negotiation was still possible, he did not personally believe there was much likelihood of a nuclear war developing. Though he had little respect for Russian leadership, he did not consider them to be maniacs. They would demand a high price for peace, perhaps even the re-unification of Germany under Soviet control, and it would then be for politicians, not soldiers, to decide if the

120

ransom should be met.

On the situation maps of the NORTHAG battlefront, General Sir Alexander Dormer could see clearly the present extent of the Warsaw Pact advance; the maps were continuously being adjusted by his staff, brought up-to-date the moment information became available from the various fronts. The battle computer system had removed much of the guesswork from strategy, though the early loss of many of the NATO reconnaissance satellites had proved very damaging.

At the moment, the Soviet forces had done little more than straighten the old frontiers. In the north, they threatened the city of Lübeck in a push towards Kiel. The largest immediate loss of territory had occurred between Lauenburg and Bergen, where a peninsula of Federal Germany, the Wendland, had been attacked simultaneously from north and south, west of the river Jeetze, and a heavy Soviet air drop at Hitzacker had unexpectedly established a bridgehead. The Elbe at this point was wide, and it had been thought the NATO defences were adequate, but a complete airborne division from the Mongolian Peoples Republic of the USSR had been used in the assault. It had been one of the possible contingencies of modern warfare; the Americans had proved the feasability of flying airborne troops into battle from great distances, and the Soviet command had been quick to see how it could be exploited to overcome problems caused by competent enemy surveillance in battle areas. The sudden involvement of unexpected numbers of men and fighting vehicles could easily disrupt the calculations of planned defence. The loss of the Wendland was Dormer's only present regret. It had been expected, but he had hoped the river Jeetze, which cut south across the whole peninsula of land and then east towards the border, would have proved more of an obstacle to the Soviet advance, and further increased their heavy casualty figures.

It had long been admitted it was impractical to consider

establishing a main line of defence at the Eastern German border. With an increasingly mobile type of warfare, and against the great strength of the Warsaw Pact countries, a solid wall technique would tend to produce near matching losses for both attackers and defenders. By using more flexible techniques, reserves could be held in readiness until the inertia was lost from the Soviet invasion, their shock troops no longer effective, and their supply lines stretched. At such a time, the Warsaw Pact armies would be at their most vulnerable, and the NATO powers at their strongest.

Dormer read the decoded message just received from SACEUR – Supreme Allied Commander Europe. 'Reference use of chemicals in various sectors, retaliatory action is in order.'

The message had been carefully worded to ensure the final decision rested with him...not only the decision, but the responsibility! Reports of chemicals had reached headquarters on several occasions throughout the day, but there appeared to have been no concentrated attacks. And in no instances had the use of chemicals been sustained. It had been difficult for him to decide whether it had been deliberately used but in limited and almost experimental circumstances, or released by pure accident; perhaps the destruction of a vehicle equipped with chemical weapons.

The communications officer knew the contents of the message and was waiting for Dormer's reaction. 'Do you want me to pass it to divisional levels, sir?'

'No, not yet.' Not until I'm damned certain, he told himself. It was all too easy to begin an irreversible escalation towards the use of nuclear weapons.

ELEVEN

Studley had been blindfolded, he thought unnecessarily, and then made to lie spreadeagled face downwards on the ground. His feelings were too mixed to be identifiable: dismay, humiliation, disappointment, bitterness. He had never before understood suicides – except as a form of patriotism where death was used as a shield to protect colleagues – he considered it now. If he were to leap to his feet, attempt to run, then his guards would shoot. But it might not be death, simply more pain; a useless gesture. Lt Colonel James Studley felt helpless. After years of exercising authority, it was not easy for him to accept degradation.

The helicopter swung down above the trees, the gale of its rotors stripping the remaining leaves from the thin twisted branches, ruffling Studley's clothing and hair. He was pulled to his feet and almost thrown into the aircraft. There was a guard close to him, the man announcing his presence by pressing the cold muzzle of a rifle against Studley's neck. The feeling of lift was brief before the machine levelled out above the trees and swung across the plain. The flight lasted less than ten minutes.

His blindfold was removed when he had been half-dragged some fifty meters from the helicopter. Its engine roared; he felt the wind of its take-off and heard it slip into the distance. He was inside a rough canvas tent, its square shape disguised by camouflage netting. Three radio operators were sitting beside their equipment, one speaking

123

rapidly in Russian. A number of officers were bent over maps on a long wooden table in the centre of the tent, and clerks and infantrymen were busy around them. They ignored him for several minutes; the guard, a thick-set man in brown combat clothing, rigidly at attention by his side.

Eventually, one of the officers straightened himself, stared at James Studley and walked towards him. The guard saluted and handed over a small cloth-wrapped bundle. The officer tipped its contents on to a narrow desk, and Studley recognized his own belongings and identity papers. The officer examined them for a long time in silence, referring frequently to notes on a clipboard beside him.

Studley knew the man's uniform, dark green with gold and olive epaulets; a captain of the Soviet Army Main Intelligence Directorate, the GRU.

'You are a lieutenant colonel in the 4th Armoured Division of the 1st British Corps,' said the captain. His English was good, too good to have been learnt only in the USSR. The man must have had embassy experience.

'I am Lieutenant Colonel James Studley, and my number is 457590...'

The captain interrupted him. 'Colonel, you have been watching too many war movies. I know what you consider to be your rights. I am also aware of your name, rank and military identification number. I know also you are commanding officer of a battle group which you have named Cowdray, and that your group consisted of part of the Kings Hussars, a company of mechanized infantry, self-propelled guns and missile launchers. I say consisted, Colonel, because regretfully it no longer exists. It has been wiped out.' He paused to allow Studley to digest his words. 'We have also destroyed your field headquarters.'

Studley said, 'I would like to join my officers.'

'I doubt if that is the truth, Colonel. There were no survivors.'

So Max must be dead after all, thought Studley. It seemed impossible.

The captain continued. 'Colonel, like yourself I am a professional soldier. You and I do not make wars, we only fight them at the command of our politicians. We realize you were under orders, and naturally you obeyed them; that is good...it is how a soldier should behave.'

Studley felt himself swaying, his vision was blurring.

'Colonel you must excuse me...of course, you have been injured; it is always a shock to the nervous system.' The captain shouted in Russian and a chair was placed at Studley's side. 'Please sit down. I will make sure you have medical attention as soon as possible. And now...' The captain picked up the clipboard from the table. 'Colonel James Studley, born in Hastings Cottage Hospital, Sussex, 16 June, 1941. Mother, Margaret Elizabeth Studley. Father, James Howard Studley, veterinary surgeon, formerly a captain in the British Army Veterinary Corps and awarded the Military Cross in action in Italy, in 1944. Quite unusual for a veterinary officer, Colonel! You were educated at Winchester, and then accepted in to the British army in August 1959...I have quite a lot here on your military career. Very successful, Colonel...'

Studley felt the rare chill of fear. He had been aware of the depth of Soviet intelligence, but this was frightening; the ability to pull such detailed knowledge out of the computer files so quickly. His capture must have been reported by radio within minutes and the request for all information on his background sent immediately to some distant central military computer.

The GRU captain read his thoughts. 'You are naturally a little surprised, Colonel.' The man smiled without humour. 'I would like to claim we had such information on *every* NATO officer, but of course you would realize this could not be so. We are satisfied with confining our efforts to those in senior positions of command, Colonel. After all, such knowledge is part of the skill of modern computerized warfare. Know the man and perhaps you know something of the manner in which he will fight. And, Colonel, much of

125

our information is easy to find; your army has a habit of cataloguing most things...promotions, postings...and much of a man's history can be learnt through your public records offices. The more personal things? They are...tricks of our trade.' The captain turned a few more sheets of paper. 'Your medical record...appendicitis in 1981...' he glanced at Studley. 'Fully recovered by now, I hope, Colonel? Unmarried...you have lost both your parents, I see...sad...and you maintain your parents' house in Winchelsea. Tidbits, Colonel, just tidbits that enlarge our knowledge of our opponents. Here, for instance: 1980...September...a military exercise, Crusader '80...one of your biggest for some time, I believe. When it ended, you went back to Britain on leave, Colonel. But not alone. I see you were accompanied by a lady who was also returning to Britain. A Mrs Jane Fairly. There is a note here that she is the wife of another officer serving with your regiment, a major...of course there is nothing unusual about people travelling together...it is sensible, economical when you are both travelling in the same direction. Also economical that you spent a night in the same hotel and the same room, in Amsterdam. And then shared a cabin on the overnight ferry.' The captain was suddenly apologetic. 'No, Colonel, please be calm. I am suggesting nothing...such things are of no importance to me. What possible use is such information to me, when you are here and they are there?' He pointed to a wall of the tent as though it were a frontier.

'Colonel, it will not be long before we require large numbers of skilled administrators...there will be much work for us all, and it will be easier for everyone if we work together. This is not a territorial war where the victor will oppress the vanquished. This is a war of liberation. It is our desire to establish lasting friendship with our British comrades once the existing corrupt system has been removed. The sooner this terrible business is ended, the fewer lives will be lost and life can return to normality once again. We should work together towards this end.' He spoke confidentially, his eyes meeting those of Studley. 'I don't want an immediate answer. Think it over for an hour. Here...' He passed Studley a typewritten sheet. 'These questions...simple ones. Relatively unimportant. Read them in private. You can help me with them later. Afterwards, I'll arrange for you to see one of our doctors. Then you can wash...I can find you a change of clothing...and a good meal, eh, Colonel.' He signalled one of the guards near the tent door, and Studley was led outside. There were several BMPs parked beneath camouflage netting at the side of a broad woodland clearing. A pair of MAZ-543 cargo carriers with their huge bodies towering above him, were standing only a few meters away, while at the side of the tent was a truck mounted with a tall radio relay pylon with dish aerials.

Distantly, Studley could hear the sound of artillery.

He was taken to one of the BMPs and ordered to climb inside. The guard closed down the hatch above him. It was gloomy, the only light filtering through one of the gun ports. The interior fittings were spartan, the seats thinly padded. It would be an uncomfortable vehicle for the infantry who used it.

Studley felt for his watch; it was missing. From the low angle of the sun when he had left the tent he thought it must be late afternoon. He held the paper he had been given towards the gun port. 'Questions,' the captain had said. 'Simple ones. Relatively unimportant.' There were no questions on the sheet of paper, simply NATO code names. Studley recognized them. Code names for the map references of the division's positions, rendezvous points, laagerings, field headquarters of all the units, the H hour time code. Relatively unimportant? With the code broken the Russians would be able to anticipate every movement the division made. All the Soviet artillery would need to do would be to wait until a few minutes after the time given in the division's orders, then plaster the area.

But the information was only good for the next seven

hours or so. At midnight, the codes would be changed. Studley felt relieved. If he could hold out until then he would be of no further use to Russian intelligence. He screwed the paper into a ball and tossed it into the corner of the vehicle.

His body felt as though it had been crushed and squashed. Every muscle was bruised and aching, his joints felt as though they were arthritic. The wound in his leg had stiffened and the blood had seeped through the dressing and hardened. He hadn't seen the wound, but didn't think it could be very serious...unless it became infected.

He stretched himself out and lifted his legs on to the neighbouring seat. He was exhausted, but knew he wouldn't be able to sleep.

Their intelligence on military personnel had startled him. It was better than just good. He had heard that over one hundred and eighty thousand people worked, in one way or another, for the American CIA. The Soviet agencies probably employed even more, collecting a mass of information and passing it back to their directorates for storage in their computers. Feed in a name and three minutes later, by radio, you had a full dossier; damn them, they were too efficient. Where did they start and end with the NATO army? Not at lieutenant...major, perhaps...everyone from the rank of major upwards, filed away in a Russian computer...every scrap of information they could lay their hands on; information from countless sources, civil and military, classified and non-classified, clerks in NATO offices who were working for the Russians...in military offices...civilian mess staff...bar staff...

It was incredible they knew about Jane. The Russian GRU captain had been right, maybe they couldn't make use of it but nevertheless they knew. War was a dirty game, and intelligence its darkest corner! Would they have ever made use of their knowledge if there hadn't been a war? Perhaps. They might have tried to blackmail him...threatened to ruin his career...expose him. God, thought Studley, expose what? Tell Max I'm having an affair with his wife? I wasn't some businessman on a week's jaunt in Moscow, or Leipzig. They didn't photograph me with a whore in some third-rate hotel...or produce pornographic tape-recordings. Jane and I are in love; we've been in love for years and we've kept quiet, bottled it up; kept it from Max and young Paul.

It hadn't been easy when they had all been together. It had been unpleasant at times, watching Max with his arm around Jane, knowing it was Max who would be taking her to bed, caressing her, sleeping beside her. Now poor old Max was dead, and thankfully he had never known. He couldn't be hurt. The thought of his death made Studley feel guilty; he had never wished it. He would have done almost anything to prevent it.

What a balls-up! He had expected casualties in the fighting, but somehow hadn't thought he would be amongst them. How many of the men had been lost? Who had survived? Maybe it wasn't too bad after all! If they'd put up a stiff fight and taken out plenty of the enemy, it was worthwhile. Had what they'd all done been enough? Had he somehow let his men down? Christ, he didn't know!

And what now? Would the GRU officer just question him again, and then pass him back through the lines until he ended up in some POW camp? There were bound to be other prisoners, he couldn't be the only one! There would be other officers, taken in similar situations along the front...the Russians would get them all together somewhere. God, he felt miserable! It would be bad for Jane, too. Her husband dead, and her lover a prisoner...and Paul, her son...trapped in West Berlin with very little hope of escaping. Damn Berlin. Damn the little red train that was its military artery. And damn Tempelhof, a vulnerable airport which a dozen rockets could put out of action. Christ, it would be bad in Berlin now; surrounded, impossible to defend against missile attacks, and too isolated to break out from. A Stalingrad, perhaps.

Escape. Perhaps that was what should be done? It was

wrong to sit around waiting for the worst to happen...escape...it might be possible. But what about his leg wound? He could walk, even though his calf muscle was stiff and aching. Plenty of men had done it before. He remembered talking to someone who had escaped after Dunkirk. 'Take the very first opportunity you get,' the man had advised. 'If you wait for the second, then it's too late...the second chance may never come.' Studley could remember the man clearly. He limped badly, broke his thigh when he jumped from a train, crawled several miles at night hiding in daytime in ditches full of water and mud. He had spent weeks in some French farmhouse before returning to England on a fishing boat. But he'd made it. He hadn't fought again, but he'd done a useful training job for the remainder of the war. He had survived.

Survival. That was what Studley was going to do...survive. One way and another...any way, he'd survive. Jane would need him; they'd need each other.

Jane...God, dear Jane. For twelve years they'd loved each other. It was hard to know exactly when it had all begun, or even how it had started. There wasn't a particular hour or even day when he'd suddenly thought he loved her, wanted her. There had been mess dinners, mess balls; the three of them always seemed to to together. Sometimes he took a lady guest with him, but it wasn't too easy to meet single women as you got older. Sometime during the evening he would find himself dancing with Jane; Max preferred to remain near a bar. The number of dances seemed to grow...the number of times she was in his arms. Even then, neither of them had said anything nor made a positive move. It was just that somehow over the years it changed; the way they held each other while they danced...the way their arms had linked as they walked from the floor.

One night they had stood together on the mess terrace; it had become too hot inside, after midnight. It had been the summer ball, and quite a grand affair...three bars, a disco

130

for the younger officers, the regimental band in the main hall. He and Jane were close enough for their bodies to be touching and he had automatically put his arm around her waist. He felt at the time it had been a protective movement, not suggestive. She moved even closer and he had felt the firmness of her hip against his thigh, and known at that second they both wanted each other desperately. Jane had felt the same, he knew, for instinctively their eyes had met and he had seen her quickly hide the emotion.

'Let's go and have a drink. I'm very thirsty...something long and cool.' Her voice was over-flippant, sounding very young, uncertain. He noticed she avoided his eyes now and shook her dark hair back over her shoulders, nervously. She and Max had married young. Paul had been born before she was twenty, he was seven only a few weeks before the ball.

'I don't know if I can face the crowd for a few minutes.' He intended it as an excuse to delay her, but she had misunderstood him.

'I can't either.' Her voice had been flat, weary. 'Sometimes I think they're watching us...their eyes following us everywhere. Sometimes I think they can read my mind.' She became angry. 'I hate these evenings. I hate the dressing up, all the gold braid, the artificial camaraderie and the inane conversations...I hate anaesthetizing myself with gin and tonics so I've got the guts to dance with you all night in front of them, and the courage to let you leave me at the end.' She had turned away from him and stared across the dark lawns and rose beds. She was gripping his hand tightly.

'What can we do?' Her outburst had startled him, forcing him to acknowledge his own feelings.

'Nothing! If I'd once loved Max and now I hated him, it would be easy; I'd be strong enough to leave him. But I never loved him, so my feelings haven't changed. I've always liked him, and I still do. And you can't hurt someone you like so much.'

They avoided each other during the following weeks, until

131

it became obvious to Max. 'You and Jane had a fight?'

'Jane? Good heavens, no!'

'We haven't seen much of you.'

Studley had lied. 'It's not been deliberate, Max. I just don't seem to have got around to socializing lately.'

'Dinner, Saturday evening then? Drinks about eight. Bozy and Felicity will be along. Jane and I thought we should invite Challace, introduce his wife to some of the other ladies of the regiment. It's never easy for a new officer's missus.'

Max, always friendly, concerned and dependable. He wasn't even built like a soldier, stocky, rounded. Gieves and Hawkes found it difficult to get a military cut to his suits. In civvies he always managed to look like a contented country vicar; perhaps he should have been, it would have suited his easy-going temperament. 'Thanks, I'll be along.'

There was another evening, later, in the mess. He and Max were alone. 'Ever think of getting married, James?'

'Thought, once or twice.' He had attempted to change the subject, but Max persisted; he had downed several drinks.

'You should look around.'

'It's hardly possible here in Germany.'

'When we're in Ireland then. Daughter of a wealthy Irish landowner.'

'For God's sake, Max...what opportunity do we get for socializing in Ireland?'

'The Queen Alexander's Nursing Corps; there are some smashers amongst the nurses. Point one out to me and I'll get Jane to invite her to dinner. Being a batchelor is no life for you, James.'

'It suits me.'

'It'll make you sour. You need a wife and a couple of kids.'

'Something I wanted to mention; the MT, sheds...there's a hold-up with...'

'Have you ever met Charlesworth's daughter? I know she's quite young, but...'

'Max!'

It had been a full year after the incident at the ball before he and Jane had become lovers. It hadn't been planned. Again, it was summer...long and dry, the grass scorching brown and the leaves becoming dusted on the trees near the roadsides. Max had suggested the trip into the mountains south of Hildesheim; it was an easy run down the autobahn. 'Find ourselves an inn and stay overnight. Get some good food and a breath of fresh mountain air. Take a rod, James, there may be a decent trout stream.'

It had been too tempting to refuse; not the thought of being with Jane, but the chance to get away from the barracks and the countryside around Bergen.

Saturday morning came and with it the unexpected arrival of a friend of Max's from the Royal Tank Regiment at Herford, passing through on his way to a NATO posting in Denmark.

Max's apologies. 'Go on ahead. I'll have lunch with him here in the mess, and we can meet this evening at Salzdetfurth. Take rooms at the *gasthof*, and I'll be there in time for drinks.'

'It doesn't matter, we'll wait...we'll travel together later. Or we can put the whole thing off until another weekend.'

Max wouldn't hear of it. 'Jane can't stand the fellow. Hates him! Didn't even like him when we were at college together. No, you two go ahead.'

They had driven down the long highway, busy with weekend traffic. The holiday season had not yet ended, and there were families heading south with camping trailers, their cars heavy with luggage. Repair works slowed the journey, funnelling the traffic across the central barriers, reducing the cruising speed. They had stopped for lunch at an autobahn restaurant south of the Hannover intersection, and been happier once they had left the main highway after Hildesheim and taken the narrower mountain roads.

They stopped near a wooded stream, a tributary of the Leine near Bockenhem, and sat beneath the rowans and beeches. There was a kingfisher hunting the shallow pools, and the cool sounds of water bubbling amongst the rocks. They were both cautious, shy, avoiding any physical contact, aware of the dangers of such a trigger. They talked a little. Jane dozed, while Studley rested with his back against the bole of an old beech and let the problems of the week slip away.

It was five by the time they reached the *gasthof* and booked rooms; almost seven when Max telephoned from the mess at Bergen.

'Damn him, Max. We're booked in here.' Studley could hear Jane's voice, peeved with the knowledge Max was probably only delayed because he couldn't deny his hospitality. 'James and I will have dinner, then drive back...pretty crowded but they'll have cleared...no, of course not...well, I'm not exactly delighted...Charles should have given you warning, anyway...well, yes, it would probably be better...about eleven...if we've gone out, we'll leave a message for you. Yes...I'll see you then...' She hung up and spoke to Studley. 'Charles has decided to stop over for the night, and Max is having dinner with him.'

'I suppose I'd better unbook our rooms.'

'No need. Max suggests we stay. He'll be down in the morning, about eleven.'

He knew by her tone of voice she had decided that some time in the next few hours they would make love. He was uncertain for a while if it was because of her annoyance with Max or a decision to relax the tight control she had maintained over her feelings for the past months. There had been occasions when he had considered that some time in the future this kind of situation might arise, and he had wondered how he would deal with it. The simple answer was to avoid it, but now it was happening. He didn't feel like a gentleman, but neither did he feel guilty.

'I noticed a prettier restaurant further down the road, shall we give it a try?'

'I'd like that, James.'

134

She had hooked her arm in his, affectionately, once they had left the *gasthof* to stroll through the town. The restaurant had been small, intimate, Bavarian in its conception. He couldn't remember what they had eaten, only her face; her eyes watching him across the candlelit table.

Sometime after midnight they had returned to the *gasthof*, its stone-flagged hallway smelling of cigar smoke and beer, echoing their footsteps. It seemed deserted.

Their two rooms were adjoining. He had opened the door to his own, and she had walked inside, there had been no suggestion, no invitations. There was moonlight in the room, and for the first time they kissed. It was gentle, tender. He could taste the perfume on her neck and shoulders as he undressed her, the light summer clothing slipping away until she was naked; there was a moment of awkwardness as he stripped, then she was in his arms, her body small, warm against his own.

She was slender, and he felt her pelvis against his thighs and let his hands trace her soft curves. The bed had been only a step away in the small room, and she had lain in the bright square of moonlight that shone through the uncurtained window.

He remembered how careful the lovemaking had been, unhurried, almost measured at first as though they were both inexperienced, then intensifying, gathering urgency and excitement as he entered her and felt the heat of her body envelop him. She had cried out with her orgasm and her fingers had dug deep into his muscles.

The thoughts of her normally warmed him, but now, trapped in the gloomy interior of the enemy vehicle and filled with an inescapable sense of failure, he felt even more lonely and despondent.

There was no retreat from the present. The metal hatch above his head was pulled open, and a thick-set guard gestured that he should climb out. The rich orb of the autumn sun had already dropped below the tops of the trees, and the clearing was streaked with lengthening shadows. Studley began to walk towards the tent where he first met the GRU officer, but the guard stopped him and pushed him in the direction of the woods with the barrel of his AKS-74.

Studley's calf wound made it difficult for him to move quickly, and the guard was impatient. Studley didn't understand the man's Russian, but knew he was being cursed. He wondered if he were about to be shot. It was a frightening thought. He wouldn't make it easy for them. He decided to wait until he was further into the woodland and then tempt the guard to get closer to him. If the man was foolish enough to prod him with his rifle again, there was a chance he might be able to overpower him and with a weapon in his hands his chances of survival were greatly improved. But there was no opportunity for him to begin to put his plan into operation for only a few paces into the woods, hidden beneath carefully draped branches and netting, was an armoured vehicle. Unlike the BMPs this was wheeled, and Studley thought it was probably a version of the BTR, perhaps a modified command post.

The GRU captain was waiting inside, impatiently, the clipboard of Studley's details beneath his arm. He spoke brusquely, making no attempt to maintain his apparent former respect for Studley's senior rank. 'You have had the hour I promised. Where is the paper I gave you?'

Studley met the Russian's eyes and held his gaze. 'I threw it away.' He could feel the muscles of his shoulders and back tightening, a childhood defence against anger which he had not experienced for many years. He straightened himself deliberately into a military posture he knew would make him appear arrogant.

The Russian noticed the action but ignored it. 'I have another sheet prepared. We shall work with that.'

'You're wasting your time.'

'We shall see.' There was the hint of a threat in the man's voice. He was twenty-nine or thirty years old and clean-shaven. He wore his peaked hat pushed casually back off his forehead, and the hair above his ears seemed longer than the normal Soviet military style. His face was sallow, angular, hollowing sharply beneath the cheekbones; hinting at an ancestry in the eastern regions of the USSR. 'You must realize it will be better for you to assist me. All senior officers of your military services will be required to face a Soviet People's Court in due time. The decisions they reach will be influenced by our reports. If your records show you have attempted to help us, then the People's Court will be lenient. If not, your punishment will be greater. At the very least you will face a long term of imprisonment. Do you understand me?'

'I am not a criminal, I am a prisoner of war. I have committed no atrocities.'

'The killing of Soviet citizens is an atrocity, regardless of circumstances. A claim you were only obeying orders has been proved to be no defence in war trials; Nuremburg established that fact of law. Many of those found guilty were hanged. You will therefore co-operate.' Studley was silent, but he shook his head. 'Very well. I regret that in these circumstances, we do not have time for sophisticated interrogation.' He spoke to the guard. Studley turned, expecting to be led away, but the man rammed the butt of his rifle into Studley's side. He felt ribs crack as all the wind was driven from his lungs by the force of the blow, and a spear of pain drove itself across his chest. As Studley doubled forward, the guard swung the weapon again, this time at his face. The slab of the metal breech smashed against his lips and teeth, a blue-white light exploded behind his eyes.

He was on his knees, his throat full of blood, his torn lips and gums feeling as though they were burning. He put his hand to his mouth; his teeth were broken stumps and there were sharp splinters in the wounds. His nose was bleeding.

'As I warned you, there is no time for finesse. Now. Do you wish to help us? If you do so, there will be immediate

137

medical assistance for you. You have simply to identify the code words.'

Studley coughed the blood from his throat. The GRU officer's voice sounded distant, and the floor beneath him felt like the swaying deck of a small boat. He attempted to concentrate his mind on a single thought...Jane. He tried to block the pain with memories.

The guard stamped down on to the wound in Studley's leg.

TWELVE

There were a group of military police on the road ahead of Sergeant Davis, their tempers frayed as they attempted to funnel the civilian refugees to one side to allow the passage of convoys of military vehicles towards the battle area. The number of refugees astonished Davis. He had expected some, but it seemed all the people from the town of Schöningen and villages near the border were trying to get away from the advancing Russian armies. There were queues of every kind of civilian vehicles, barely moving at walking pace along the entire length of the road. He had seen newsreel pictures of the Second World War when refugees had similarly blocked the movement of troops, but hadn't expected it to be like that now. Cars and lorries had broken down, run out of fuel, and been abandoned at the roadside still piled high with family possessions. Trucks and farm wagons, tractors and their sugar-beet trailers, people on foot or on bicycles, moved in a slow but determined procession towards the west. Davis followed the route of the road, but kept to the fields except where boundary ditches or irrigation dikes forced him back. Angrily, the refugees paused to let him by, and he knew from their contemptuous stares they suspected the two tanks, like themselves, were fleeing from the enemy.

The flood crept past the military police, obeying their desperate signals for only meters before swelling back to occupy the full width of the road. A convoy of Stalwarts was making only a few kilometers an hour eastwards,

139

despite their drivers' attempts to make use of the verges at the roadside.

A harrassed young corporal, red-eyed with fatigue, clambered on to Davis's Chieftain. 'Who the 'ell are you?'

Davis told him.

The corporal checked a list. 'Okay, Sergeant. Your regrouping area is three kilometers on...you'll see crossroads after Kissleberfeld and then your divisional number on a black sign — that is if some bastard hasn't moved it. Turn right there; it's unsurfaced. And keep off this road as much as possible.' He stared at the scarred hull of the tank, seeking an excuse for further conversation to keep him a few moments longer from his near-impossible task. 'Was it bad, mate?' Davis nodded. It was too early yet to find adequate words to describe the previous few hours of battle. 'Bastards,' the corporal swore. 'I'd hang every fuckin' Russian we catch. Watch out for their bloody Floggers; they've been brassin' the roads every hour or so...civvies, everything. Murdering swine. A bit north of here the convoys are driving through swamps of pulped bodies, it's the only fuckin' way they can get the supplies up.' He pointed towards drifting smoke three hundred meters across the fields. 'See them...AFVs they caught in the open. And this soddin' lot...' He jerked his head towards the slow-moving river of people. 'Get 'em out of the way, and a minute later they're all over the road again...they're fuckin' deaf...daft. It's all fuckin' murder. We heard it's even worse towards Hannover.' His conscience nagged him as he heard shouting from his colleagues. 'Take care, mate. And when you're in there again, give 'em one up the arse for the Redcaps. So long.'

It took Davis half an hour to travel the last three kilometers. He managed to shorten the distance a little by taking a more direct route across country. Where possible he used the cover close to the fringes of woods, and well away from the roadway. He kept his eyes open for aircraft, but it wasn't easy; there were plenty in the skies but he couldn't always identify them. A few screamed over at little more than tree-top height heading eastwards; they were NATO planes, but even had they been Russian he couldn't have reacted quickly enough to take evasive action. It wasn't the low-flying aircraft he feared, for they came and went in seconds with their pilots concentrating on targets many kilometers ahead of them; the greatest danger was from those who stooged at a high altitude, risking the anti-aircraft missiles or attacks from NATO planes, as they searched for vehicle concentrations.

There were more military police near the regrouping area, a roadblock overlooked by a machine gun post. Again Davis was stopped, and this time his identification was carefully scrutinized by an officer before he was allowed to continue. Enemy sleeper groups had been reported to be making use of captured NATO vehicles to infiltrate depots; an incident a few minutes earlier, at one of the airfields, had brought renewed warnings. The police and guards were nervous of any vehicle which showed signs of combat. The MP officer pointed with his swagger-cane. 'Over there to the right, Sergeant. Follow your number. When you get to the harbour area, get your vehicle out of sight fast. Cam' it, and report to the command vehicle at once...PDQ...on your way.'

The roll of camouflage netting which had been lashed to the Chieftain's hull was missing, as was all of the external equipment, jerry cans, tools, cable reel. The left-hand smoke grenade launchers had been torn from the turret, and the infra-red searchlight was smashed and buckled out of shape. Once the tank had been parked, the crew climbed out of the hull for the first time that day.

Shadwell was hugging his arm, his roughly bandaged hand under his armpit. His dark NBC suit concealed most of the bloodstains, but there were brown streaks down his face and neck. 'Five minutes, lad, and we'll get you to the aid-post. Can you hang on?'

Shadwell grimaced, then smiled. 'It don't hurt now,

Sarge. Not as bad as toothache. I've got blisters on my arse though, from that seat.'

' 'ere, have you seen this?' Inkester was running his fingertips along a deep scar in the metal of the turret. 'And Christ...look at these!'

'Okay lads, that's enough sightseeing. Inkester, there's spare camouflage netting over there...double across and get it. DeeJay, give him a hand. If you need more, scrounge around while I go and report.' Davis noticed Corporal Sealey lounging on the turret of the neighbouring Chieftain. 'Don't sit around, Corporal. Get your crew out and cam up. I want these two vehicles so well hidden I won't be able to find them when I get back, understand? Jump to it, all of you.' Shadwell moved with Hewett and Inkester. 'Not you lad. You take it easy. If you can't sit down, then see if you can find out where we can get some decent grub.'

Sergeant Davis recognized Captain Clarkson the operations officer in the Sultan. The officer's clothing was still barracks-clean, and Davis was suddenly conscious of his own filthy appearance, but Clarkson made no comment.

'We've been expecting you, Sergeant Davis. We've made contact with Captain Willis; he's due here shortly, too. I'm afraid we've had a lot of casualties, Sergeant. Very unfortunate.'

Davis was unable to resist the question. 'How many tanks have we got left, sir?'

Captain Clarkson hesitated. Strictly speaking he shouldn't divulge figures, but he knew Davis had as many years with the regiment as himself. 'Discounting the headquarters squadron, fourteen.'

'Fourteen!' Davis felt the blood draining from his face. Fourteen survivors out of forty-five main battle tanks...plus the colonel's and the Number Twos...'Fourteen, sir?' Perhaps he had misheard.

Clarkson nodded. 'Chieftains, yes. And we still have five Scimitars in the battle group.' He knew the sergeant's feelings exactly, his own had been identical as the figures

142

had come through; disbelief and then horror at the loss of so many men...not all exactly friends, but at least regimental comrades, colleagues. 'It's been a very bad day, Sergeant.' He added: 'For all of us. Have you been informed about the colonel?'

'No, sir.' God, not old Studley, too! Colonels were supposed to be indestructible...they didn't get themselves killed!

'The colonel's tank was knocked out. He's gone.' Clarkson made it sound as if Colonel Studley was off somewhere on a jaunt, but Davis understood. 'And Major Fairly is reported missing believed killed.'

'I'm sorry about that, sir.'

'For the time being, the figures are confidential, Sergeant. I don't want them bandied around. Wouldn't help matters. And, of course, there may be quite a few survivors; some of the men will have been taken prisoner...perhaps even making their way back out of the line on foot, holed-up somewhere.'

'Yes, sir.' There might be a few, thought Davis, but he knew Clarkson's optimism was purely for his benefit. The condescension annoyed him slightly.

'Now, if I can have your report...'

Davis told him as much as he could recall. It was hard remembering, and he corrected himself frequently. One of the clerks was jotting down notes. Davis answered the captain's questions, then said, 'That's about all, sir.'

'Good, Sergeant. Very useful.' Clarkson paused and mentally confirmed there was nothing he had overlooked in the interview, and then leant back in his chair. 'Take your loader to the aid-post, and then get some food inside yourself and the crews. Stay close to your vehicles, we'll want you back here later.'

'Yes, sir.' Davis saluted and climbed out of the vehicle. The sky towards the east was heavy with black smoke clouds; the war was seeking him out, relentlessly. There were too many vehicles moving in the laager for him to hear

143

the guns, but he knew the sounds would be there.

The crew were sitting beneath the netting beside the Chieftain's tracks. There was no need for him to suggest they should eat, they were doing so already. DeeJay was asleep, his open mouth still holding an unchewed bite of fried egg sandwich. Inkester cradled a pint mug of tea, and Shadwell a pair of cheese rolls balanced in the crook of his injured arm.

'Come on Shadwell, let's get you seen to.' Davis stared down at him good-humouredly.

'I think I'm fit, Sarge. Fit for duty.'

'Don't be daft, lad.' He understood Shadwell's reluctance to visit the hospital tent. Here, he was with his mates; there, everyone would be strangers. It was the same feeling you got when you were posted.

'It's not bothering me, Sarge, honestly.' Shadwell waved his bandaged hand. 'I'm okay now.'

'It'll bother you later. The war hasn't ended yet. We'll be back in action in a couple of hours. You've got yourself a "Blighty".'

'Lucky sod,' enthused Inkester. 'You'll be drinking beer in an English pub tomorrow. Bloody ace, Eric. You'll have smashing nurses to teach you to pick your nose with your other hand!'

'Balls,' muttered Shadwell. He followed Davis across to the field ambulance and glowered as Davis handed him over to the orderlies. 'I've left some gear in the tank, Sarge.' A delaying tactic.

'I'll get Inkester to bring it over.' Davis slapped Shadwell's back, gently. 'Thanks, lad. We'll see you soon.'

'Was I okay, Sarge? I mean, well, did I do all right?' He sounded like an insecure teenager who'd just surrendered his virginity.

Davis knew it was unlikely he'd ever see Shadwell again. He would be moved back to the UK eventually, and probably discharged. He had been a crew member for two years, and Davis realized whatever he said to Shadwell now

144

was going to be remembered for a very long time. His attempt to choose the right words made them clumsier. 'You did marvellous, son...marvellous. You're a first-class loader, Shadwell. Best I've ever had.'

He turned quickly, left the ambulance, and then paused outside. Shadwell had said he had left some of his gear in the Chieftain; Christ, he had some of Shadwell in his overall pocket...his fingers! Davis called to the nearest orderly, a young pink-faced man sterilizing instruments in a steamer outside the aid-post.

The fingers were of no use, they had been off Shadwell's hand for far too long for them to be sewn back in place, but just throwing them away somewhere didn't seem right to Davis. He sorted them out from the compo ration sweets which had gone sticky in his pocket.

'Sergeant?' The orderly looked at him quizzically.

'Here. You'd better have these,' said Davis.

The orderly held out his hand automatically, and Davis dropped Shadwell's stumpy bloodstained fingers into his palm. It took the orderly a moment or two to realize what they were, then his face paled. 'Bloody hell!' He dropped them as though they were hot.

'Pick them up,' Davis shouted furiously. They were no longer fingers, they were all his friends who had died that day on the battlefield. 'Pick them up, lad. See that Trooper Shadwell gets his ring back, and give his fingers a decent burial.'

Davis was facing a brigadier from Division HQ, glad he had managed to find himself a cup of hot water and shaved. He would have liked to strip off and shower because he knew he was stinking, but it had been impossible. However, he was relieved he had got some of the muck off his face and hands.

Charlie Squadron's leader, Captain Valda Willis, was with the staff officer and had smiled as Davis entered the command post. 'Glad you made it, Sergeant.' The greeting had held genuine warmth.

'Thank you, sir.'

'Davis!' The brigadier was glaring at him. 'Captain Willis has just put in a report of your performance this afternoon.'

Christ, thought Davis. What now?

'He tells me you personally stood-off a Russian tank battalion. Is that correct?'

Davis felt himself blush. 'I don't know about that, sir.'

'At Redstart, Sergeant. Yourself and the corporal in charge of Charlie Bravo Four. He tells me that on your own initiative you got yourself hull-defilade beside a road, and picked them off as they came across the fields. You then retired four hundred meters and did the same thing again. It has been confirmed by an officer of the 17th/21st.'

'It seemed the best thing to do, sir,' said Davis. He hadn't realized there had been an audience. It made him even more embarrassed.

'You could have simply retired, Sergeant; the remainder of your squadron vehicles were all knocked out, it would have been reasonable for you to have done so.'

'Yes, sir.' Davis didn't know what the brigadier was expecting him to say. He wasn't sounding particularly friendly, perhaps Davis was about to get a rocket for putting the tanks and men at risk.

'Good show, Sergeant. Damned good show. I see that your loader was wounded, and your tank hit!'

Davis thought he should emphasize the part Shadwell had played. If there was credit to be handed around, then Shadwell was due for some. 'Trooper Shadwell lost his fingers early in the action, sir. He kept on loading even after he had been wounded. And just now, sir, he refused medical attention until I gave him an order. He wanted to remain with the crew.'

'Excellent spirit, Sergeant. His behaviour won't be overlooked.' Davis was surprised to see Captain Willis wink at him from behind the brigadier's shoulder. The brigadier continued. 'Your Chieftain's a little worse for wear. I want you to take over a troop, Davis. We're rebuilding your squadron. On your squadron leader's recommendation, I'm promoting you to warrant officer first class. The promotion takes effect immediately. Do you understand, Mr Davis?'

'Yes, sir.' He understood the brigadier's words, but he couldn't believe him. Not yet, anyway. A warrant officer. Mister Davis. My God, WO1. He had jumped ranks. Hedda would be over the moon.

Outside, Captain Willis shook his hand warmly. 'You deserve it Mister Davis. You've also been recommended for a decoration.'

'Good God, sir!' He wondered if he was dreaming.

Willis laughed. 'You'll get used to the idea, Mister Davis. The next step is a pip on your shoulder, remember that. By the way, there's a tank delivery squadron in the woods. Here are the papers from Captain Clarkson. They're expecting you over there. You're getting a fresh vehicle. They'll introduce you to your new crew. Run through the usual POL, and checks, just to be on the safe side. When you've got yourself sorted out, come and see me. I can't exactly promise you a celebration, but I've got enough brandy for a small drink to your promotion.'

'Thank you, sir. But the crew, sir. I'd like to keep my own...just need a new loader, sir.'

'It's not always wise with a promotion, Mister Davis.'

'I understand, sir. But I know these men; they're good.'

Willis smiled again. 'Very well. Use them.'

Dusk came early as the sun dropped below the thick pall of smoke that seemed to form the horizon in every direction. Shortly afterwards the squadron moved north-west to its fresh positions behind the River Schunter. The war was more obvious again, much closer, with the undersides of some of the clouds lit by explosions on the ground beneath them. Warrant Officer Davis knew what it was like there, knew what he had to expect again within the next short hours; the turmoil and confusion, the sounds, the heaving

147

ground, and death. It hadn't been too bad the first time, not knowing; and then it had all happened so quickly there had been little time to think. Now, it was different. He had survived once, while a lot of men had died; many of his friends were there, behind the enemy lines, still in the wreckage of their tanks. Could he make it a second time? He would damn well try! What the hell was the use of a promotion if you couldn't enjoy it? He wanted to be with Hedda and the kids; wanted them to share the pleasure of a new uniform, his new rank and the privileges it would bring. There'd be more money, too...a better car, maybe.

The new Chieftain's engine was throbbing softly. The position was on level ground six hundred meters behind the narrow river, on the outskirts of the village of Süpplingen. Davis's tank was in a small garden, with a rising bank between it and the river giving some protection against artillery. The radio nets were silent.

The replacement loader, a nineteen year old, Henry Spink, was fussing about in the fighting compartment. He seemed to be polishing the gun. Davis let him get on with it; the lad was nervous. It wasn't surprising.

DeeJay was whistling softly down in his driving seat, feeling a little happier with a full stomach and a couple of hours sleep behind him. He hadn't enjoyed leaving Bravo Two standing forlorn and battered under her netting beneath the trees. He had felt he was deserting her. It took a conscious effort to turn his back and walk away. The new tank hadn't even smelt right; he had run up the engine, gunned it hard for several minutes, listening to it and trying to spot weaknesses or faults before allowing himself to rest. He knew Inkester had experienced similar doubts about the gunnery equipment. A tank is only a tank, DeeJay kept telling himself; one bit of army equipment is the same as the next. His own arguments didn't convince him. He tried thinking of other things. 'Inky?' He shouted over his shoulder, his voice distorted by the engine vibration and the metalwork of the new Chieftain's hull.

148

'Yeah?'

'Ah've been considerin',' DeeJay yelled. 'Considerin' warrant officers!'

'Oh yeah,' answered Inkester.

'Well, I reckon t' be warrant officer, tha's got to have more brains than a sergeant.' The northern accent was deliberately heavy, broad.

Davis was going to interrupt the banter, and then decided to let DeeJay finish. He didn't want to appear sensitive about his sudden promotion.

'Well, yeah, that's probably right.'

'In that case, stands to reason Inky we got to be better off than this morning, ain't we? Cus, we've got a warrant officer with us now.'

'How would you like some fatigues instead of R and R when we get out of this, Hewett?' Davis thought a little controlled annoyance might be beneficial.

'There y'are, Inky. Our warrant officer said "when we get out". See...warrant officers are bloody optimists, too!' DeeJay began whistling again, this time 'Colonel Bogey'.

Inkester twisted around in his seat. 'That's meant to be a joke, sir. You know DeeJay.'

'I know both of you; that's why you're with me.'

'We're bloody glad we are, sir.'

The moon was beginning to rise and Davis could see movement a few meters away across the corner of the field. He watched carefully. There was a hedgerow to the right, neatly trimmed, below a row of poplars that had been planted as a windbreak for the crops. A fox! He could see it better now, stalking a rabbit that was feeding a few meters out in the stubble. Everything is killing everything else, he thought. One day there'll be only one living thing left on earth, and it'll be so lonely it will have to kill itself, and that will be the end of it all. The earth might be a better place then. Green, lush, peaceful, soundless. Green? If everything killed everything else, it wouldn't be green. It would be brown...dry rock and sand...mud. It would be the

149

battlefield again.

Davis's new troop in Charlie Squadron had retained its designation 'Bravo'. Davis wasn't sure if it was deliberate or accidental, but somehow it seemed to indicate continuity; it certainly made life easier for himself. All he had to remember was that his new Chieftain was Charlie Bravo One, and that as troop leader, he might use the call sign Nine. Captain Willis' voice was on the squadron net now. 'All stations, Charlie, this is Shark. Wolf griddle five seven six zero nine two. Out.'

'Charlie Bravo One. Roger, Shark. Out.'

The radio clicked to silence again. The shorter the time a sender spent on the air, the less likely the call would be intercepted or its source located by enemy listening posts.

Wolf. That was the code name for a Soviet recce battalion. The numbers were a coded grid reference. Davis worked it out on his knee-pad, and then found it on his map. God, they were less than three kilometers away, and a recce battalion could move quickly in their light vehicles.

'How long?' asked Inkester. His voice seemed to have aged in the past hours. Perhaps it was only fatigue.

'Depends. They could try to cross north or south of us. Unless they're delayed, they should reach the river in twenty minutes to half an hour.'

'The minefields will slow them.'

Slow them! Inkester had learned fast, thought Davis. This morning he would have said: 'Stop them'. Sometimes it seemed nothing would ever stop the Russians; they'd keep rolling right the way to the Channel.

'We'll get plenty of support,' Davis said. At least that was true. They hadn't intended to hold them close to the frontier, only slow them down, inflict as many casualties as possible to the armour. Here, it was different. The defences were much stronger, the minefields denser and deeper. There had been a little more time for preparation, and information on ˙he enemy's movements and tactics was clearer.

'You been keeping score, sir?'

150

'Score?'

'Kills.'

'No,' admitted Davis. Christ, trust Inkester! The lad thought he was Von Richthofen. The first opportunity he got, he would paint a line of red stars on the side of the turret.

'Me neither.' Inkester sounded disappointed. 'I got as far as five, and then I lost count. It was more than that though, maybe eight.'

Eight, maybe eight, thought Davis. Better than the odds against them. If every NATO tank took out eight Russian tanks in the battles, then the Russian advance would soon be too costly for them to continue. Eight for one...no, God, not even eight for one. Better than that; he and the crew were still alive, still fighting. At least, three of them were. And the Chieftain was reparable. She was probably back in the workshops now, being serviced. She could be in action with another crew in twelve hours, perhaps less. Eight Russian tanks; three men to a vehicle. That was a lot of dead Russians. There were more – he remembered a BMP exploding, and that would have been carrying its full load of infantry besides the crew. Perhaps thirty men, all told. And this morning he had never killed anyone. How many things had he ever killed in his life, before today? Insects. Everyone killed insects...except perhaps Buddhists, and they probably killed some by accident. Davis could think of a dog he had killed once. An officer's dog. Ran straight under the track of the Chieftain as he drove it across the tank park at Bovvy. That wasn't intentional so it hardly counted. And there had been a squirrel under the tyre of his car, one early morning; Hedda had been upset, and one of the twins had cried. Apart from those, thought Davis, I haven't killed anything. Now, thirty men. Thirty, that was mass murder! Crippin, Jack-the-Ripper, Heath...none of them had killed that many. He would never tell Hedda about them, she wouldn't be able to understand. She knew you had to kill in wartime, she wasn't stupid, but she would

151

blank out the fact that her husband was one of the men who had done it. Perhaps it wasn't a bad thing, because it would be terrible for a woman to have to hold someone in their arms if they knew he had killed so many men.

He wondered what Hedda would be doing. It was past the children's bedtime. It seemed years since he had spoken to her; he had wanted to telephone her when the regiment had received its orders, but there were long queues at the call boxes. She would have taken the boys to her sister's house at Ahlerstedt; it was well away from the city. They had discussed the possibility of war a few months previously, and he had tried to persuade her to agree to join the other British wives on evacuation flights to Britain if a war developed, but she had refused. She had become stubborn and rejected all his arguments. Ahlerstedt was well to the west of Hamburg, and south of the Elbe estuary; it was bound to be safe there...there was nothing to bomb. Eventually he had agreed with her. But now, what if the Russian advance wasn't held? What then? What would happen to her and the children? Would they stay on her sister's smallholding, or join the thousands of refugees who would certainly move westwards just as those on the road had done this afternoon? It would be bad if that happened. What if he lost them? Families got split up in Europe in wartime, and sometimes never found each other again. They starved. Women sold themselves for food for the children. Momentarily the thought of Hedda being forced to make love to some Russian peasant soldier made Davis feel sick. She was too proud he told himself, it would never happen. Somehow, she would manage; she was a capable woman. Her family were all there, and they'd stick together. One thing about German wives, they made protective mothers.

A bright orange light illuminated the woods a kilometer beyond the river, there was the doppler effect of a full battery salvo of rockets passing overhead, then the rolling shock of the multiple explosions as they reached their target.

152

There was a shrill mewing sound beside Davis. He looked into the fighting compartment. The lights were dimmed but he could see the new loader, Spinks, huddled down between the gun and the charge bins, his arms wrapped tightly over his head, his knees drawn up to his chest.

'Spinks!'

'What's going on?' It was Inkester calling above the increasing volume of gunfire. 'Oh, shit! That's all we bloody need.'

'Spinks...' Davis struggled down beside the gun and grabbed the loader by the hood of his NBC suit, dragging him upright. The man kept his face hidden in his hands. 'Spinks, you've got a job to do, and by Christ, you're going to do it.' Davis shook him.

'We're going to die...' Spinks' voice was a wail. 'Oh God...'

Davis jerked Spinks' head back and slapped him hard across the face, then he pushed him back into the seat. Spinks was sobbing. 'You load every time that gun is empty,' Davis roared. 'You load, you understand you bastard...you load. Make one mistake and I'll kill you and throw your body outside.'

Spinks nodded, fearfully.

Davis climbed back up into the turret. He was shaking with rage. Cowardice was something he hadn't bargained for. Worse, he knew his threat to kill Spinks was real.

THIRTEEN

There was a gentle shuffling within the Scimitar unit's concrete bunker; the sound of the men preparing to move out, nothing metallic, only the brushing of cloth against cloth, webbing against cotton, the pad of rubber-soled boots on the dusty concrete. Teeth gleamed in sharp contrast against camouflaged skin as the men grinned at each other in anticipation of action after long hours of waiting, their conversations were whispered.

Captain Fellows had been watching the parked Soviet self-propelled guns since a little before dusk, hoping they would move on. As the evening light had faded there had been some activity in the line of vehicles, but the hull of the nearest was still silhouetted against the night sky.

He had commented to the SAS lieutenant: 'They're still out there.'

'Probably a reserve battery. They don't matter, we can easily get rid of the crews later.'

Bloody cocky, Fellows had thought. The damned SAS always thought they were little gods...pink Range Rovers...good God, they even sold plastic model kits of them in toy shops. SAS. They claimed to shun publicity, but somehow managed to grab more than anyone else.

He checked his watch. Twenty twenty-three. 'Sergeant!'

'Sir.'

'Keep an eye on the RTO will you? The orders will be through shortly. For God's sake make sure he doesn't send out a signal...no acknowledgement.'

'Yes, sir.'

Mick Fellows hooked off his beret and ran his fingers through his short wavy hair in one movement. Wearing a beret for several hours at a time always made his scalp itch and gave him dandruff. He had washed and shaved earlier, and changed his shirt. It made him feel fresher, more alert. He had noticed that Lieutenant Hinton had not bothered, and there was already a dark stubble on the man's cheeks and chin. It rankled with him; he would not tolerate slackness in appearance in his own officers, no matter the circumstances. Carelessness in dress and bodily cleanliness indicated a similar attitude towards soldiering; a smart soldier was invariably efficient.

Hinton didn't even look like an officer...at least, not a cavalryman. A Sapper, maybe. He was too bulky, squarer, bull-necked enough to appear the archetypal Prussian soldier of the First World War. In mess kit he would look like an all-in wrestler in fancy dress. Fellows had taken a dislike to the man the moment they had met. Hinton's rough palms during their handshake had felt like those of a labourer.

'Sir...Captain Fellows, sir.' The sergeant was beckoning from beside the radio operator. Fellows hurried across and picked up a spare headset. There were a lot of metallic clicking sounds, atmospherics, cracklings.

The strength of the transmission was fluctuating, but they could make out the distant operator's voice, each word ennunciated sharply and positively. 'Magpie this is Wizard. Apex Echo. Trophy Bacon Sunset Juliet. Repeat: Apex Echo. Trophy Bacon Sunset Juliet. Out.'

A ten second transmission, thought Fellows. It would have been damned easy for a careless radio operator to miss. The RTO had switched off the unit's set the moment the message had ended; it would remain silent for another six hours.

It pleased Fellows to think that his German CO would sweat a bit now, hoping the message that would initiate his pet project had been received. Only future events would confirm it.

Hinton was standing nearby waiting, so Fellows translated the code from memory. 'The Russians have advanced a long way. They're at Wolfsburg.' Apex was the head of the Soviet thrust, Crown the city of Wolfsburg. 'Wizard has given us one K west of Hehlingen as the approximate location of the Soviet Divisional HQ.'

'The Russians must have taken the whole of the Werder,' commented Hinton, sourly. 'The bastards haven't wasted time.'

'It's only just begun,' Fellows reminded him curtly. 'And it's obvious they're already making mistakes.'

'Mistakes?' Hinton looked puzzled. To accuse the enemy of errors without knowing their total battle plan was naive.

'Look at the map. If their 12th Guards Army are now in Wolfsburg, then it's certainly a mistake to put a main HQ so close to the front...it's too vulnerable, and not even normal planning tactics. It's more the position for a Forward Command HQ.' Fellows paused for a moment to allow Hinton to digest this observation. 'If we assume their attack has otherwise been in character, then the 12th Guards Army will have advanced on a narrow front; at most only five or six kilometers in breadth. They will have attacked in echelon, backed by strong reserves to exploit points of success. The forward command would be up-front and the main headquarters somewhere to the rear of their second echelon. But this isn't the case, Hinton...and why?'

Hinton was resenting the manner in which Fellows had arrogantly turned the briefing into a staff college lecture on tactics, but he kept his feelings hidden. 'They could be over-extended.'

'Yes, Hinton, perhaps. I believe their thrust has been a little *too* fast...deeper and quicker than they anticipated. Normally their divisional depth would not exceed thirty-five Ks...but if it were much greater...perhaps as much as fifty, and with the second echelon lagging or depleted by an airstrike...then the main headquarters might have been moved up. Alternatively...' Fellows hesitated for effect. 'They have actually lost their Forward Command HQ; that being the case, Hinton, if I can take out the main HQ, then the 12th Guards Army won't know its eyeball from its backside for the next twenty-four hours.'

'Yes, sir.' Hinton was pleased he was only serving temporarily with Captain Fellows.

'Your chaps ready to deal with the gentlemen outside?'

'Quite ready, sir.'

'Then I think you should make a move.'

Lance Corporal Mark Ellen of the 22nd SAS lay with his face only an inch above the ground. He was twenty-four years old, the son of a Ruardean lorry driver. The smell of rotting beech leaves, damp with night dew, usually reminded him of time spent poaching in the Forest of Dean, in his schooldays; tonight he was too preoccupied for memories. The air was chill after the muggy warmth of the bunker, condensing to glistening beads on the metal hull of the Russian SPG ahead of him. He was watching one of its crew leaning against the sharp bow of the tank. The man was wearing his corrugated leather helmet and had the collar of his overalls buttoned tight to his neck for warmth.

Ellen had never yet killed, but all of his SAS training led him towards this end; he had no qualms about the task. In fact he was waiting impatiently for the opportunity.

Eight years previously, he had left his Ross school with two low grade Certificates of Education and no other qualifications. He had not been particularly interested in sport, nor shown any special aptitude for a trade. There was little employment in the Ross area at that time, and the general recession in industry had made matters far worse. The first summer after leaving school, he worked as a builder's labourer; he bought a small motorcycle with the money he earned. He sold the machine during the winter, when he was laid off. It had not occurred to him to join the army until he saw the recruiting posters one Saturday afternoon after a visit to the Hereford Football Association ground at Ledbury.

He signed up for two reasons, boredom and bloody-mindedness; his father, with memories of National Service and wasted hours, had advised him against it.

Ellen signed for nine years with the Gloucesters, did two with the regiment, then completed a parachute training course and in euphoric bravado applied for transfer to the SAS. Selection was notoriously hard and he did not expect to be accepted, but for the next few days his status in the canteen bar was raised. He reported to the SAS barracks in a mood which wandered between apprehension and gloom; in a few days he would be forced to return to the regiment and admit his failure. He had already spent time inventing excuses.

To his amazement he found he enjoyed the tests. He was already very fit, and there was pleasure in being forced to push his body beyond the limits he had believed possible; a masochistic satisfaction in completing the tasks set for his fellow entrants and himself. Maybe he hadn't always been able to beat the system, but he could certainly try to beat himself and others like him. Lying for hours half-submerged in icy water, or slogging twenty miles across the Brecon Beacons in deep snow, was easily tolerable if you were proving yourself tougher than the men weakening beside you. He passed all the tests and became a member of the unit. He had thought he was already an experienced soldier; the SAS proved him wrong, and began his training again. At the end of a further year he had trebled his number of parachute drops and learnt how to handle a dozen different weapons and explosives. He learnt how to canoe, and slide his way silently across a pebbled beach or through deep undergrowth. He could dive into a darkened room, and hit a man-sized target illuminated for only five seconds with four shots from a Browning pistol. But real action seemed to

158

elude him. His unit was used several times during the next years; there were jobs for the SAS even in peacetime, but he was never chosen. It was the luck of the draw. He was promoted as his expertise increased. Four and a half years of dedicated training had led up to this particular moment. He was determined to enjoy it.

There were five Russian SPGs remaining in the woods. There had been eleven earlier in the day, but six had apparently moved on. Three SAS soldiers would deal with each vehicle. The orders were explicit; quick job and no noise. It was essential the Soviet radio operators should give no warnings.

The two men with Ellen were already in position, one crouched against the turret beside the gun and the second lying flat on his stomach above the driver's hatch.

The Russian SPG commander Ellen was watching struck a match and lit a cigarette. In the fraction of a second that the match flared, momentarily blinding the man, Ellen was on his feet. As the man dragged on the tobacco, Ellen clamped his hand over cigarette and still-burning match and crushed them against the man's mouth, at the same time driving the slim blade of his knife upwards beneath the ribs. The Russian struggled but Ellen pulled him off balance backwards, then cut his throat twice just above the stiff collar, using a quick sawing movement of the razor sharp blade. It was almost too easy; he had practiced it many times.

The two remaining crew members of the Russian SPG were already dead. Both killed while they slept. The driver's back had been within reach of the soldier lying flat along the hull, while the gunner had taken no notice of the man who had silently dropped in through the turret behind him believing, if he had awakened at all, it was his returning commander.

Ellen lowered the Russian's body to the ground. A non-smoker himself, he could smell the faint coppery scent of the man's blood; it gave him a sense of elation. His hands were sticky, he wiped them on the dead man's overalls. He had made his first kill. Never again would he have to stand at a bar and listen enviously to the tales of his colleagues who had been in action. Now he was truly one of them; a fully-fledged member of the elite corps.

Welbeck, who had been the one to tackle the gunner, seemed to be a long time inside the tank. Lance Corporal Ellen should have waited beside the track, but didn't. He reached the turret just as Welbeck climbed out. Welbeck reacted instinctively to the dark figure that appeared unexpectedly in front of him. His bloodstained knife was still in his hands. He drove it straight into Ellen's chest.

Ellen felt the blow, realized what had happened but felt no pain. He had time to say quietly: 'You stupid bugger.' Then his legs weakened and crumpled. He dropped to his knees and felt the cold of the metal against the palms of his hands...and then nothing. His body dropped backwards from the hull to land on the corpse of the Russian he had killed only a minute earlier.

'Everything satisfactory, Sergeant?' Lieutenant Hinton had been waiting beside the bunker's secondary exit.

'Yes, sir. The area's clean. I've posted guards. One casualty.'

'Wounded?'

'Dead, sir. Lance Corporal Ellen.'

The first of many yet to come, thought Hinton. 'How?'

'Bloody carelessness, sir! Disobeyed orders.'

There was no point in delving further at the moment, and Sergeant Welbeck was obviously unwilling to volunteer details. Hinton knew he would learn in time. 'Thank you, Sergeant. Get the doors open will you.' He gave a thumbs-up sign to Fellows and swung himself into the nearest of the APCs. The sound of the Scimitar's Jaguar engines made the air of the bunker vibrate.

There was nothing that could be done to disguise the appearance of a FV107 Scimitar; its sharply angled turret and sloping bow resembled no armoured vehicle used by the Warsaw Pact armies. Protection for the tanks and the SAS APCs was the night itself, their speed and manoeuvrability, and the direction of their travel -- westwards towards the battlefront. From a distance, in the poor light, they might be mistaken for reinforcements moving forward in support of the Soviet advance.

Hehlingen was twenty kilometers from the bunker; little more than fifteen minutes at top speed on a good road. There were no longer any such roads, and a fast direct route was impossible.

Fellows, standing half-out of his hatch, watched the night sky towards the west. Flashes of distant light flickered like summer lightning along the horizon, and the sky itself was coloured as though it reflected the illumination of a vast city. It was almost beautiful, smoke clouds glowing scarlet, violet and a continuous pyrotechnic aurora borealis shimmering above the fields. He was feeling alert, self-confident; it had been far more of a strain on his nerves while they waited cooped up in the bunker. He still found it hard to believe that this was war, though there was plenty of evidence. Every small village or even farmhouse they passed had been destroyed, tumbled and blackened stone, crazily-angled window frames, fallen roofs, deserted...still smoking. Wrecked vehicles, some unidentifiable, others which looked as though they had simply been abandoned, littered open fields. There were bodies, corpses lying awkwardly in the wreckage; a line of uniformed men arrayed beside a hedge, neat and tidy as though ready for inspection, weapons beside them, the night hiding the bloodstains and the wounds. Shell and rocket craters, dark irregular patterns in the fields; shattered tarmac and cobbles, sewer pipes and drains, burnt woodland.

He was surprised they had seen no Russians as yet. He had expected the odd patrol or company of Engineers, but decided they must be working further north, more directly behind the main stream of the 16th Guards' attack.

Two kilometers east of Hehlingen he led the convoy into the shattered remains of a pine wood and deployed them amongst the few undamaged trees. Now that the engines were silent the sounds of gunfire were loud; only a few kilometers towards the west. The coloured sky which at a distance had looked attractive, was now heavy, ominous.

Hinton was waiting with his platoon. 'Don't hang about,' Fellows told him. 'I don't want my Scimitars around here too long. In and out fast, that's the name of the game. You've got two hours to find the exact location and report back to me, that should be enough.'

'Yes, sir.'

Fellows watched the men jog silently into the darkness, fading like ghosts amongst the stumps of the trees. More waiting, he thought. The whole damned war for me seems to be waiting. He almost envied the men who had remained with the regiment or who were operating as recce squadrons; they would have been in action since the first shell was fired. But this waste of time, this waiting... waiting.

FOURTEEN

Master Sergeant Will Browning thought he now knew why the Black Cavalry Squadron's counterattack had failed. During the past hours while he and the crew of Utah waited for darkness there had been time for him to think over the possibilities. When the squadron's Captain Harling had given the order to advance, the intention of HQ must have been to strike at the flank of the Soviet spearhead. By ill-luck, poor intelligence or plain bad timing, and Browning was unable to decide which, the counterattack had met the head of the second echelon of Russian armour and, worst of all, at a point on the battleground where the enemy artillery could give it the best possible cover.

The second wave of Soviet tanks, reforming after crossing the river, had been fresh into battle and received sufficient warning to enable them to deploy in readiness for the counterattack. The Soviet divisions' main artillery, still in its positions on the eastern side of the border, was able to treat the American armour in exactly the same way the Russian artillery had dealt with the British charge of the Light Brigade, at the historical battle of Balaclava. And with the same decimating results. The losses to the Russians had been negligible. Maybe it wasn't entirely the captain's fault after all, Browning decided. The officer was bluff, often blustery, but West Point didn't turn out fools; and it

163

certainly couldn't be the troop lieutenant's responsibility either, because he would just have obeyed orders like the rest of them. If a mistake had been made, then it was at headquarters. Wasn't it always!

Browning peered at his watch. He could just see the glow of its luminous dial; it was twenty-one twenty-seven. In three minutes Podini would come down off the hill where he had relieved Adams as guard, and then it would be time for them to move out.

There was plenty happening. Adams had watched a build-up of Soviet logistics on the west bank of the river. The two bridges had been in constant use for the past four hours. It appeared, in darkness at least, that the Russians were unconcerned about the threat of air attack, although the movements of their supplies column should have shown up on NATO infra-red detectors. It suggested to Browning that the Russians were feeling very confident about the present lack of NATO air surveillance, and as he hadn't seen any US aircraft overhead since late afternoon he thought that, for the moment anyway, their efforts must be concentrated on the forward combat zone.

Ginsborough nudged Browning's arm urgently, and whispered, 'Out there...'

Browning could hear noises on the hill twenty meters away, the rolling of a small stone through frost-dried leaves, the snapping of a thin twig. He aimed his Remington into the darkness, and eased off the safety catch.

An off-key blackbird whistled an unlikely first two bars of 'John Brown's Body', and the scuffling on the slope above them increased.

'Podini?' It had to be!

'Who else?'

'You gink,' swore Ginsborough, the tension had made him feel sick.

'Will said half after nine, and it's half after,' hissed Podini.

'What did you see going on over there?' Browning asked.

Podini's eyes glinted, catching the light of the rising

moon. 'Same as Mike said. They're still building up. Man, some heavy stores!'

'Like what?'

'Rear service equipment. About twenty MAZ cargo carriers...fifteen tonners...ammunition I'd reckon, by the way they spaced them out. Plenty of trucks.'

'Any armour?'

'Nope...some artillery on the other side, waiting to get across. There's an MTU laying another bridge. That'll make three.' He paused and then said casually, 'I saw a nuke.'

'A nuke?' It was Adams, incredulously. 'A nuke missile? You're kidding!'

'How d'you know it was a nuke?' demanded Browning.

'I don't know. All I know is that it was one hell of a rocket.'

'How long?'

'I'm guessing...it ain't too easy to see down there. Maybe ten meters, a big eight-wheeled transporter like a fire truck.'

'It's probably a Frog-7,' said Browning, 'with a conventional warhead.'

'You and your fucking nuke,' grunted Ginsborough. Podini seemed determined to make him throw up his rations.

'Okay, let's move out,' ordered Browning. He wanted to get clear of the open ground before the moon rose any higher.

Gunthers was still smouldering, burning in places when the light breeze stirred up ashes and fanned new life into the embers. Rubble spread across the streets from shattered houses and stores. The volunteer Bundesgrenzshutz infantrymen who had defended it with their Dragon and Milan missiles had drawn heavy artillery and tank fire, and because most were local men defending their own homes, they had fought bitterly. The bodies of many of them now lay amongst the ruins, but the wreckage of the Soviet tanks,

165

twisted and blackened hulks in every street, was evidence of the ferocity of the battle.

Browning was feeling despondent. Now he was away from the Àbrams, it seemed even more unlikely it could ever be repaired. Maybe it was best to write Utah off, and try to make it back on foot even though it might be difficult. The smell of war and death was getting through to him; it had done so at times in Vietnam. It was familiar, a recurring sickness that made him ill for a time, and like 'flu he would get over it. Only there was no medicine he could take to ease his present discomfort. The only rapid cure he knew was in a bottle on the shelf of a bar, in some town as remote from war as maybe Las Vegas.

Adams was a few meters ahead, flattened against a crazily tilted wall that was overhanging the sidewalk. He was signalling frantically with his arm. When Browning reached him, he jerked his head towards the interior of the wrecked building. Browning listened. For a few moments he could hear nothing, and then there was a faint scratching sound.

Browning whispered: 'Civilians, leave them.'

'Maybe they can help us.' Adams dropped to his knees and crawled over the rubble into the darkness.

'Come back you damn fool,' hissed Browning, but Adams ignored him. Browning squatted beside the doorway, his automatic ready; behind him Podini and Ginsborough waited tensely.

Adams was gone a full minute before he reappeared. 'I was right,' he said, 'it's a woman and some kids.'

'If they'd been Russians, you'd have got us all killed,' said Browning angrily. 'Don't ever do that again.'

'They can help.'

'*Maybe* they can help!'

It was a few moments before his eyes became accustomed to the darkness of the shelled building, then he saw them, huddled together in a narrow wedge of open space between a fallen wall and a staircase – a middle-aged woman and three young children.

The woman asked nervously, '*Soldat...Amerikanish?*'

'Yes, ma'am.'

'*Gott sei Dank.*'

'Don't thank me yet, there are only four of us. D'you speak English?'

'*Bitte...verstehen sie nicht!*'

'I can speak.' It was one of the children, a boy of about twelve, pale beneath the grime of brick dust that coated him.

'We're an American tank crew,' explained Browning. 'We got outselves knocked out this afternoon near the river. We need repair equipment. Can you show us where there's a garage.'

'All garage is bombed,' said the boy, staring at him.

'We know they're bombed, son. We're not looking for service. We need a metal cutter...a gas cutter...you know gas, big fires, very hot!'

'Gas...I think I know.' The boy spoke quickly to the woman but she simply shrugged her shoulders. 'I come show you.'

'What about your mom?'

'Not mother...I come with you.'

'Okay,' agreed Browning. 'But you tell this lady to stay put. We're the only Americans there are around here. If she hears anyone else, they're probably Russians.' He saw the fear in the woman's eyes as he turned away. He followed the boy to the doorway, then stopped and walked back towards her. He raised his automatic.

She misunderstood his action, twisting herself sideways to protect the two children beside her, shielding them with her body.

Browning spoke gently. 'It's okay, lady. Here...' He reversed the pistol in his hand and held the butt towards her.

She relaxed, then smiled guiltily. She took the weapon slowly, then placed it in her lap. '*Danke.*'

'Good luck.'

There was something wrong; Browning could sense it. It was the feeling that things had somehow got beyond his control. The boy was hurrying them despite Browning's warning there might still be enemy soldiers in the area. As they moved into a broad alley between two old half-timbered barns, he realized it was a trap. The boy suddenly dived behind a pile of rubble, and shouted loudly. There was a quick burst of automatic rifle fire from the darkness ahead, the bullets hissing past them.

Podini was already firing as the men dropped, the crisp sounds of his Remington echoing from the high walls on either side. Bullets from the automatic rifle were ricochetting from the brickwork.

The boy was shouting again, his words punctuating the rifle shots.

'Jesus Christ,' Ginsborough swore beside Browning, 'the lousy little fucker.'

Browning's German wasn't much good, but he'd understood enough to hear the boy yell that they were Russians and still alive. If they were supposed to be Reds and someone was firing at them, then whoever was at the other end of the rifle was likely to be a friend. He called out, 'We're Americans...Americans...'

The shooting ceased but then nothing happened for a few moments until a voice said, 'Stand slowly. With your hands up.'

'Real slow,' Browning warned the crew. He stood, cautiously. Out there in the darkness someone had him in their sights. A slight twitch of a finger and he would be blown away.

'Put your weapons down,' said the voice.

'They're down.'

There was movement. Browning thought he could see several men at the far end of the alley. A barrel glinted in a window a few meters above them.

'Walk forward.'

Browning and his crew did so.

The boy had scrambled from behind the rubble and now ran past them. He spoke quickly to the soldiers. One, a lieutenant, walked over to Browning, keeping a rifle aimed at his chest. He said a few words which Browning assumed to be Russian.

'I'm sorry, I don't understand you. We're American...Black Horse Cavalry. Our tank's out of action...the battle near the river, this afternoon.'

'Be quiet.' The lieutenant spoke to one of his soldiers. The man searched Browning, and then the others. 'No...don't move. Keep your hands up.'

The officer looked through the identification papers, then shrugged. 'These don't mean anything. There are plenty on the battlefield.'

Adams said: 'Shit, man, you think I'm Russian?'

'You could be Cuban, Angolan.'

'Assholes...that's worse than being called nigger.'

'Steady Mike,' warned Browning. If Adams lost his cool then everyone was likely to end up dead; and Adams was particularly sensitive about his nationality.

'Who's your commanding officer?'

'Mickey Mouse,' answered Podini. He was angry with the way the man had spoken to his friend.

'You know we can't tell you that,' said Browning. 'How the hell do we know *you* aren't Russians?'

'We got a stand-off situation,' added Ginsborough. 'Only we ain't got guns.'

The boy spoke from behind them, excitedly.

The officer levelled his rifle at Browning's forehead. 'One of you still has a pistol...which one?'

'None of us,' answered Browning. He hoped he was right.

'The boy says you all had one; he has found only three.'

'I gave mine away.'

'Lying is a good way to die.'

Browning spoke quickly. 'It's the truth. I gave mine to the woman who was with the boy. You can check.'

'Why would you do that?'

169

'I was sorry for her.' It didn't sound convincing.

The lieutenant spoke to the boy who turned and ran from the alley. 'We will find out. Now move.'

They were led into the barn and then down a narrow flight of steps to a cellar. At the side of a stack of boxes was a narrow door partially concealed behind a concrete pillar. They were pushed inside. The room was lit by an oil lamp. Resting on benches along its length were more than a dozen infantrymen, Bundesgrenzshutz, their faces worn and tired, filthy with camouflage and the dirt of battle. Their weapons were across their knees or resting on the ground beneath the seats. Several looked up as Browning and his crew entered, but most ignored them. The lieutenant pointed to the far end of the room with the barrel of the rifle: 'Go sit there.'

Browning and the crew did so.

'What now?' asked Adams.

'What the hell what now? Why d'you always ask what now?' grumbled Podini. 'How the hell do I know what now?'

They waited for several minutes, and then one of the soldiers who had been outside in the alley came into the room and handed the German lieutenant Browning's Remington. He said a few words to the officer, then left. The lieutenant examined the pistol, slid out the magazine and worked the round from the breech. He examined the bullet slowly, turning the case in his fingers close to the light.

'It's a live one,' said Browning. 'You can test it.'

'On your head,' suggested Adams.

The lieutenant grinned sheepishly, and for the first time sounded friendly. 'I believe you. No one but an American is going to be so stupid as to give his only weapon away. Chivalrous...but stupid. Don't forget, Sergeant, the Russians have been in Germany before; our women learnt how to survive. A pistol, for them, is the shortest route to the execution ground. And if you were a soldier of the Heer, such a generosity in wartime could get you shot. However...thank you for the gesture.'

'So okay,' said Adams. 'Now what about my gas cutter?'

Browning explained about the XM1's track, and how they had become isolated after the battle.

'And what will you do if your tank is repaired?' asked the lieutenant.

'Get back to our unit, if we can. Try to find a place where the Russians are thinnest, and break through, rejoin the war.'

'You have enough fuel?'

'We've a three hundred mile range; we topped-up before the attack.' Browning studied the German's face. The man was very young, not much more than twenty-five years old. He looked like a student.

'We will help you. We know the village. We can find the equipment you need.'

'Once we get the Abrams repaired, maybe we can give you guys a lift someplace,' suggested Browning.

The lieutenant grimaced, then shook his head. 'We're staying. The Russians will be back to consolidate the area, and we will be waiting for them.'

Lieutenant Colonel Studley had blacked out, fainted with the pain when one of the guards stamped on the wound in his calf, but it was the agony which dragged him back to consciousness, pulsing, searing, encompassing his entire body.

Studley heard himself scream, and the sound horrified him. There was still only darkness, and the sounds which came from his throat were uncontrollable, unreal, making him feel disembodied. Once, in childhood, he had broken an arm and been taken to hospital to have it set. He awakened on the operating table while the doctor was still manipulating the bone, and there had been the same combination of pain and sound...but then it had ended abruptly with the introduction of more anaesthetic, and became nothing more than a nightmare he remembered

171

later. He tried now to find reality but for a long time it refused to appear, drowned by the spasms which shook his body and mind.

The bright glow was a small light above his head; faces blurred. He thought at first he must be in some medical centre where they were tending his wounds; his head throbbed violently. He found his arms were pinioned, pulled backwards so far his spine was arched away from the ground beneath him. His legs were spread wide.

There was a voice, persistent, questioning. It echoed inside his head, distorted, strident. He was being forced to concentrate on the words, the threats. He remembered.

'You have no more chances. I warned you it would become unpleasant. You are throwing your life away for no purpose.'

I am not here, thought Studley. He tried to blank the recent past from his mind. This is not reality; reality is Jane...brown eyes, long dark hair slipping between my fingers...her gentle body.

The agony returned, electrical, twisting at his bowels, jerking at strained and torn muscles, contorting his body and exploding like a thousand white-hot needles in his brain.

'The code, Colonel Studley...only the code...the code...the code...only the code.'

The code? What code? There wasn't any code...isn't any code. The word doesn't exist. Nothing I am experiencing exists in my real world; only Jane exists. Jane...dear God, Jane.

He felt her lips on his neck, and the round warmth of her breasts against his body. He could smell the scent of her hair. She was gripping him tightly, her thighs clasping him...he was losing her...the pain tearing her from his grasp.

'The code, Studley...a few simple words...' The agony and the shouting repeated a hundred times, gathering momentum until all his senses spun together in confusion.

The screams – they were no longer his own and he found

172

he could ignore them. He could see her face again...the gentle mouth smiling, her eyes moist.

He realized his arms had been freed; it was part of the dream again. He refused to allow himself to be tricked. He was upright; body sagging, legs useless, his head lolled as if the neck muscles had been severed. Hands supported him, controlled him.

He heard the voice of the GRU captain, but didn't understand the words. The light had gone, his feet dragged across rough ground. Cautiously he allowed his mind to return; it was reluctant.

He tried to shake himself free of the hands, attempting to support himself, but there was little co-ordination yet in his movements; it was returning slowly. There were voices beside him, unintelligible.

He began to recognize his surroundings, the woods. He was stumbling through beds of autumn leaves, over fallen branches, trunks. He could not distinguish between the night sky and the dark outlines of the trees.

They let him drop. He felt the damp ground beneath him, and pushed himself on to his hands and knees. He saw the flash of orange fire from the muzzle of a gun a meter away; a deafening burst of sound as he fell sideways, rolling, tumbling down a steep incline.

He knew they had shot him; he was dying. He lay on his back, and he could see the stars above him. He recognized the Great Bear; found the beacon of infinite north, the Pole Star. He wondered how long he would be able to watch it before his senses faded. And what then? Perhaps he would still be able to see the stars. Perhaps, after all, something followed death. It would have been better to have died somewhere else. Beside a good river; in the warmth of a summer afternoon. There was no romance about death in wartime; that was the myth old men told the young, a lie to feed violence...religion...was there even a God? It was all very convenient, a God to control the people while they were alive, blackmail them into submission with threats of

173

godly vengeance...provide them with an after-life to remove the fear of death, and what did you have then? A disciplined army who would fight.

If there is a God, thought Studley, if you are up there and can hear me, just remember please that all I want is Jane. Not now, but in time.

Max would want her, too. How would a God solve that problem?

There was a dark shape beside him, the fallen trunk of some great tree. He could smell it rotting; the fungi. We'll rot together, he decided, here in this hollow in the ground. The beetles and the worms will share us. You didn't die peacefully either, tree, but you probably took longer. Perhaps you took fifty years to die; more than my lieftime.

He closed his eyes for a time, and tried to conjure warmth; it wouldn't come, nor would the images of Jane. It was almost as though he had expended them while he was resisting the torture. There was satisfaction in that...in the endurance. He had won, and the GRU captain had lost. It had been a small individual war between them, and the knowledge the Russian would have to live with defeat pleased him.

The Great Bear had moved a little, tilted slightly towards the heads of the pines. Studley wriggled his hand sideways until he felt the soft bark of the dead tree. It took him several seconds to realize he had done so. He clenched the other hand and felt it grasp moist earth.

Experimentally, he lifted his head.

No one survived a close-range burst from an AKS-74, and that was what he remembered the guards carrying. He thought he had felt the blow of the bullets, their impact throwing him sideways down the steep bank through the undergrowth until he pitched against the tree trunk. Soviet 5.45mm bullets had the reputation of going in small, but doing a lot of damage on their way out. If he attempted to move too much perhaps he would burst apart, spilling his blood and entrails beneath him. He cautiously flexed a leg, and the pain from his calf wound was startling, seeming to awaken every nerve in his body.

He collected together his memories of the past hours; his capture, interrogation, torture. He set them in order. Miraculously, he was still alive. Alive? Why? How? He tried to understand, and realization brought a strange bitterness. He had meant nothing to the soldiers who had been ordered to shoot him; an insect to be squashed. They hadn't even bothered to make sure they had done the job properly. He was of no importance, simply rubbish for disposal.

He pushed himself upright and into a sitting position, his back against the fallen trunk. The exertion made him dizzy and sick. Carefully, he examined his face with his fingertips, by touch. It was unrecognizable, swollen and tender. His teeth were broken stumps, and his lips torn, caked with congealed blood. He could not open his jaw. The cracked ribs in his side ached as he breathed, a reminder of the blow from the guard's rifle butt.

His leg was throbbing, the rough bandaging over the wound seeping blood. He tightened it as best he could in the darkness. There was some sort of injury to his upper back; he couldn't tell what, it was painful but it didn't prevent him moving his arms.

They had wanted him to give them the code, and he had refused. They had tortured him and then tried to kill him, and he had survived. The thoughts strengthened him. He would get away; he would drag himself deeper into the woods, find somewhere he could hide out during the daylight, clean and examine his wounds. When he was stronger, he would work his way south-west and attempt to find a way through the lines, perhaps into Switzerland. If not, he would seek out one of the guerrilla groups that would certainly have been formed. Somehow, eventually, he would get back to Britain and Jane.

He thought of the GRU captain; the man's angular face becoming more twisted by fury as Studley had remained silent. He would torture others who came into his hands. For Studley, the code would change at midnight, but for the GRU captain there would always be a new daily code to be broken along with the will and bodies of his prisoners.

Studley remembered his own words to his officers less than a week previously. 'We will be outnumbered...perhaps by as many as five to one...a lot of us won't survive. But we *can* hold them, *if* we make it too costly for them to win. Fight like hell...to the last shell or bullet or man. Never surrender...take out as many of them as you can. It'll be bad, bloody bad, but it all depends on us. It's *our* job to stop them.'

Stop them. That was what it was all about. Fighting until you couldn't fight anymore. Then what the hell was he doing smugly assuming he had done enough? Just because he had been wounded and got himself battered didn't relieve him of any responsibility. Just because he'd managed to survive for a few hours didn't permit him to believe his war was ended. What of the other men? His men. They would still be fighting somewhere...wounded or not, they'd damn well fight on. So must he.

He had crawled the steep slope above the fallen tree, to the point where the guard had shot at him. His movement had been slow and painful, but it was easier to crawl than attempt to walk at the moment.

He could hear the sound of an engine, a generator in the distance through the trees, and worked his way towards it. The sky was brighter, the moon rising beyond the tall horizon of the woodland. A few feet to his left leaves rustled; he froze, then relaxed as a terrified rodent scurried away through the undergrowth. There were other hunters in the forest beside himself.

He could smell diesel fuel, exhaust fumes, and the throbbing of the motor was louder. There were men beyond the clumps of bracken and bramble that skirted the clearing.

He could see the head and shoulders of a guard patrolling the edge of the woods. He knew there must be others concealed throughout the forest.

It took a long time to inch his way forward until at least he had a clear view of the encampment. The clearing itself was almost empty, but there were vehicles parked close to the trees on the side farthest away from him, and bivouacs beside them. He recognized the radio vehicle, with its dish aerials, seventy meters ahead. A few meters from it was the BMP in which he had been imprisoned before his interrogation; the GRU officer's truck, the BTR command post, was on the left of the clearing, isolated.

There was a lot of activity. The radio vehicle was operating, a dim glow showing through its open doors. A group of cooks were working in a halo of mist around a field-kitchen beneath the trees, and there was a small queue of infantrymen waiting nearby. Camouflage was being improved over several of the BMPs, as though the men intended to remain in the present position for some time.

To his left, beyond the BTR command vehicle, was a slit trench. He noticed it only because one of the guards paused and spoke to the men inside, before continuing his patrol. Studley crawled towards it.

He was only a few meters from the trench when one of the men it contained stood, stretched himself and then climbed out. He said a few words to a man below him, laughed, then walked away across the clearing. Studley watched him go. The man joined the end of the queue waiting by the field-kitchen. Studley wriggled his way closer to the trench. He could see the helmet of another guard; there might be a third man stretched out beside him, but it was a chance Studley realized he would have to take. He had already decided that if something went wrong, then he would fight with his bare hands until they killed him; they would shoot him anyway if he were captured again. And this time there would be no carelessness.

He slid closer, keeping low in the shadows of the thin

scrub. The man was an arm's length away now, and if he looked over his left shoulder would be staring into Studley's face. Studley pushed himself silently to his knees. The Russian infantryman was sitting on a box behind a machine gun. His head was cupped in his hands, the strap of his helmet was beneath his chin.

Studley took a deep cautious breath, paused for a fraction of a second gathering his strength, then grabbed at the front of the helmet with both hands, jerking it fiercely backwards. The man's legs kicked away from him and his hands clawed at Studley's arms. As with the advice he had been given about escaping, Studley knew there would be no second chance. A combination of anger and determination made him stronger. He ignored the pain of his injuries, and swung himself around until he could get his knees against the man's back, then with as much power as he could find he wrenched the head and helmet sideways.

Bone snapped. For a moment Studley thought the strap of the helmet had broken. He changed his grip quickly to gain more purchase on the man's head; it moved strangely, loosely in his hands. The infantryman struggled weakly for a few more seconds as his life died away, and then was still.

Studley felt exhausted; throbbing agony had returned to his wounds. His clothing was soaked with sweat. He wiped it from his eyes with a sleeve, and felt it stinging in the cuts of his lips and face. Every movement of the past few seconds had sounded terrifyingly loud and he expected at any moment to hear shots and feel the thud of bullets ripping into his body.

He glanced towards the field-kitchen, the queue had lengthened, the cooks were not hurrying their work. Men stood chatting while they waited, swinging their arms across their bodies or stamping their feet to keep their circulation moving in the night air. They were far enough away from the front lines to still feel secure; in probability, they had not yet seen any action, he thought. Men who had faced shells and bullets did not relax their vigilance so easily.

178

He quickly examined the machine gun: a 7.62mm PK on a bipod, simple to operate unless it jammed. If it did so, then he would discard it instantly; there was no time to study its mechanism.

He moved the body of the dead guard. The box on which the infantryman had been seated held additional magazines of bullets, and to Studley's greater satisfaction contained ten RGD-5 grenades. Beneath the body he found a loaded AKM rifle.

The slit trench overlooked a long valley sweeping down towards the west. Studley debated quickly on the choice of weapons; he would not be able to carry them all. He pushed half a dozen of the grenades into his pockets and then dragged the machine gun with him over the brow of the hill, where he was able to move around the perimeter of the camp out of sight of the guards.

He was within twenty meters of the radio vehicle when there was a shout from across the clearing in the direction of the slit trench. Studley jerked the pin from a grenade then hurriedly tossed it underhand through the open doors, scurrying back into the undergrowth like a disabled crab as it exploded inside the armoured vehicle, belching flame and smoke through the buckled and split metalwork. The tall radio mast collapsed sideways into the trees. He threw another with all his strength towards a running group of men near the centre of the clearing, and several crumpled bodies were hurled away by its blast.

The camp was panicking, the men unable to identify the whereabouts or nature of the attack, mistaking the grenades for mortar bombs. Studley limped towards the nearest BMP. Its crew were scrambling inside, and the troop hatches were fully open. Studley's grenade bounced off the rear of the turret and exploded within the hull. A sheet of fire roared upwards as the fuel tanks ignited. He caught a glimpse of the driver, crawling away from the hull, his overalls alight.

There were no more close targets for his grenades.

Studley dropped behind the machine gun. He worked the first round into the breech with the bolt, and mentally crossed his fingers.

On the far side of the clearing were a group of men huddled around the BTR command post. It moved, its driver reversing it towards the woods. The men moved with it, using its hull as protective cover. Studley squeezed the trigger and felt the satisfying shudder as the gun reacted. He kept the burst short; it was unlikely he would have more than two hundred rounds in the magazine, and this gas-operated weapon would get through more than six hundred and fifty a minute. As the bullets struck, the BTR began smoking. He gave it a second burst, low alongside the driving compartment. The smoke became flame which billowed and swelled like the fireball of a miniature atomic bomb. He raked a longer burst through running figures then scrambled deeper into the undergrowth, moving further to his left, dragging the machine gun.

One of the BMPs was thundering blindly towards him, crashing through the light woods, its tracks slapping and squealing. He threw himself aside and the vehicle roared past. There were shots crackling viciously in the trees...unaimed, indiscriminate, shouted orders, more explosions. Vehicles were revving, moving. A wounded man was screaming.

'Bastards...you bastards,' yelled Studley. He knew he was invincible; better than invincible, he had become death itself. He grabbed the machine gun under his arms and staggered into the open, firing it from his hip at a BMP that was dragging itself out of its camouflage, trailing the netting. Its rocket exploded in the launcher, ripping the vehicle's turret off backwards as neatly as if it had been removed by a cutting charge. Fires had brought eerie daylight to the clearing, the contorting shadows and smoke adding to the stygian chaos. One of the BMPs exploded for a second time as its ammunition overheated, scattering flaming debris high into the air. A UAZ Jeep bounced out of the woods and spun in the open ground. Studley caught it with his final burst, firing until his gun stopped. The Jeep accelerated for a few meters, hit the wreckage of one of the BMPs and rolled on to its side.

Studley dropped the machine gun and pulled out his two remaining grenades. He removed the pin from each and stood waiting defiantly. The only remaining undestroyed target he could see was the field-kitchen.

'I'm here, you bastards...' The reply was the digestive sound of the fires, the sharp crack of small-arms ammunition as it exploded amongst the burning wreckage. The madness left Studley. He said, quietly, 'I'm here.' There was a sense of anti-climax, unrealness.

He stared around him; nothing moved but the shadows.

The fatigue, exhaustion, and the pain were returning. He must get away; find somewhere where he could lick his wounds. He needed a weapon, though. Not another machine gun, something convenient, light, a pistol. He could see a holster on the belt of a body lying beside the upturned Jeep. He staggered over to it. It was the GRU captain; the man was unconscious. Studley looked at the two grenades he was holding in his hands; the pins were lost somewhere on the far side of the clearing. He had never expected to replace them. He considered tossing the grenades into the woods, then changed his mind.

Carefully he wedged them beneath the GRU captain's body, the man's weight holding the levers against their casings, then he took the pistol from the man's holster.

He was about a kilometer away down the long slope of the woodland when he heard the two grenades detonate. The sound gave him no more satisfaction than had he killed a rabid dog.

FIFTEEN

DAY TWO

A canopy of ponchos hid the white-blue light of the cutting torch as the men worked on the jammed track of Utah,. the Abrams of November India Squadron. The Bundesgrenzshutz platoon, with the exception of one engineer who was helping Adams, Ginsborough and Podini, were scattered on the lower slopes of the hill above the crippled tank. Master Sergeant Will Browning and the BGS lieutenant lay below the crest of the ridge and watched the activity on the three bridges now completed across the river.

The engines of the Soviet vehicles muffled the sound of gunfire, but distant fires were colouring the sky towards the west.

'There's one hell of a lot of supplies down there.'

The lieutenant nodded. 'Too many. It should not be so. They are holding them...waiting for something.'

'Reinforcements?'

'No. I do not think they need them yet. I think they wait because they have delay.'

'We're holding them?' It was a good thought, but Browning wasn't convinced.

'Maybe, yes. How far do you think it is to the combat zone?'

Browning studied the horizon. It was difficult to estimate distance at night, but the gunfire he could see was well below the rim of the night sky. 'Eight or nine kilometers.'

'Not much more than this afternoon. I think the American and German corps begin counter-offensive.'

'Counter-offensive? Jesus man, we don't have the strength. You've seen the amount of their armour.'

'We now have French armour...and French aircraft.'

'French? When the hell did we get the French?'

'Yesterday morning. They join us.'

'Could they get their armour up this fast?'

'It is possible. The distance is not so great.' The German was lying on his stomach, his chin resting on his forearms. 'You know what we must do?'

'If I had any sense, I'd tell you we should get the hell out of here while we've got a chance.' Browning stared down at the bridgehead and supply dump. The loss of ammunition, fuel, food and vehicle supplies would be a serious blow to the Soviet division, and if it could be achieved at the expense of a single NATO tank, then it had to be justifiable. The trouble was, it was his tank, his crew and his life; and he had already made himself a few promises. He attempted to weigh up the odds.

The lieutenant misunderstood Browning's hesitation. 'How do you want to fight this war, American? From twenty kilometers the other side of the front line...firing shells at an enemy you can't see? In a tank, you fight close, like infantry. And sometimes it is necessary to die.'

'I know my job, Lieutenant, and I know about dying.' Browning was silent for a while. A lot of memories he had forgotten had been revived in the past hours, and almost as though it were Armageddon ghosts had risen from graves. He had called Adams 'Jackson' during the battle, but Jackson had died near Dong Ha; he had looked out through the episcope in the earlier minutes of the counterattack and for a few moments been unable to recognize the XM1s of the squadron, he had expected sand-coloured M48s. Dying? He was an expert. They had offered him a commission once...suggested he train to become an officer. He had

183

refused, because he knew too much about death. As an officer you decided how a battle should be fought, and then you gave the orders to your men to fight it. As a sergeant you took the orders, but then made decisions to try to keep your men alive while you obeyed them. He preferred the latter responsibility.

'You have visited my village before, Sergeant?'

'Gunthers?' Browning saw the German officer nod. 'I passed through it a couple of days ago. It was a nice place.'

'Yes, a good place. Small, but good. And my school was good, too. I took my last class three days ago.'

'Teacher?'

'Yes, I am a teacher, art. I took my class on Tuesday afternoon. Boys and girls, fourteen years old. And they painted the bridge across the Ulster, from memory. I should have taken them down there, and let them sit by it...by the bridge. Now, it has gone, and with it the old *gasthof*, many memories. Yesterday morning, I blew them to pieces.'

Adams had repaired the track; cut it loose, replaced the severed link, repositioned the track on the sprockets and adjusted the tension. The XM1 was operational. There would be no opportunity to warm up her engine; once it was started every Russian within a kilometer would know there was an armoured vehicle somewhere close by. For a while they might think it was one of their own, but it wouldn't be too long before someone decided to investigate. The sound of Utah's Avco Lycoming turbine was distinctive.

Podini and Ginsborough had cleared most of the rubble from behind the tracks and with luck the Abrams would be able to reverse straight out. The men were waiting now for Browning's orders, anxious to be moving.

The BGS lieutenant asked: 'Well, Sergeant?'

'How long will it take to get your men in position?'

'Four minutes.'

'Will you be using your missiles?'

'It's not easy in the darkness...but yes, we will try.'

'Okay,' agreed Browning. 'You have exactly four minutes.'

Podini's voice was anxious in Browning's earphones. 'What's going on? How many minutes to what?'

Browning had pulled down the hatch and was settling himself in his seat. 'We're going back to war.'

'I thought we were going home...'

'Afterwards, Podini...'

'You had to mention a nuke,' interrupted Adams, wearily.

'It ain't no nuke...I made a mistake. You're kidding us, Sarge.'

'Two minutes,' warned Browning. 'When you get her out of here, Mike, go right. Keep her close to the wall below the hill. After three hundred meters the ground dips below another section of wall that runs towards the river. I want her hull-down there for three shots, all HE...you get that, Mike...just three shots? You with me, Podini? Okay! There's a fuel bowser this side of the bridge...that's your first target. The missile you saw is under net some three hundred meters further up the bank, in a grove of trees, that's your number two. I want that rocket taken out...so no mistakes. It may need a couple of shells...otherwise, we'll see what we've got afterwards. Mike, once you move, move fast. Head straight into them...Podini, you're on your own, I'll be using the point five; and keep it cool, guys.'

'Cool? Shit!'

Browning said, 'Okay...let's roll.'

Browning was watching the scene ahead of the XM1 through the light-intensifying lenses. They did not bring daylight, only dusk. There was no colour, soft shadows...the light of the minutes before nightfall.

The XM1's turbine had started with a roar that Browning

knew must have been heard clear across the border. If anything was calculated to jerk the Soviet ground radar operators back into full alert, nothing much more suitable could have been invented. At any moment he expected shells to begin bursting around them.

Adams quickly settled the tank in the dip of the ground behind the low stone wall. Browning would have been happier if the hollow had been deeper, but it was the best cover available; the near three meters height of Utah didn't make her the easiest of armoured vehicles to conceal.

Podini hadn't wasted time. He wanted to get it over so they could leave the area. He was talking nervously to himself, running through the firing drill. 'Target...laser range-finder...firing-switch on...computer adjusts...fire!' The M68 gun roared, lifting the XM1's bow. A fraction of a second later the fuel bowser, a thousand meters away, exploded into a billowing wall of fire that turned the river into brilliant gold. 'Target...where the hell is the nuke...?'

'It ain't a nuke...' Adams' voice. 'Please God that ain't no nuke.'

'Left some,' advised Browning. He was thinking along much the same lines as Adams, but didn't think there would be a nuclear explosion even if the missile was armed with a nuclear warhead, which he doubted. Aircraft had crashed when they were carrying nuclear weapons, and hadn't exploded. 'Left more...eleven o'clock...yeah...'

Podini said: 'Countdown begun...ten...nine...'

'Very funny you Wop nut...' Adams wasn't amused.

The explosion of the bowser had stirred wild activity into the area; a group of infantrymen were hurrying across the open ground in front of the nearest of the bridges. A twin automatic anti-aircraft gun with a high rate of fire began loosing off indiscriminate bursts into the hillside above the XM1. It wouldn't take them too long to find their target...the Abrams had got off the first shot without being seen, but plenty of eyes would be scouring the darkness watching for the source of the second.

Podini fired. The explosion of the shell was

unspectacular. 'Come on Gins...come on...move your
ass...'

'Loaded...'

'Go you shit...' The XM1 surged as Podini fired again.

'Okay...move out, Adams,' shouted Browning.

Adams slammed the Allison transmission into reverse
and spun the XM1 sideways, then ten meters back along the
gulley into the open field. As he did so the hull vibrated to
the rapid explosion of a dozen high explosive rounds in the
hollow where they had been hull-down. Adams changed to
forward gear and accelerated fast. He hit the low wall and
the XM1 bucked wildly, the stone glancing off the hull like
shrapnel and scattering into the darkness.

Browning hadn't seen the gun's third shell strike. Near
the first bridge the fuel bowser was still blazing furiously.
He thought he could make out the position of the anti-
aircraft gun, and was bringing the .5 to bear when the entire
strip of ground that was his night vision horizon burst
upwards in a blinding flash of white fire. He saw trees
blasted out of the ground, and huge pieces of unidentifiable
debris hurled from the centre of the explosion. The light was
so fierce he was forced to cover his eyes with his hand, but
the vision of the towering explosion remained. The XM1 hit
the shock wave as though it were being driven into a deep
snow drift.

'Christ!' Browning didn't know whether Podini was
cursing or praying.

Adams had his feet on the brake and the XM1 was
almost stationary.

'Keep her going, Adams...move the cowson...'
Browning found that so long as he was looking directly
towards the raging fires near the bridges he could see, but
the remainder of the landscape which had formerly been
twilight through his night-sight was now pitch-black.

The whole stretch of woodland beyond the dump where
the missile launcher had been concealed was blazing, as
though a hundred napalm bombs had been dropped within
the small area.

187

'HE, I told you it was HE,' Podini was shouting joyfully. 'Boy, see that rocket go...Jesus Christ...'

A Russian truck was being driven furiously but blindly on a diagonal collision course towards Utah. Browning expected Adams to change direction; he didn't. Utah struck the truck a third of the way along the body, tore it apart and tossed the wreckage high into the air. The tank shuddered. Behind them the front end of the truck somersaulted across the field shedding bodies, and then burst into flames.

Browning began using the .5 machine gun, concentrating on the riverbank where some of the anti-aircraft defences had been positioned. He could not see a clear target, but hoped his bullets were encouraging the AA gunners to keep their heads down. 'Adams...right a bit...Podini...go for the bridges...' As he spoke the nearest bridge erupted into a mass of fire and twisted metal. 'Forget it...leave them to the BGS...hit the transports.'

Podini was firing as fast as Ginsborough could get shells and charges into the breech, and Adams had cut the speed again, keeping Utah close to the cover below the hill. The first of the PG-7 anti-tank rockets exploded three meters ahead, followed by a second more to the right. Adams accelerated. He saw a group of infantry twenty meters ahead and drove for them; three chose the wrong direction and were pulped beneath the XM1's tracks.

Two shells fired by one of the twin 23mm anti-aircraft guns shrieked off Utah's Chobham armour, the third exploded on the turret ring, failed to penetrate, but jammed the Cadillac Cage turret drive.

Podini yelled, 'Let's get the fuck out of here...'

Utah rocked as an anti-tank grenade exploded close to the hull. Browning could see a platoon of enemy infantry charging towards the hill. 'Okay, Mike...let's go.'

Adams spun the tank, the violence of his action tossing Browning against the equipment which surrounded him. Adams, like Browning, had lost most of his night vision. Now that Utah was heading into the darkness he could see

188

nothing, and they were closer to the river than he realized.

The NATO bar mine, ploughed into the riverbank the previous night by US Engineers, exploded under the rear of the tank, tearing off the track, rear bogeys and drive wheel, and rupturing the fuel tanks. The driving and fighting compartments were filled with a fine mist of diesel fuel. Utah stopped dead as the transmission locked solid.

Browning knew they had only seconds before the fuel would ignite and Utah burst into flame. He yelled: 'Bale out, guys...' He rammed the hatch open and climbed on to the hull. He could see Ginsborough pulling himself from the loader's hatch nearby. Podini's head and shoulders were close to him, he grabbed them and lifted the man clear of the turret, pushing him off the hull before jumping down beside him.

'Where's Mike?' Podini shouted the question wildly.

'Get down...she'll go any second.' Browning tried to drag Podini further away from Utah but Podini wrenched himself free and ran towards the front of the tank, pulling himself on to the sloping foredeck. He reached the driver's hatch and tried to open it. It was jammed. Browning heard a burst of machine gun fire and saw Podini spin back against the turret, his body jerking with the impact of the bullets before it folded over the barrel of the M68. Smoke billowed suddenly from the hatches, and ignited with a dull roar.

Browning was on his knees. He could see Ginsborough to his left, crouching, watching, his eyes wide and his mouth open as though he were screaming silently. Silhouetted against the fires of the supply dump the body of Podini hung across the Abrams' gun-barrel, his clothes burning. Four Soviet infantrymen were running towards the tank.

Browning stood up. There was nothing more to be done; it was all over. He raised his hands, saw that the Russians had stopped and were watching him in the light of the flames, and felt a strange sense of relief. He took a step forward, and as he did so the infantrymen began firing. Will Browning's second war had lasted his lifetime.

SIXTEEN

Second Lieutenant Robin Sache-Worrel was feeling very uncertain of a situation which had developed in the stay-behind unit 'Magpie'. For the past three and a half hours he had been sitting in the fighting compartment of his Scimitar questioning his own memory. He had been standing near Captain Fellows when the orders had come through from headquarters. He heard Fellows repeat the radio message. 'Apex Crown Echo... Trophy Bacon Sunset Juliet area.'

Then the captain had translated for Lieutenant Hinton: 'Wizard had given us one K west of Hehlingen as the location of the Soviet Divisional HQ.'

Things had happened so quickly after the unit received its orders that Sache-Worrel gave them no more thought until the SAS had left to reconnoitre the area and determine the exact situation of the enemy headquarters the stay-behind-unit were to attack. Sache-Worrel's mind had been keyed up by the thought of the coming action. He had no experience of death or pain in war, and there had been no sense of fear to dull his anticipation. He knew its dangers only secondhand.

His present uncertainty had nothing to do with his own future in a physical sense. It had arisen during the waiting period, when the adrenalin level had eventually dropped and his thoughts became more reasoned. Captain Fellows' translation of 'Trophy Bacon Sunset Juliet area', had been incorrect.

'Bacon' was not Hehlingen; Sache-Worrel was certain it was Bisdorf.

He had run through the day's codes a hundred times in his head. The more he did so the more positive he became that the code-name for the town of Hehlingen was 'Brandy'; 'Bacon' as Bisdorf was a full ten kilometers further south.

Sache-Worrel was very aware he was the most junior of the Scimitar commanders in the stay-behind unit. It was unusual for all commanders, within what was virtually a troop, to be commissioned. But it had been thought by HQ that, with a high casualty probability, this would enable the unit to continue to function regardless of losses. Sache-Worrel was only a second lieutenant, and above him in rank were two first lieutenants, Roxforth and Gunion, and then Captain Fellows.

If a mistake had been made by the captain, Sache-Worrel thought, then surely one of the others must have noticed as well as himself. As a junior officer, he could hardly accuse his unit commander of something which amounted to at least carelessness, perhaps worse in wartime.

He had now begun to doubt his own memory. Perhaps *he* had learnt the codes incorrectly...perhaps *he* had misheard the message. It wasn't doing much to help his self-confidence. What would happen if he made similar errors in battle? Mistakes were even more possible in the clamour and confusion! Supposing he forgot something vital? This was no longer a training exercise...he might write off his whole crew as well as himself...perhaps jeopardize the entire scheme.

But if Captain Fellows had made the mistake, then everything was a cock-up anyway.

He had known Captain Fellows almost a year, though it had only been during the past three months that he had served under him in the unit. Fellows was normally pleasant enough, finicky perhaps; the captain didn't have to rely on his service pay for his cash, he had a good private income which allowed him to run a couple of polo ponies and live extremely well, but that was his good luck. He seemed to have few friends in the regiment, but talked as though he

191

had plenty outside. In fact it was generally agreed amongst the younger officers that Fellows was really waiting for dead-men's boots, his father's, and the estates in Bedfordshire that went with them. But Sache-Worrel had never heard the captain criticized for any lack of ability as an officer, only for his obsession with tidiness.

'Bacon' *is* Bisdorf! It was there in his mind again, nagging like a persistent fishwife.

Silently he pushed himself out of the Scimitar's hatch. Captain Fellows had suggested rather than ordered them to stay with their vehicles, but nevertheless Sache-Worrel felt guilty as he jumped from the hull, and almost expected to hear the captain's voice question him.

Gunion's Scimitar was the closest, thirty meters away to his right at the easternmost corner of the square formed by the four tanks. The two SAS APCs were concealed within the square. Somewhere in the darkness of the woods beyond the tanks were the SAS guards Hinton had posted before leaving with his patrol; they gave Sache-Worrel the same feeling of safety his father had spoken of when discussing the operational value of Gurkha riflemen in the Second World War.

Sache-Worrel's background sometimes inhibited him. It did so now as he stood below Gunion's turret. He felt he should knock rather than simply trespass on his neighbour's territory by clambering uninvited on to the hull. He tried a discreet cough, but although Gunion's turret hatch was open, no one appeared. After a moment's hesitation, he pulled himself on board.

'Ben?' The interior of the Scimitar was a black pit, but Sache-Worrel could smell the usual combination of oil and sweat. 'Ben?' He was keeping his voice low, confidential. He was about to reach down into the darkness when Ben Gunion's face appeared very close to his own, like a surprised jack-in-the-box.

'Good God!'

'It's me...Robin...'

192

'Damn you, Robin, I almost pissed myself. What on earth are you creeping about for?'

'I was thinking...'

'For God's sake don't think,' advised Gunion. 'It's contagious. Want a quick snort? Here...' He handed Sache-Worrel a quarter litre flask of Asbach. 'I've got a decent bottle of claret in my locker, but it's probably too shaken about. Wasn't going to leave it for the bloody Ruskies, though. Well, drink up...'

'No thanks, Ben.' Sache-Worrel passed him back the liquor.

'You sound ill. Nervous?' Gunion was sympathetic. He liked Sache-Worrel. 'Don't be. It won't be as bad as you think. Pre-match nerves – they'll disappear as soon as the balloon goes up.' Sache-Worrel was the same age as Gunion's younger brother, and always made the first lieutenant feel protective. 'We'll give them hell. Just remember the training; keep your head down and whenever possible attack the command vehicles. In and out fast, before they've a chance to recover.'

'It's not nerves, Ben. It's just...well, something else.'

'Girls? I say, you haven't got yourself into a spot of bother! Now that would be a fine thing.'

'No, it's not a girl...it's to do with Captain Fellows.'

'Well, spit it out.'

Sache-Worrel told him. Gunion took another sip of his schnapps before he made any comment, then he said: 'I didn't hear the message. Bugger! You're certain you've got it right? Bacon is the correct code for Bisdorf, but was Bacon the word in the message? Are you *sure* you heard Bacon and not Brandy?'

'I *was* positive; now I'm not so certain. That's the trouble. I've been thinking about it so much I've confused myself. An hour ago I'd have staked my life I was right, now I don't know.'

'We could all be staking our lives on it,'

'What can we do?'

'You, nothing! It's Sandy's job as senior lieutenant. God! I wondered why we hadn't seen anything of Hinton's lot, they're probably chasing halfway around the Hassenwinkel on a wild goose chase. They were due in an hour ago, and working with the SAS is like working with robots; they usually programme themselves to the second.'

'You'll tell Sandy?'

'Yes, I'll tell him. If you see a flash of blue light from his tank, it'll be him reacting.'

Roxforth was experiencing some of Sache-Worrel's feelings on hearing the information passed him by Gunion. It wasn't easy to tell your commander he was wrong and, like Gunion, Roxforth hadn't heard the original coded message. He was tempted to let the matter slide; sooner or later Fellows himself would realize he had made an error and would probably correct it. The only trouble with that line of reasoning, Roxforth knew, was correction might be impossible if too much time was lost. A Soviet division's main headquarters was as mobile as the battlefront itself. The opportunity to knock it out might never occur again...there were too many contingencies involved to guarantee the survival of the stay-behind unit for more than a few hours. One surprise attack during the darkness of the first night was all they could count on; with a lot of luck, they might even manage two. But by daylight , the Russians would be looking for them. Even if they remained where they were now, every hour that passed brought a greater chance of discovery as more enemy troops entered the area and the Soviet consolidation and mopping-up began.

Although Roxforth liked Sache-Worrel, he was hoping the second lieutenant was wrong. It would be much better if Fellows could simply shrug his shoulders and say: 'Nothing to worry about, everything is fine.' The entire incident could be passed off as normal anxiety in this kind of situation. It would be forgotten immediately.

Mick Fellows was standing beside his Scimitar when Roxforth found him, staring out into the darkness of the woods. 'Sir?' Fellows was as twitchy as the rest of them, and turned quickly. 'Can we talk for a minute?'

'I shouldn't wander around too much,' suggested Fellows. 'I'd rather you all kept to your tanks until the recce patrol gets back. What's the probelm?'

'The message from HQ. I didn't hear the original code.' Roxforth found himself speaking over-quickly.

'Having doubts, Sandy? Don't worry. These damned SAS are taking their time, they're overdue. It shouldn't have taken them so long, we put them down within a couple of miles of the location. This waiting makes all of us edgy. It doesn't help hearing the sound of battle all the while; makes you want to get in there and do something. Bloody frustrating. How are the crews?'

'Fine. Most are sleeping.' He knew he was going to have to persist even if Fellows did get angry with him. 'What was the code, sir?'

Fellows replied sharply, 'Trophy Bacon Sunset Juliet. What's on your mind?'

Oh Christ, thought Roxforth, there *has* been a mistake! The thought dismayed him though he hadn't spent too much time dwelling on the consequences of the error. He said, 'I'm sorry, sir. I think there's been a mistranslation.'

'Nonsense!' Fellows was immediately defensive, and annoyed. 'The translation is correct.'

'Bacon, sir.'

'Bacon is Hehlingen.'

'No, sir. Bacon is Bisdorf. Hehlingen is Brandy.'

Roxforth could sense Fellows bristling in the darkness. 'Now see here, Roxforth...' Fellows paused, thought for a few moments as his doubts grew then spoke more softly. 'Damn...damn!' He had been showing off in front of the SAS lieutenant...if he had taken just a few more seconds to check the message.

'It was a mistake for HQ to choose neighbouring towns

with code names beginning with the same letter,' said Roxforth, offering his commander an excuse.

'No need for eyewash, Sandy. Which one of you spotted the error?' Fellows answered the question for himself. 'Only Sache-Worrel could have heard the original.'

Roxforth realized the knowledge it was the junior lieutenant wasn't going to make it any easier for the captain.

'I wish to God he'd spoken up at the time,' said Fellows, quietly.

'I don't believe he thought about it until we reached here...then he wasn't certain how to handle it.'

'Are the crews aware of this?'

'Of course not.' Roxforth could see no point in reducing the men's confidence in their commander. Everyone could make mistakes, and he could appreciate the captain's feelings.

'One kilometer west of Bisdorf would put the Red HQ about three K's from the A2 autobahn.'

'Or thereabouts,' agreed Roxforth.

'And we've lost three hours.'

'We may be able to recover time,' Roxforth said, encouragingly.

'Nonsense. There's no way you can recover lost time. Damn and blast! Get the crews ready to move out. The minute Hinton is back, we'll get going.' He studied his watch. 'I'm giving him another thirty minutes.'

'Yes, sir.'

'You don't need to "sir" me, Sandy, just because I've made a bloody fool of myself. And by the way, I'll make out a report of the matter afterwards.'

'I don't think that will be necessary.'

'It *is* necessary. Thank young Sache-Worrel for me will you. Tell him he did the right thing, Sandy. Late, maybe, but right.'

Fellows watched him walk away through the shadows of the woods. He felt angry with himself; not only angry, but ashamed. He had prided himself that his career had been

196

near-faultless, no errors in training, always the highest marks; a close runner-up for best cadet at Sandhurst. He had never put a foot wrong, until now. And this had been what all the training had been about – war. He had made a balls of his first command in real action. Why? Because he had been unable to trust the judgement of a superior officer. He still believed his German CO was wrong; if you were going to have armoured stay-behind units, then they should be Chieftains with more protection and heavier weaponry, not lightly-armed Scimitars. But as he had always felt this, then he should not have accepted the command; he should have had the courage to refuse. His lack of conviction in the practicability of the scheme had led to his carelessness. Responsibility now for its failure was totally his own. It was not going to be easy to live with in the future; he rejected imperfection in others, but had discovered it in himself.

Hinton's patrol had been unsuccessful. He returned feeling dispirited. They had probed further than he had originally intended and still found no indication of the enemy main HQ. They had seen Russians; a field hospital, a number of engineering units, and two kilometers west of Rosche a motor-rifle company. He was surprised by Fellows' casual acceptance of his failure, it seemed out of character with his own experiences of the tank captain.

Fellows said, simply, 'Bad luck, Hinton. We'll try again to the south...to the west of Bisdorf. Get your lads on the APCs briskly, we don't want to waste any more of the darkness.'

Fellows led them south-west for several kilometers, then crossed the Wolfsburg Neindorf road and swung east. Movement was difficult. Whereas on their first run from the bunker they had been travelling almost due west and in the general direction of the Soviet advance, now they cut across the main supply line of the enemy division. The Russian commanders were making use of darkness to move up their supplies and reinforcements, and those south of Neindorf were coming within range of the NATO howitzers sited west of Köningslutter. The ground the Scimitars and APCs were now covering bore signs of heavy battle activity. Every dip in the fields, every wood and copse, farmhouse and village had been defended. Damaged and wrecked military vehicles and equipment littered the fields and roadsides, some of the vehicles still alight, their metalwork twisted and blackened, the corpses of their crews around them. There were wounded men in the ditches and shell craters; sometimes they moved or signalled frantically at the Scimitars. Fellows knew that many were NATO soldiers, but there was nothing he could do for them, and therefore no gain in slackening the speed of his unit. Some would survive, but they would have to wait until the Soviet medical units had attended their own men.

Fellows had slowed the unit two hundred meters from the ruins of the small village of Almke when they came under fire. The first indication was the explosion of the second in line of the SAS APCs. In open ground a little to the rear of the Scimitars, it burst into flames, swerved to the left and overturned. Sandy Roxforth, in station sixty meters to the right of the APC, had been standing in his Scimitar with his head and shoulders out of the hatch. The attack was unexpected, accurate identification was difficult at night and Soviet troops would be taking care not to fire on their own armour.

Roxforth dropped into the vehicle and as he did so heard machine gun bullets rattling off the aluminium hull. The lieutenant had just sufficient time to realize its significance when a 120mm shell, its point-blank range confirmed by the ranging machine gun, penetrated the Scimitar hull just below the top run of the track and exploded directly behind the driver.

Sache-Worrel saw Roxforth's tank destroyed. The way in

which it blew to pieces was terrifying, and he realized instantly there was no possibility of survivors. He was praying for someone to break radio silence and tell him what he should do. It seemed sensible to use best speed to get out of the immediate area of the village and away into the darkness; at fifty miles an hour it didn't take long to get a Scimitar out of trouble. But Captain Fellows, to Sache-Worrel's right and eighty meters ahead of him, had not changed course and appeared to have stopped.

Sache-Worrel saw a burst of flame from Fellows' Rarden; a single shot, then two in rapid succession. He was getting too close to Captain Fellows' tank so ordered his driver to swing away further to the right and increase speed, intending to draw around in an arc beyond the leading Scimitar.

Fellows' Rarden fired a three-round burst, then his Scimitar accelerated. The captain had left it a fraction of a second too late. A shell exploded beneath the tank's square stern, lifted the hull upwards and threw it completely on to its side. It ignited immediately, its fuel spreading around it so it appeared to be floating in a lake of flames. Sache-Worrel caught a horrifying glimpse of a small dark figure staggering within the incinerating fire, then heard Gunion on the net, his voice urgent.

'Magpie Sierra Echo...this is Ben...three o'clock, woods,...go like hell!'

'Wilco...' He felt the Scimitar surge across the ground as his driver swung it away.

'Magpie Sierra Delta...this is X-Ray Nine...we're going in to neutralize.' It was Hinton.

'Roger X-Ray Nine, we'll stand off.'

The net was silent again for several minutes. Sache-Worrel brought the Scimitar around two thousand meters beyond the village, and waited.

'Magpie Sierra Delta this is X-Ray Nine. It's okay here now.'

'Roger X-Ray Nine, out to · you. Magpie Sierra

199

Echo...white farm building four kilometers back...small lake...rendezvous there.'

'Roger Magpie Sierra Delta.'

The HF died. Sache-Worrel was stunned by the happenings of the past few minutes. Half the SAS unit wiped out...and two Scimitar crews...Sandy Roxforth...Captain Fellows...all in seconds. A body thrashing in the petrol fire, Fellows' or his gunner's? There was no slow introduction to war and death, one moment it was peace and the next all hell had broken loose around you. And he had not even seen the enemy although he had kept his eyes to the L2A1...Fellows must have spotted them though, he had managed several shots with the Rarden.

McLeod the gunner shouted by Sache-Worrel's right shoulder, 'We hit the shit, sir...bloody shame!'

Hit the shit! That was understatement thought Sache-Worrel. Everything had gone wrong since the moment they left the bunker! He could see the farmhouse ahead of them now. Before when they had passed it the ruins had looked serene in the darkness, and the carp lake bordering its grounds had appeared calm and peaceful. Now he wasn't sure; it might hold an enemy gun...death...nothing would be as it seemed for him ever again. At least, not in war.

Gunion had stayed with the remaining APC, and then escorted it back. The vehicle was now in the shadow beside the tumbled farm building, and the men were stationed in the rubble. The two Scimitars were parked in what had been the farm's orchard and a carpet of apples covered the ground.

Hinton was angrily discussing the tragedy. 'It was a Leopard! A bloody Heer Leopard. Hull-down in the wreckage of a supermarket.'

A Leopard! Good God, thought Sache-Worrel, we lost all our men to a NATO tank. Is war *all* mistakes? It was beginning to look like it.

'You sure it was a NATO crew?' asked Gunion. 'It might have been captured!'

'It *should* have been bloody captured,' growled Hinton disgustedly. 'It would have been better for us. I lost eleven men, good men...you've lost six...every one dead.'

'Who were the Leopard crew?'

'There was a 7th German Armoured Division flash on the back of the tank,' said Hinton. 'And what I could see of their equipment afterwards was all West German.'

'What did they say when you told them we were British?' asked Sache-Worrel.

'I'm afraid we didn't have time for a conversation. They were fighting with the commander's hatch wedged partly open...we dropped them a message and shut the hatch.'

'A message?'

'A British ordinance mark on a grenade!'

The second transmission from HQ, due to be made at 02.23 hours, did not materialize. Again the men experienced the now familiar feelings of uncertainty. Had the radio message been transmitted an hour earlier than they had expected? Would it be transmitted an hour later? The message was supposed to give a new target for the unit. But even more important, it was a form of contact with their comrades. Gunion had decided against any further attempt to pursue the first target of the Soviet Division's HQ, by now they would probably have been moved, and there was less than four hours until dawn. He didn't want the last two Scimitars caught in the centre of the main Russian troop movements in broad daylight.

The SAS were free to operate as an independent unit after the first night, and Hinton had already explained his plans. He intended to abandon the APC and work on foot. Men were easier to conceal than vehicles, and he would travel for the remainder of darkness into the sector occupied by the

Soviet logistics column and operate there. He had a potential rendezvous with a Bundesgrenzshutz unit in forty-eight hours, and would link up with them if they still existed. Supply points of additional weapons and explosives were already available to him when he needed them, and he would be organizing a guerrilla force.

Hinton could make it all sound so casual and easy, thought Sache-Worrel. The man was much harder than himself, brutal in his attitude even to friends, though there weren't more than three of four years' difference in their ages. Listening to him made Sache-Worrel feel like a new boy at prep' school.

He realized now that everything he had ever done in his military training had only been a game. Of course it had been tough and essential...the best that could be given to the officers and men. But behind every training action was the knowledge that someone somewhere was giving the orders and knew what they were doing; within a very few hours you were always clean, warm, and ensconced back in the comfort of the mess with your friends, laughing over a few gin and tonics. And in the background were your families, girlfriends, wives, keeping the whole thing in perspective.

Ireland? It had felt dangerous at the time, but it had been a pushover; border patrols in the open countryside south of Armagh, and the faintly hostile attitude of the people, which you knew was seldom genuine but enforced by the IRA activity in the area. In resrospect, the former tour of duty seemed like a holiday.

He remembered a conversation with his father a few days before he had left for Ireland. 'Don't try to be a hero,' his father had said.

He had laughed at the well-meant advice which was almost a cliche. 'Chance would be a fine thing.'

'That's exactly what I mean. Don't look for the opportunity. Heroes have a tendency not to survive.'

'It's not a war, Dad.'

'It's active service, and the nearest thing to a war you may ever have to fight. Don't be tempted to use your tour of duty to test your courage. That's not its purpose.'

'Things have changed in the army, Dad. It's a lot more organized than in your day; modern communications are very sophisticated...satellites, advanced radio techniques. We have computers...we just feed in the information, and the instruments come up with the answers. Our intelligence is first-class...radar...infra-red detectors...electronic sensors...we know every move an enemy can make. It's all very organized and technical. About the only decision I have to make, is when to clean my teeth.'

Everything had seemed so neat and orderly. Then. Clean smart uniforms, instructors who fed you their information lucidly and with assurance, orders given and immediately obeyed.

'This is a Scimitar.' The usual army practice of treating everyone in training, even young officers, as complete idiots. 'Welded aluminium construction. Fast, light and manoeuvrable. Pretty, gentlemen, very pretty. First-class reconnaissance vehicle. Crew three. Length 4.743 meters, width 2.184 meters, height 2.115 meters. Maximum road speed eighty-seven kilometers an hour. Range, six hundred and forty-four kilometers. It will climb a vertical object of half a meter, or a trench two meters wide. No nasty habits, well-bred, and a little on the fancy side. A nice smart charger for a Lancer gentleman. Treat her right, and she'll look after you. And what appears to be a punt-gun on her turret, is a Rarden cannon; ninety to a hundred rounds a minute. Single shots, or bursts of up to six rounds. Cases ejected outside the vehicle, so they don't scrape the burnish off your toecaps. Interesting ammunition, the round doesn't arm until it is twenty meters from your barrel, and if it doesn't hit the target in eight seconds, blows itself to pieces. Very convenient...tidy. You are going to learn *everything* about it, gentlemen, and I am going to teach you.'

'This is your ammunition: TP; TP-T; MINE HEI-T;

SAPHEI, APIC-T.'

'A Helmgard helmet, Mister Sache-Worrel. And what is it fitted with? Accoustic valves to protect your delicate eardrums! And what else? Right! Your communications facilities. And these are part of...? Yes, Clansman...your communications system. Eight hundred and forty channels available, gentlemen; HF and VHF; frequency coverage from one point five to seventy-five point nine seven five MHz, and two hundred and twenty-five to three hundred and ninety-nine point zero MHz.'

'This gentlemen, is the ZB 298 battlefield surveillance radar, which can be fitted to reconnaissance vehicles...the thermal imaging sight...lasar range-finder...the night vision gunner's sight...you need to know about mines, gentlemen; this is a film of the Ranger mine discharger system; the discharger holds one thousand two hundred and ninety-six mines in one load, and can fire out eighteen mines a second...bar mines are laid by ploughs; seven hundred an hour...note the angles of your smoke grenade dischargers; a full hundred and eighty degree smoke screen...gentlemen, this is not a cage for the display of baboons, though I sometimes wonder, this is the Morfax gunnery simulator...'

So much information, but still confusion...

Would his father have been confused, too, wondered Sache-Worrel? His own war had lasted less than twenty-four hours and he had no idea what was happening. His father's war had lasted five years. Could doubt and uncertainty last that long, or was it eventually overcome? And fear? War had not really begun for him yet...it was early days...hours...and yet he had already been terrified. He had seen death at a distance but not yet touched it. He realized how condescending he must have sounded to his father...wars were all the same. You might fight them with different weapons, in different places, but they were the same.

'Robin...'

'Yes, Ben.'

204

'I think we should try and make ourselves useful. Hinton's moving out now. We'll head back towards the west and have a go at the Ruskie engineering units; create a bit of mayhem with their soft-skinned transports. Strike, cut and run, keep on the move. Are you game?'

Sache-Worrl nodded. 'Yes, I'm game.' What was it Mister Hatton his schoolmaster used to say? Don't think you've lost, just because you're fifteen points down at half time; you can still win.

SEVENTEEN

It was different now, thought Morgan Davis; working better. The battle groups were holding the Russians! The minefields on the eastern bank of the River Schunter had been carefully laid with plenty of depth. The NATO gunners, covering it from well to the rear of the armour, had wiped out the first of the Soviet recce squadrons with a spectacular copy-book strike.

A large number of sensors, still operative deep in the ground through which the Soviet division was attempting to move, were feeding information back to the artillery observers and continuously giving them new targets. Unfortunately, in many cases, blanketing the area where an electronic sensor detected and reported transport movement also meant the destruction of the device. But nevertheless they were proving effective. The Soviet division had for the moment lost its momentum; the head of the attack had weakened.

Warrant Officer Davis still knew little of the progress of the war outside the Elm Sector. He had heard rumours that the Russian forces had captured Lübeck and Hamburg in the north, and the Americans in CENTAG, supported by the French and German corps, had pushed the invaders back into East Germany as far as the town of Nordhausen. He realized however, the stories were unlikely to be fact, as he felt certain the NATO forces would not be permitted to advance into Warsaw Pact territory. Everyone was guessing, and those with the most fertile imaginations guessed the wildest. Stories grew in wartime, and everyone liked to think they knew something special or had experienced something unique; like the Angel of Mons. Angel of bloody Mons. Christ, we could do with one here, he mused. But the Angel of Mons had been only imagination, too...no one had even mentioned one until years after the First World War when some London journalist wrote a fictional short story about the battle and the intervention of a host of Heavenly warriors; then everyone remembered – or thought they did. The Russians in Hamburg? They might well get there eventually, but by God they would have had to shift to be in the city by now. Hedda and the kids? They'd be okay. Hedda would see to that. Bloody good bird, Hedda. Bird? Lady. Warrant officers' wives weren't birds. And the kids, too. They were nearly officer's kids now. And he wouldn't be spending the rest of his army career as a warrant officer, there would certainly be more promotion ahead...a commission to lieutenant...captain...major? Christ, it was impossible. Hedda the wife of a British major, hell, she would lap it up. It would be great for them all.

There had been a lull for the past half hour, following a rocket barrage that passed beyond Charlie Squadron's present positions, and landed harmlessly in open farmland. There was still artillery fire from both sides, but it all seemed to be aimed behind the front lines. There was nothing to be seen moving in the vision-intensifying lenses...the Russians were somewhere in the darkness...they were there...but they weren't coming right now.

There was a ripple of movement in the ground and the sky far across the Schunter glowed briefly.

'There's another, Sarge...sir,' said Inkester. He was still having problems remembering Davis's new rank. 'What you reckon they are?'

'Lance missiles.' Damn, thought Davis, I've joined the guessing game!

'Hell of a warhead, sir! Did you see them SPs go in a

while back? Glad I wasn't on the receiving end. Bloody hell, it's like fucking bonfire night a million times over. Wish I knew what was going on though.' He raised his voice. 'Here, DeeJay, you bleedin' awake?'

'Yeah...' DeeJay's voice was muffled, hollow.

'You want an egg banjo?'

'Don't be daft.'

'I've got one...got two. Put 'em in me pocket, back at the reform.'

'Christ, a bloody cold egg banjo!'

'They ain't cold. You want one?'

'Stick it!'

'What about you, sir?'

'No thanks,' answered Davis. He could imagine it, slimy in his mouth, the fried egg sandwich covered in oily thumbprints. He sighed, it would be dawn soon. Another dawn; it had to be better than the last one. Just twenty-four hours, and everything had changed. What would happen next? What were the bloody government doing? Talking! The government always talked, and usually ended by cutting back on defence funding. Well, they'd soon know if they'd cut their bloody budgets too hard; they probably knew now. A couple of thousand more battle tanks along the frontier would certainly have helped matters. How many had been lost? God, it must be hundreds already. 'Spink?'

'Yes, sir.'

'Knock us out some char.'

'Yeah, earn your bloody living,' called Inkester.

'Give the lad a chance. How're you feeling now, Spink?'

'A bit better, sir.'

'You don't smell better,' said Inkester. 'You're like a big tart, pissing yourself when a gun goes off. They ought to 'ave issued you with a nappy...'

'Inkester, shut up! One more remark like that and you're on a fizzer. I mean it, lad.'

'Yes, sir.' Inkester decided to think of something else; something pleasant. What was the name of that bird he had

208

met in Bergen, in Angie's Bar? Irma. The same as the one in the film...the musical...bloody bore that was...Had her didn't I, the night we were celebrating Weeksie's promotion; she wanted a length Irma did, and she got it in the back of Weeksie's Volks! Wonder what happened to that? It wasn't a bad jam-jar. Nicked by now, or bloody full of shrapnel holes. Gone the same fucking way as my stereo, and all the tapes...and my civvy gear. Wonder if they'll pay us compensation; bloody should, we didn't start the fucking war.

God, Davis certainly came up fighting to defend Spink. Fancy him threatening me like that. Flaming charge. Bloody hell, for a moment he sounded just like my old man. Christ, Saturday nights in Scotland Road...beer and a punch up the throat, or a boot in the side of your bloody head. A bloody boot...God, it was a boot that got me here now.

'This is the second time you have been brought before this court, Inkester.' Bloody pompous old sod; just a butcher in a backstreet round the corner from Lime Street Station. Who the hell does he think he is? 'There's no reason why we should be expected to tolerate this disgraceful hooliganism. If you were a year older, I would have no hesitation in sentencing you to six months in jail. A few years ago, I would have ordered the birch. I am recommending a period in an approved school which I hope will bring you to your senses...'

It was *his* fault, thought Inkester. The magistrate's bloody fault he was out here now. Bloody old shit. No it wasn't, he decided suddenly, it was his own. He'd been a bit of a tearaway and he had been caught. It was fair enough.

'Sorry Inkester, we can't take you at the moment. The army's not that easy. Prove yourself first. You hold a job down for two years, and re-apply. If you've got a good reference, then we can use you.'

Two years. It had seemed a long time. 'You'll never hold a job down two years, you little bugger.' His father sometimes worked in the markets, but was more often on the dole.

Where the hell did you look for a job that would last two years? 'Struth, it was on the way to a pension. Two years...and if he so much as batted an eyelid at the boss and got sacked, the two years would have to begin again. Bloody hell!

'You may as well piss up a wall, kid!' His brother was a year younger and still at school. 'What the hell do you want to join the army for? Someone must have hit you on the 'ead!'

'It's good; you can learn a trade. There's opportunity.' He had seen a recruiting film and sent off for all the pamphlets, before visiting the recruiting office. Even the sergeant who had turned him down had made it sound worthwhile.

'Opportunity! Look at our old man...a toolmaker until he gets called up for his National Service, then he's a batman and half the time in the glasshouse...hasn't bloody worked since. Army fucking ruined him. You've heard Mam go on about it.'

'Yeah...it's a load of cobblers. He doesn't work 'cus he's too bloody idle.' Where the hell was he going to find steady employment; there weren't a lot of jobs around Liverpool. He tried a dozen different places before Woolworths. What if he were absolutely honest about his reason for applying for work there? He tried it!

The manager was sympathetic: 'Two years, Inkester? Normally, we prefer to train staff who intend to stay with us longer...young men like to go on to managerial posts. We can afford to be selective; there is a lot of responsibility in a company like this. What sort of work would you be prepared to do?'

'Anything, sir. Anything at all.' The man hadn't said no; it was the closest he had got yet to a job.

'In the warehouse? It's tiring and I doubt if I could promise any kind of promotion.'

210

'Would it last two years, sir?'

The man had smiled at his anxiety. 'It'll see you into the army young man, if you work hard...'

Two years in Woolies. Afterwards, when he had been accepted, it had felt like extra time on a sentence, but it hadn't really been like that. The two years had gone quickly. They had even held a small party for him the day he had left; turned out to be a good lot of blokes, and girls. It wasn't bad. Dickenson the manager had seen him right...first man who ever did. Not bad for a Wallasey poofter!

Catterick! Jesus Christ, the first weeks of training...the first two. He had cried at night, like a bloody baby.

'What the hell do you lot think you are? You terrify me...all of you! How am I expected to make soldiers out of you? Trooper! What the hell are you grinning at?' A face three inches from his own.' Pull your chin in, Wacker...square your shoulders, you ignorant bloody maggot.'

'You with the big ears...weasel head...yes, you, Trooper. Swing your arms smartly down to your side, don't let 'em drift in the bleeding wind like a fairy...and don't bloody 'sir' me...I'm a corporal...what d'you call me, Trooper?'

'Corporal...'

The face, leering again, the breath on his cheeks still smelling of the beer that had been drunk the previous evening. 'No you don't, Wacker...I know what you bloody call me. You call me a Manchester bastard! Now right dress...*as you bloody were...Squaaad. Right dress.*'

It had begun to get better; he had cottoned on to what was happening. The corporals and sergeants didn't hate them...it was all an act. And the act worked. It turned raw individuals into soldiers, into a unit, a team...made them think and work together, get annoyed with themselves and each other if something dragged them back. Christ, it began to look clever. The NCOs treated them like humans when the day was over; accepted them, talked to them, gave them

211

private advice. He made more friends in the first four weeks than in all his previous life. And what was even better, he trusted them; they were proper mates.

'Any idea what you'd like to do, lad?' The sergeant leant across his desk, genuinely interested in him.

'I'd like to be a gunner, Sar'nt.'

'You'll have to work hard for it...it's pretty technical, and important. A lot of responsibility. Think you can handle it?'

'Yes, Sar'nt.'

There was a moment's hesitation that made Inkester doubt himself, and then the sergeant's reply: 'I'll see what I can do for you.'

He *had* worked; it had been like being back in Woolworths in some ways...proving yourself for someone else's benefit...not entirely; for your own as well. It hadn't been easy. He had wasted a lot of his time at school, and had to make up for it now; but there was a good reason for learning.

There had been a great week last year, he remembered. A week's package in Calella, Spain, with a couple of the other lads, Weeksie and Lovell. They had tried to persuade three of the WRAC girls to join them, but one had suddenly become engaged to a civvy, and the other two got chicken. Pity, because he had quite fancied one of them, though her Glasgow accent got on his nerves a bit; smashing figure, though. They hadn't found one girl between them in Calella. Every bloody English girl wanted to go out with a Spaniard. And the local girls just giggled like fourteen year olds when you tried to chat them up. But, God, they had shifted some drink in the six nights and seven days. They tried to keep count of the bottles of wine, but in the end it became impossible, there was always a bottle floating in a kind of mist in front of them, stuck in the sand, or balanced on a table.

Irma. That was the last bird he had screwed. What a bloody carry-on! She had one leg over his shoulder, and the

212

other under his arm, wedged against the rear window so tightly he thought the bloody glass would pop out. When was it? Two months ago? Shit, it was barely one week.

The sky was brightening with the dawn, turning the vision blocks of the episcope in the Chieftain's turret into bars of soft green light. To the left of the Chieftain, fifty meters away, were the crew of a machine gun, lying beside the weapon sited in a break in the stone wall. Davis could see them clearly for the first time; twenty meters on were another group, but they were still difficult to distinguish from the low shrubs in which they were waiting.

He sat watching them. It was chilly enough inside the tank, it would be perishing cold out there. The infantrymen would be feeling stiff and uncomfortable, their clothing wet with the dew, their helmets dripping the condensation on to their shoulders. Jesus, who'd be a foot soldier!

'Tea, sir.'

'Thanks...' It was hot, sweet. He heard Inkester mutter something and thought, well, they'll get on together in the end. It was always difficult for a new crew member for the first few days. First few days? Charlie Bravo One and its crew might not last that long. A few days. Another two and maybe, if they were still lucky enough to be alive, they might get pulled out of the line for R and R. That would be good. That's something to aim for...aim to stay alive just two more days.

'What you doin' down there, DeeJay?' Inkester was leaning forward below Davis's knees, trying to peer into the driving compartment.

'Shaving.'

'You what?'

'Shaving!'

'In yer tea?'

'In maiden's water...what the hell do you think?'

'You're bloody mad...you'll be changing your shirt next.'

213

'I've done that.'

'I wish Stink would change his trousers...'

Davis had been watching the machine gun crew in the growing daylight. There was a kind of sadistic satisfaction in sitting inside the Chieftain with his mug of hot tea cupped in his hands, while the infantry shivered outside. One of the soldiers was standing, stretching, shaking his arms. He was taking a risk, a good sniper with a Dragunov and telescopic sight could pick him off from across the river. What the hell was he doing? He had stripped off the upper part of his NBC suit and was waving his helmet above his head. Another of the members of the GPMG crew was going to get him...no, was ignoring him...what in God's name were they doing with the machine gun? A man was lifting it off its bipod...he dropped it...picked it up, then threw it at one of the soldiers on the ground. They were laughing. One stumbled to his knees, then lay on his back, kicking his legs in the air like a crippled insect.

'Christ!' Davis shouted in horrified realization — tossing his half-finished mug of tea out of the way under his seat. 'Gas...gas...gas...All stations, this is Bravo One...gas...gas...gas...check all vehicles and close down.' He switched quickly to the squadron net. 'Hullo Shark, this is Bravo One...gas...gas...gas...Over.' He rammed on his respirator and blew out hard.

'Shark here...Roger Charlie Bravo One.' Captain Willis's voice was reassuringly steady. 'Do you have casualties? Over.'

'The infantry...I'll check the troop.' Davis's voice was slightly muffled, but he knew it would transmit.

'What kind of gas?'

'Chemical...unidentified.'

'How was it delivered?'

'No idea...no shells over...haven't seen aircraft. High altitude rockets, maybe.'

'Roger Charlie Bravo One...out.'

'DeeJay,' shouted Davis, 'you got your hatch clamped

down and your respirator on?'

'Yes.'

'Spink...check yours, lad.' Davis peered out through his lenses. The infantrymen he could see were hunched on the ground, curled into grotesque foetal postures; one was convulsing rhythmically, but the others were now all still. God, it was nasty...bloody terrifying. An unseen, unheard form of death that drifted in without warning. He could have been out there...leaning out of the turret for a breath of air when it arrived. The bastards; those bastard Russians. What about the rest of his troop?

'All stations Bravo, this is Nine...acknowledge. Over.'

'Bravo Two. Over.'

'Bravo Three. Over.'

Davis waited. Where the hell was Four? 'Bravo Four, this is One...acknowledge. Over?'

'Bravo Four. Over.'

Relief made Davis angry. 'Bravo Four, this is Nine. When I say acknowledge, I mean acknowledge...and fast okay? All Bravo Troop standby...and for God's sake stay closed-down. Any casualties near you? Over.'

Only one of the troop replied to his question. 'Bravo Three...report Milan squad knocked out here.'

'Roger Bravo Three. Out.'

PBI, they used to nickname them; poor bloody infantry. It was appropriate. 'Inkester, keep your eyes peeled.' DeeJay had already started the Chieftain's engine. 'Everything okay down there, DeeJay?'

'Ace, sir.'

'Spink? Spink, wake up, lad!'

'Yes, sir. I'm all right.'

'Fucking stay that way,' warned Inkester. 'Shit...look at that...' Four stub-winged aircraft in a tight diamond formation were swinging up above the distant woods, rising into a steep climb. Below them the ground was already a seething mass of napalm flame. 'What the hell are they, sir?'

They had come in so fast Davis had not seen their

215

approach dive. 'Tomcats maybe...Yanks...ours anyway.' The aircraft were already only small dots; the formation broke, sunlight glinted on perspex and they were gone.

It's begun again, thought Davis. As though in confirmation, the hull of the Chieftain began to quiver with the shock of exploding missiles. Overhead, the shrieking roar of heavy artillery shells rose above the throb of the tank's engine. Two more days, please God...that's all, just two days...keep us alive for two more days until we're pulled out.

Floggers! He saw them in the distance against the dawn sky, chunky, menacing, only a hundred meters above the ground. They seemed to be aiming themselves directly at Charlie Bravo One. He lost them for a second and they were suddenly terrifyingly close...one disintegrated into a vast orange flame; a comet spewing flaming debris as it fell. The others...he saw missiles briefly...heard the explosions somewhere to the rear. Smoke! Shell bursts ahead of him. Ethereal dark serpents writhing from the earth, to envelop the fields and swell along the riverbanks. The ground leapt, trees and shrubs flattening beneath the sharp aerial detonations of canister, aimed against infantry already incapacitated by the gas; steel pellets hammered the Chieftain's armoured body, shot-blasting the paintwork from polished metal.

Davis wondered what it was like for the Russian tank crews. Perhaps in some ways better; at least they were moving forward. But into what? Minefields! The leading tanks armed with rollers and ploughs to clear the treacherous and deadly ground...wedged up against ditches and streams where they became stationary targets for the Milan crews or the gunships. And here against the well-prepared defences, unable to use the natural cover until it was cleared of mines by their engineers. No, it wasn't better for them, and it was probably psychologically worse...they had everything to lose, and not much to gain...only someone else's piece of ground to die on.

216

Imagine being up there watching, he thought. Up there, not like God, but just up there. In a command helicopter well up out of harm's way if there was such a place; looking down and seeing it all happen. Like the time he had flown into Berlin, and seen the East German minefields stretching as a dark ploughed road as far as he could see in both directions from the windows of the aircraft; only now the border would be a band of fire and smoke cutting Europe in half. How wide was the devastation and destruction? Would it go on expanding until the whole world was one huge smoking ruin?

Inkester called, 'Infantry...I think I can see Russian infantry!'

Davis swept the ground through the smoke with the 7.62mm machine gun, pleased to give himself something to take his mind off the devastating artillery bombardment. He stopped firing, and watched through the episcope as a British Saracen disgorged its men sixty meters to his left; ten infantrymen, clumsily-suited and cradling their SLRs, alien in their respirators, comforting. Replacements; infantry to fight infantry. Davis wanted more of them to appear, supported by some fresh armour to charge forward and roll it all up, get it over with. They wouldn't come, it was a waste of time even thinking about it.

'Charlie Bravo One...this is Shark. Soviet air-drop to the rear...about two Ks back, at Cyanide...some light armour. We'll hold here until it gets too hot, then move to Potash...out.'

'Roger, Shark,' acknowledged Davis.

Air-drop, bloody hell. And behind somewhere. That was bound to be the way they'd do it; they weren't going to get themselves shot to hell in order to ford some pissy little river; they'd just put up a diversionary artillery barrage, and then air-drop their troops past the defences. Sod crossing minefields and bridging ditches. They would secure the bridgehead by an airborne assault first. Gas! That was bloody obvious, too. Someone should have had those poor

217

infantry bastards in their respirators since first shot yesterday...bloody disorganization...too many bosses up top...too bloody far away from the battlefront. No, that wasn't true. The colonel had been right up there with them...Colonel Studley in his Chieftain, out there in the battle like his crews. Bloody good for him; he was...had been the sort of colonel you wanted to fight under...poor sod.

'Armour! What the hell?' Inkester's voice, anxious. 'Range six hundred...' The Chieftain lurched on its suspension as Inkester fired. 'What was it, sir?' The wreckage of the vehicle was hidden in the smoke.

'An MT-LB...worry about what's coming, lad, not what's gone.'

EIGHTEEN

12.00 hours. Day Two

'They look like dead rats, Jesus, they look like rats!'
Inkester was staring ahead at a heap of Soviet paratroopers'
bodies beside the shattered walls of a derelict barn. The
corpses, twisted, torn and bloody, were still dressed in their
NBC protective clothing and long brown-muzzled
respirators.

Only minutes before the Russian paratroopers had been
alive, manning a pair of RPU rocket launchers; the guns of
Charlie Bravo Troop's tanks had opened up on them and
Davis had driven the Chieftain into the courtyard of the
farm buildings with his machine gun blazing. You could
demolish a wall, row by row of bricks, with a 7.62mm. It
did terrible things to the human body.

The squadron had pulled back from the river...retired
five kilometers in a series of leapfrogs; tank protecting tank,
troop protecting troop. Today, thank God, there had been
fewer losses so far. Only two tanks gone from the squadron,
and Bravo Troop still intact. It was the infantry who were
having the hardest time, sweating blood as they fought in
their clammy suits, dying from the bullets and shrapnel, or
the gas when the blast of a nearby explosion stripped the
protective clothing from their bodies.

Davis had watched them die. First the infantrymen beside
the Chieftains at dawn, then their replacements, killed more

219

horrifically by a mortar bomb, screaming, shrieking, with the combination of broken bodies and searing gas droplets in open wounds. It was macabre to Davis that men should end life as they entered it, bloody and reluctant.

How many men had Davis killed this morning? Thirty. No, thirty was yesterday! Yesterday? Today? Not men today...brown-muzzled rats...giant rats...vermin. He would never count victims again.

'Fuckin' compo rations! Stodgy steak and kid...glue soup.'

'If you can eat cold egg banjos, you can bloody eat anything.'

'What about tea, Stink?'

'Piss off, Inkester. I ain't your batman. There's no time for food.'

'Don't you piss off to me, Stink my lad. Get your grubby finger out and mash char.'

'Bollocks!'

Back six more kilometers; three villages defended until they were blown to ruins around them. Lost, Bravo Three and another five tanks of the squadron. Eight tanks gone...every crewman dead. There was no survival. When they baled out it was too late, the gas had got them through punctured hulls. A brief respite now, there were two villages between Bravo Troop and the Russian armour...and in the villages the other troops of the squadron waited, and with them the infantry with their missiles and mortars. Somewhere, always in the rear, was the battalion's artillery; their guns red hot, the paint burnt from the barrels. The gunners trying to cool their weapons with buckets of gas-contaminated water, to prevent the charges exploding prematurely in the breeches as they were loaded.

' 'Scuse me, sir. I've got to have a shit.' Inkester wriggled sideways in his seat below Davis's knees.

'It's those bleeding egg banjos...' DeeJay's observation was unsympathetic.

'For Christ's sake, DeeJay. I'm not doin' it so's I can play with myself. It's fucking urgent. There's no sign of gas on the suit indicators.'

'Get it over with,' suggested Davis. 'And make it quick. Anyone else want to relieve themselves? We may as well all get it done at the same time.'

'Don't miss the bloody bag, Inky. Your bare arse is just above my head. And don't toss your gash into my driving compartment. Cor, bloody hell, stroll on!' DeeJay made exaggerated gasping noises.

'You may as well break out some rations, lad,' Davis told Spink. He was thirsty, his mouth dry and tasting as though he had spent the whole of the previous night drinking. Night? He looked at his watch. It was 16.00. The second day had almost gone. Another four hours and it would be darkness again. It had been dawn when he had last had a drink. 'Better make tea, lad.' When had he eaten last? Sometime during the night! But he didn't feel hungry. Had he slept at all? An hour at the reforming area.

'I could do with a ciggy,' Inkester had shrugged his overalls back on to his shoulders, stowed away his waste bag and settled himself into his seat again.

'Forget it.'

'These seats give you piles, sir...well, a sore arse. What's happening, sir?'

Davis ignored him. 'What ammunition have we got left, Spink?'

'Eight rounds, sir.'

'Eight!'

'Yes, sir. Plus what we've got in the driving compartment.'

'DeeJay, help Spink with the ammunition. Pass it back to him.'

'There isn't any down here, just a lot of old rag in the lockers.'

'Jesus Christ! Inkester, you're supposed to have checked the ammunition.' Inkester didn't answer. 'You should use your mouth less, boyo, and your brains more.' There was no point in making a bigger issue of the matter, as commander it was basically Davis's responsibility. In future, he would check everything himself. How the hell could they defend the village properly with only eight shells? He called up the other two tanks of Charlie Bravo Troop. Fourteen shells in Bravo Two, eighteen in Bravo Four. He reported to the squadron leader.

'We're all in the same boat, Charlie Bravo One. I requested more from Group two hours ago. God know's where they've got to.'

Somewhere ahead of the squadron was the city of Braunschweig. Warrant Officer Morgan Davis guessed it must lie beneath the rose-tinted pall of smoke on the western horizon and having witnessed the destruction of the small towns and villages through which he had fought in the past twenty-four hours, he had no difficulty in imagining the devastation. Braunschweig was a sacrificial victim, a city whose death had been planned long before the outbreak of the war; a lynch-pin. Situated at a point where the Mittellandkanal and several tributaries met the winding river Schunter, it was a crucial pivot to swing the Soviet advance towards the north and into the river-latticed plain east of Hannover. Those parts of Braunschweig that had remained undamaged by the bombs, long-range shells and missiles of the Russians, would by now have been systematically demolished by the NATO engineers. For the second time in its recent history, its centre, the smart shops, offices, cinemas, theatres and restaurants would be only smoking rubble. Its suburbs of neat and orderly houses had become armour-snarling traps, blocked streets and mined parks; a lethal maze.

To the north of Braunschweig, and on the right of the

222

squadron's tanks, was the low range of hills, some forested and now sown with many thousands of bar and anti-personnel mines. Almost impenetrable to heavy tracked vehicles, it was the kind of ground that could only fall to slow, tedious and costly infantry assault; every hill-top and ridge defended and contested. An invader's nightmare.

Davis had learnt you could defend every river, canal, pass, village and town, but no matter how well your men fought, sheer weight of numbers always beat you in the end and made the terrible loss of life mean nothing.

Too many times, it seemed like a million in the past forty hours, he had wanted more military strength around him. Too few tanks attempting to defend so much ground. Never enough of them to give security in depth. Soft defence was sound thinking, but it seemed to Davis to be based on an original weakness – lack of equipment. Make the most of what you have. Eight tanks the squadron had lost today and they hadn't stopped the invaders, only slowed them down. And now, they were out of ammunition and pulling back again...back, always backwards. Always more frustration. So bloody unnecessary; wasteful.

How many kilometers abandoned today? Fifteen at least. And yesterday? And how many tomorrow? Fighting for what? Fighting for time. Time for reinforcements to arrive? For politicians to talk and negotiate? And negotiate what? The surrender of Germany to the Warsaw Pact countries? The promise to disarm and behave like good little boys?

The ammunition should have been up where it was needed, but it wasn't. The gas had made things difficult for everyone. Good God, it wasn't as though it was a possibility that had been ignored. Gas attacks had been expected; practised.

The wooded hills were already in shadows as the sun dropped behind their peaks. They looked peaceful enough, if you ignored the smoke over the horizon or didn't look back towards the battlefront barely a kilometer away. Just a month previously the hills and woods had been filled with campers, hikers, and the evening bars of the towns and villages had been noisy and happy places. It was all another world; history.

He saw the decontamination unit sited beneath the trees and followed the squadron leader's Chieftain across the open ground towards it. The operators in their NBC clothing fired turbine powered blasts of liquid decontaminant over the tanks as they drove by. Fifty meters on they were stopped, while a final cleansing took place with hand-held sprays.

Less than a kilometer along a firebreak the squadron leader brought the squadron to a halt beside a line of fuel bowsers. Davis could see ammunition being unloaded from a trio of Heer Transportpanzers a little way ahead. Everything was taking too much time. The squadron had been lucky not to have been attacked while moving in the open, but they were even more vulnerable now.

He jerked open the front of his NBC suit and pulled the front of his sweater away from his chest. The air felt cool, refreshing. His sweater and vest were soaked with perspiration and he could smell his own sweat, stale and sour, mingling with the rubberized scent of the protective clothing. He would have liked to climb outside and stretch his legs in the open, try to get his bowels working; at the moment his intestines were cramped and made him feel as though he had gorged himself. But the crews had been ordered to remain inside their tanks as they queued for fuel and ammunition. The decontamination of the vehicles had been hasty, and it only needed a few drops of nerve gas liquid on a man's skin to incapacitate him, perhaps kill. All the tanks carried injection kits, but whether or not these would be of any real use in counteracting the effects of the unknown Soviet gas was debatable.

Davis wondered what was being planned for the squadron. Knowing the captain would contact HQ, he tuned to the battle group net and felt guilty as he eavesdropped.

'Valda?' Davis recognized his squadron leader's first name, but not the voice using it. 'Where are you?' The voice was languid, as though its owner had just climbed from his sleeping bag. Some bloody officers, thought Davis. They spoke so far back it was a miracle they didn't swallow their tongues.

'Postmark.' It was the squadron leader.

'Good fellow. Casualties?'

A stupid bloody question, Davis cursed the man mentally. 'Eight...I've reported each as it happened,' said the squadron leader, and Davis was pleased to note an edge to the captain's voice that matched his own feelings.

'Just started my stag, haven't caught up. Any problems?'

Christ! Any problems? What the hell was facing a Soviet army if it wasn't a problem. Davis could feel his irritation swelling towards anger, but resisted an overwhelming urge to interrupt the conversation and give the officer a piece of his mind.

'Of course we've got problems...God Almighty!' Good for you, sir, thought Davis as Captain Willis allowed his irritation to show. 'I called for ammunition two hours ago...where the hell was it? We've had to fall back to a depot. Falcon's squadron moved in from the flank.'

'I'm sorry.' The officer's voice was more subdued.

'How much gas is there about?' Willis asked curtly.

'It's being used along the entire front as far as we can tell. Wherever the Russians are being held they're using chemicals. There have been chemical attacks on most of the airfields they can reach, and any supply concentrations.'

'What about the civilians?'

'What about them? Gas? We don't know.'

'Bastards!'

'I'm a bit out of date.' Like a hundred years, you berk, thought Davis. 'I'd say, nasty. Not going too well in the north...that's all I know.'

'Okay, thanks.'

'We want you at Capricorn, soonest.'

'Thirty minutes.'

'Roger, Valda. Good luck.'

Capricorn. Davis switched back to the squadron net, then checked his code and maps. Capricorn, one kilometer north of Gardessen. Another step towards the Channel. It was always backwards, and it always felt as though it was Davis himself who was being forced into the corner.

21.00 hours. Day Two

The mortar bombs were coming over at precise intervals, a pair every ten seconds on to the squadron position, exploding simultaneously, but sometimes just sufficiently separated for the double concussion to be noticeable. Whatever types of mortars were being used they were damned big, sending a shockwave through the ground which moved the Chieftain on her suspension and made the hull vibrate. Davis didn't know enough about Soviet equipment to be able to identify them, but thought they must be at least 160mm, perhaps even the giant 240s. The regularity of their arrival was nerve-wracking.

The troop's position was below the western ridge of a low hill, little more than a gentle rise in the ground. Three thousand meters to the front and right was a village, and to the troop's left, another. It had been night for almost an hour, but the steady mortar bombardment had been taking place since dusk. The village ahead was burning, bright flames colouring the smoke, sparks swirling upwards into the sky. But although it was night there was no real darkness. Parachute flares, fired at intervals almost as precise as those of the mortars, were swinging down above the battleground bringing colourless daylight.

In the ruins of the village ahead the infantry were fighting. Several times Davis had seen the trails of missiles hurtling from the rubble; and occasionally he heard the sounds of

120mm guns which he could recognize as those of one of the other reformed troops, Alpha. He didn't know who was throwing up the flares. It was impossible to judge from this distance, they were drifting northwest along the length of the battlefront, and they seemed to offer little advantage to either side. Someone, somewhere, must have thought they were being helpful. It was like watching an old black and white film – *All Quiet on the Western Front*. Christ, there was nothing quiet about this battlefield!

Inkester was humourlessly acknowledging the arrival of each pair of mortar bombs, his voice flat with fatigue. 'Miss...miss...miss...' A monotonous monosyllabic chant.

'Charlie Bravo One this is Charlie Alpha...standby. We're pulling back.'

Davis acknowledged, and passed on the information to his remaining two tank commanders. He could not put names or faces to their voices yet, but their radio techniques were already familiar. He kept his eyes on the outline of the village. With the magnification of his light-intensifying lenses, he could see movement; the occasional dodging infantrymen scurrying between the piled rubble, silhouetted, stooped, bent almost double. A dark hull, recognizable as a Chieftain, passed in front of a blazing building, looking like an identification cut-out at a training lecture. He knew how its crew would be feeling; they had survived for a little while longer. If they could retire now behind Bravo Troop, then they would have another small respite...perhaps the opportunity to catch a few minutes' sleep...a hot drink. And like Bravo One, the interior of their vehicle would be stinking, fetid. You pissed or shat in bags, if it were possible. Sometimes it wasn't, and you held on as long as you could. Eventually, in some unexpected moment of stress, you let it go. That kind of stress never presented itself in training, so if you lacked battle experience you were always unprepared. Davis's NBC suit was still dry inside, but the fighting compartment of the Chieftain stank, and it probably wasn't all the responsibility of the new loader, Spink.

227

Three thousand meters from here to the village, and the Russian armour is probably skirting the place now. That means we should see something of them pretty soon. Christ, not again! Davis's head was throbbing; it was the continuous noise, a never-ending reminder of death. He saw some of the infantrymen double across the edge of a field sixty meters to his left, heading for the cover of the nearest buildings; an APC lurched its way past him on the right, followed by two of Alpha Troop's Chieftains, one belching heavy smoke from its exhausts. Its driver would be sweating keeping it running, praying he would be allowed to drive it back out of the line, to one of the rear servicing units.

Davis was staring so hard in the direction of the enemy that when he momentarily closed his eyes he could still see the same scene imprinted on his retina like the negative of a photograph. Nothing but the flames of the village, and the drifting flares overhead, moved now.

'The sods aren't coming...' Inkester's voice made the comment sound like a wish. The lad was tired, exhausted, Davis knew. Christ, how much did they expect you to give? Almost two days of continuous fighting...two days of willing your mind to concentrate, ignoring the discomfort, the stinking heat of the fighting compartment, the cramp that wrenched at your muscles. 'Come on...come on...' It wasn't bravado, Inkester was as nervous as all of them, but he wanted to get it over with...defend this village and then leapfrog back to the brief rest somewhere to the rear; the next village, river or wood.

Davis had sometimes prayed, but he had never been convinced by religion; he was even ashamed that during the past hours he had resorted to praying to a God in whom he did not believe. But consoled himself with the excuse that you tried everything at times like these. It was no worse than being an atheist all your life, and then demanding absolution a few minutes before you died, just to be on the safe side. It was human nature. And what if I *was* wrong, though, thought Davis. Christ, it would make you feel bloody stupid if you were killed, and suddenly opened your eyes to find yourself in a far better place...all peaceful, birds singing, warm sunlight, flowers...someone standing there with a cool pint of bitter in their hands. You'd think, Jesus, I've been shit scared for days, for no reason. It's great here, wherever I am. Maybe there'd be a long warm beach, shallow water where the kids could play safely, where you could strip off and just lie in the edge of the sea with the waves lapping along your body, a bit of soft music somewhere in the background, a cool-drinks bar a few meters up the sand behind you, sort of Pacific island scenery.

They said you never heard the shot that killed you; Davis heard the rocket salvo for a fraction of a second before the massive explosion...the roar of their propellants drowning out every other sound, destroying thought and reason. A salvo from thirteen Soviet BM-21 multi-rocket launchers; five hundred and twenty rockets fired together and landing on Charlie Squadron's positions, betrayed by infra-red location equipment in a Soviet robot observation helicopter hovering four kilometers behind the Russian side of the front-line.

The immense blast totally surrounded Davis's Chieftain, and though it was fully closed-down the hull transmitted the shockwave like a hammer blow through the air of the fighting compartment, dazing and numbing the crew. There was a shrill whistling in Davis's ears...sharp pains shooting through his head. Debris and rubble clattered against the tank's hull. Davis could hear his men shouting, distantly, their voices thin, feeble, confused.

'Shut up...all of you shut up...' It hurt him to speak, his chest felt as if it had been crushed, every rib fractured, his lungs raw. 'Everybody okay...DeeJay? Inkester? Spink?' It could happen again, at any moment. What was it? A full missile salvo of some sort. God knows how many have landed. 'DeeJay, is the engine okay?' He couldn't hear it running. 'Can you see down there?'

229

'Fuck all, sir!'

'What the hell was that?' Inkester's questioning voice was tremulous. 'Christ I've got no vision...'

The smoke was hanging over the ground drifting only slowly in the light breeze, heavy, sinister. Miraculously the episcopes were undamaged, but condensation in the lenses made the smoke appear denser. He wiped the glass with his beret. The haze was thinning a little but it seemed an eternity before Davis was able to see more than a short distance. The flares, the bloody flares were making it worse; turning the mist opaque, like fog in car headlights.

'Shark, this is Bravo One, over.' Only silence on the net. 'Shark, this is Bravo One, over...' Where the hell was Captain Willis? 'Shark, this is Bravo One, over.' No response, not a sound on the squadron network, only the crackle of atmospherics and the low oscillation of a jamming attempt. 'Charlie Bravo Three, this is Bravo One, over.' Nothing! God! Check the tuning...'All stations Charlie, this is Charlie Bravo One, over.' Bloody dead air...everywhere!

Battle group? He was beginning to feel desperate, isolated. 'Quebec this is Charlie Bravo One...over.'

There was an instant response that made Davis weak with relief. 'Charlie Bravo One, this is Quebec.'

'Charlie Bravo One...we have lost squadron and troop contact.'

'Roger Charlie Bravo One...the same situation applies here.'

'We've just taken a time-on-target on the squadron position.'

There was a moment's silence that made Davis wonder if he should repeat the last part of the message, then: 'Do you have visual contact?'

'No visual contact.'

'Roger Charlie Bravo One. Rendezvous Orchid. Tiber open Causeway.'

'Wilco, Quebec. Out.'

230

Davis checked through the code...Orchid was Rüper...Causeway, Braunschweig; he knew Tiber was bridge. He could still use the bridge at Braunschweig, but where was Rüper? He switched on the lights and studied the map...the page appeared almost white, and the aching in his head made it difficult to focus his eyes. Rüper...God, it was ten kilometers west of North Braunschweig. What the hell was happening along the front? They had told him to pull back twenty-five kilometers. Maybe they were resting him? God, that would be a relief. 'DeeJay...can you see yet?'

'Yeah, reasonably, sir.'

'Then get us out...and go easy, Christ knows what the ground is like.'

The Chieftain slewed, then straightened as DeeJay corrected the steering and accelerated. It was comforting to feel the movement of the tank once more. The Russian armour must be close now, thought Davis nervously. Maybe only meters away through the smoke. Their infantry would be on foot between the villages, they would keep their BMPs a bit further back until the ground opened up again. Infantry. What the hell had happened to the NATO troops? He had seen nothing of them since the rockets had landed...poor bastards, they didn't stand a chance...they would be lying amongst the rubble, the lucky ones already dead, the others dying.

Dying. Death. What had happened to the others; all the tanks of Charlie Squadron? There had been nine of them. Surely Bravo One wasn't the only one remaining in action? It wasn't possible. Hopefully he tried the radio nets again, but there were no replies. He stared out through the vision blocks but could see only rubble which held even darker wells of mist in its shadows. DeeJay swerved the Chieftain, a hulk of twisted wreckage barely recognizable as a tank lay tilted in a crater; black fumes wreathed over Bravo One's hull as they passed. Had Davis seen bodies? He wasn't certain...men weren't always easy to recognize when they were killed violently. He hadn't even been able to identify the vehicle; it was another Chieftain, that was all he knew.

Alpha Squadron? They should be here somewhere. What was their net wavelength? He found it. 'Alpha Nine, this is Charlie Bravo One.'

'Alpha Nine...what's your problem Charlie Bravo One?'

'We're coming through you. Battle group orders.'

'How many tanks?'

'One.'

'One? What the hell happened?'

'TOT.'

'Poor sods...okay Charlie Bravo One, we'll keep our eyes open for you.'

There were two dull explosions in the wreckage of the village now to the Chieftain's right quarter; they were followed by long staccato bursts of GPMG fire just audible above the sound of the engine. DeeJay accelerated again as they reached more open ground.

'Where they sending us, sir?' Inkester asked the question with an obvious note of detachment in the query. He was talking for talking's sake.

'Back twenty-five kilometers.'

'Twenty-five?' There was sudden interest. 'R and R, sir?' Optimism showed in the gunner's voice.

'Maybe.'

'Thank God, sir...Christ, thank God! You hear that DeeJay, we're going out of the line...back twenty-five kilometers...Yoweeee! Fucking good, eh?' A pause...'Stink...Stink you shit-arse...you hear the WO? We're going out...buy you a beer, Stink,...buy you a dozen.' Excitedly to Davis: 'Sir, whereabouts they sending us?'

'Orchid, Inkester, and cool it. Do your job, lad, don't chatter.'

'Sir?' Spink's voice. 'What about the rest of Charlie?'

'They'll be pulling back, too...'

'You couldn't contact them?'

'Maybe radio malfunction!' No point in talking about the losses now; there would be plenty of time later, perhaps too much time.

'Sir, I've got mates in...'

'Concentrate, Spink, the damned war isn't over yet!' God, it certainly wasn't; he could still hear explosions close behind the Chieftain...it only took one shell to knock out a tank, and they were still in range...one fast troop of Soviet recce PT-76s, and Bravo One could get hers. 'DeeJay see if you can pick up what's left of the road...should be on the lower ground to our left.'

He glanced behind; the war was everywhere. The entire horizon to the east glowed, spat flames and fire trails; the night sky was not black, but the colour of blood.

Five times Charlie Bravo One had been stopped at roadblocks or check-points, twice by infantry and three times by MPs of the traffic control organization. And most of the traffic Davis encountered was travelling in the same direction as himself; very little moving towards the battlefront. All he had seen heading eastwards in the past hour were two motorized companies of German anti-tank infantry, and a solitary armoured reconnaissance unit. The villages through which Bravo One had driven were already wrecked, demolished by bombing or long-range missiles. They were still defended by infantry, but seldom by any visible armour. Davis had noticed engineers and their mine-laying equipment, a few supply vehicles, but little else. He had seen greater concentrations of equipment during peacetime exercises. Where the hell was it all now? He hoped it was somewhere hidden in the darkness, waiting. If not, dear God, NATO defences were pathetic.

Bravo One was approaching Braunschweig, the tracks scattering sparks from the surface of the road. Davis was startled by the changed appearance of the city's outskirts; every building was flattened, blasted. Craters in its surface had been roughly filled with the bricks and concrete of its wrecked houses, and only a narrow track, kept clear by engineers' bulldozers, allowed the passage of the vehicles.

DeeJay cut the speed. Ahead of Bravo One was a line of transports, heavily loaded Stalwarts forming a slow-moving convoy that, even at night, was such an obvious target their company made Davis nervous. Had he been certain there were other bridges still open, he would have been tempted to continue by another route.

There were no refugees this time, at least he saw none who were alive. Further back, towards the battlefront, there had been many dead at the roadside. Their bodies lay tumbled amongst their possessions, scattered and crushed by the wheels of heavy vehicles, victims of the drifting gas clouds, machine gun bullets of Russian fighter planes strafing the roads to add to the confusion and make the movement of NATO troops and supplies even more difficult.

Bravo One at last reached the bridge, and yet another roadblock. Military police again, and supporting them a platoon of infantrymen in their protective clothing behind a sand-bagged machine gun post. Davis watched the MP sergeant examine the hull of Bravo One with his flashlight; there were no identity marks. The man walked to the rear of the tank and used the infantry telephone. Davis was astonished it still operated.

'Where the hell do you think you're going all on your own? Give your identification!'

His temper's as worn as mine, thought Davis. Sod's probably been on the go for two days. 'Charlie Bravo One. Battle Group Quebec. Warrant Officer Davis...you want my fucking number, too?'

'You've no insignia or markings on your hull.'

'Replacement tank. We've worn one bugger out already.' Davis made his tone of voice friendlier. There was no point in aggravating the man, it would only cause more delay.

'Where are you from?'

'If you want the name of the village, I've no idea. We've

234

been ordered to Orchid, from somewhere west. If you want to know who gave me the order, I can't help you; I was too busy at the time. Check back to Quebec.'

'You contaminated?' It seemed as though the thought had just occurred to the sergeant.

'Of course we're bloody contaminated. The whole battlefront is contaminated. We've been washed down once, but we had to go back in.' Forty hours of fatigue and stress had sharpened Davis's temper. The effort to remain polite was too much.

'Okay, take it easy, I'm only trying to do my job. We've had deserters attempting to get by in vehicles, as well as on foot. Bastards! I wouldn't waste time with a court-martial!'

Deserters? They hadn't occurred to Davis before. Now the thought didn't upset him too much. Perhaps they were the only sane ones. 'Can we go ahead?'

'If you wait, we'll check you out. Sorry, we have to do it.'

It took several minutes while the MP radioed Group HQ.

'You're okay, Charlie Bravo One. Your blokes are building up west of the Mittellandkanal and the Ise. Heard about the north, sir?'

Davis shook his head wearily. The north? Christ, there was enough going on around here. The north was a million miles away.

'The Belgians and Germans are holding the Lübeck suburbs, and the south bank of the Elbe as far as the River Luhe. The Dutch are doing pretty well across the Lüneburger. We don't know much else though.'

'Thanks,' said Davis. 'We'll push on then.'

The man's voice held him. 'For God's sake take it easy on the bridge. The structure's not too good...bombs...had raids most of the day, they keep getting planes through...the rockets are the worst...long-range...you hear them coming after they've exploded. There's a decontamination unit beyond the city, on the 214 just before you reach Watenbüttel. You won't miss it, nor the route through Braunschweig — it's the only cleared road. Just follow it. On your way, sir.'

NINETEEN

Day Three

Davis could smell the decontaminant, antiseptic, drying on Bravo One's hull as he pushed open the hatch. The fresh air was sharp, chill, inviting, clearing the fumes and the stench of body filth from his nostrils. He stood and directed DeeJay to the camouflage netting bay that was already in position. When DeeJay cut the engine, Bravo One settled as though it were as fatigued as the crew.

He reported to the Command HQ, but no one seemed interested in him, and a lieutenant ordered him to return in two hours' time. Exhaustion was making him feel old, indecisive. He checked his watch; it showed half an hour past midnight. It took him a little time to work out it was now the third day of the war. It was Saturday morning, and he was still alive. He didn't want to return to the Chieftain, at least, not yet. The tank was too closely linked to death and the horror of the past hours.

It was a clear night above him, and for the first time since dusk he was able to see the stars. They were things that never changed, could be related to memories of better times. Everything else might be different, altered, except for the fine pattern of the night sky. Looking at the stars now was like watching old friends. They were always there; even when there was cloud you knew they were resting somewhere above it all. Towards the south-east some were hidden now...the rising smoke of the battlefront? No, cumulus. Davis looked more carefully. It *was* cloud, dense clouds, thunderheads building to the south; rain clouds! He sucked his finger and tested the breeze; it seemed southerly. 'Let it rain...please God let it rain.' He was speaking his thoughts aloud.

'I've been making the same prayer for the last hour.'

Davis hadn't noticed the man standing nearby in the darkness, and the unexpected voice made him jump.

'I didn't mean to startle you.' It was an officer's accent. The man moved closer and Davis could see a white collar beneath the combat jacket; a padre. 'I think our prayers might be answered. I've modified mine now; I'm praying it rains quickly, and heavily.'

'It's what we need, sir. Something to bog them down...prevent them bringing up reinforcements and supplies...hold their armour.'

'Yes. Is that your Chieftain?'

'Yes, sir.'

'I went over there a few minutes ago; thought perhaps the men might like a chat. I think they were all asleep.'

It didn't take them long, thought Davis. Rest was more urgent than food for them at the moment. 'They've only had a couple of hours kip since it all started, sir.' He could make out the padre's face now, he wasn't as old as Davis, perhaps in his late twenties. Apart from his collar and badge, he could have been any officer.

'You've been at the front the whole time?'

'Most of it, sir.'

'I was there briefly this afternoon, with an infantry company. They tolerated me for an hour, then sent me back here again. I suspect I was in the way.' He sounded amused, but then his voice was more serious again. 'It's all madness...total madness. I was with a Roman Catholic priest, both of us in NBC suits; he gave the last rites to a Russian soldier who couldn't even see what he was...perhaps didn't even care...wouldn't be able to hear him behind his own respirator and hood. We both prayed...it's all madness!'

Davis was uncertain what he should say. Army padres usually attempted to raise men's spirits, but this one...'You're probably right, sir.' He stared longingly in the direction of the Chieftain. Waves of fatigue were flowing through his mind.

'Would you care to join me in prayer?'

'I'm sorry, sir. I have to sort out a few things, if you don't mind.'

'Perhaps tomorrow morning?'

'Goodnight, sir.' Davis walked away. He felt uncomfortable; he had a feeling the padre had needed him, wanted his help. Perhaps it had all been too great a shock for the man, at least an active soldier's training provided some form of cushion against the reality of war.

There were three bundles lying close to the Chieftain's right track; the crew, well-wrapped, their heads covered, but preferring the open air to the tank's clammy interior. They hadn't even bothered to erect bivouacs. Davis looked down at them. Hewett, Inkester and Shadwell...no, not Shadwell any longer, Spink. Good lads, all three. And somehow still alive, but God only knew how! Twice now...twice they had survived when most of the others hadn't. Why? Luck! If any of the Russian gunners who aimed the launchers had made just an infinitesimal part of a millimetre difference to their adjustment the crew and himself might be dead...all of them. Earlier it could have been their tank and not Lieutenant Sidworth's that was brewed-up by the aircraft...it was luck, all luck, and there was no profit in attempting to rationalize the fact.

Davis found his sleeping bag and crawled inside. 'Return in two hours', they had told him in the command vehicle. An hour and a half, now. Just an hour's sleep, he ordered his mind; his subconscious would obey, it always did, the military years had seen to that. Somewhere inside his head was a built-in alarm clock which never failed. It was handy.

238

He wedged himself against the track a few feet from the nearest of the crew. Although he couldn't see the man's head, the snores sounded like those of Hewett. Davis closed his eyes but sleep wouldn't come, hovering seductively close but driven away by his thoughts. Count sheep? Count tanks! Soviet tanks...BMPs...it was too easy to see them driving forward out of the smoke.

He tried to find a more acceptable peaceful subject that might lead to rest. Hedda and the children? No, he didn't want to think about them...he did, but...they had been in his mind a lot during the past hours, Christ, of course he was worried about them...worried bloody stiff about them. In the background was the continuous sound of artillery to remind him of the future. It was like your heartbeat, always there but so familiar you didn't notice it until you remembered, and listened.

He dozed only briefly, fitfully, and by the time he was due to report felt even more exhausted.

Reform. Again. This time not just battle groups, but entire divisions. No one talked casualties in terms of numbers, but it was obvious they had been far greater than expected. Davis was uncertain how many fighting survivors there were left from his own regiment, but knew it wasn't more than a dozen tanks; it was horrifying, unbelievable. Men he had worked and trained with for years, drunk with in the messes and bars, his friends, Sergeant Harry Worksop who had been the best man at his wedding...Colonel Studley, Major Fairly, Lieutenant Sidworth, Captain Willis, Lieutenant Burrows...Sealey...too many to name. Yesterday the operations officer had said perhaps they weren't *all* dead; there might be some wounded, even prisoners. It made little difference, they were all gone. Apart from his own crew, he had spoken to only one man he already knew...there were others, but he had not met them, yet. It had been a lieutenant, a troop commander of Alpha Squadron.

'Sir...'

'Sergeant Davis...' The lieutenant seemed as relieved as Davis to see a familiar face, and grinned a welcome.

'Warrant officer, sir...promoted yesterday...' Was it yesterday or the day before? Davis couldn't remember.

'Good man...I'm pleased.' The lieutenant had two days' growth of dark beard. Davis had watched him bring his tank in, its hull as scarred and blistered as that of his own Chieftain. 'By the way, do you know where I can get POL?'

Petrol, oil, lubricants...and then ammunition; always the first thoughts in the mind of a good tank commander. 'They've told us to wait, sir. There are a lot of infantry around...sleeping everywhere. They don't want us moving our vehicles in the dark until they've got them all safely out of the way. There have been one or two accidents already. Have you reported yet, sir?'

'No. I want to clean up a bit.'

'There's a lazyman boiler in the trees; over there...you can just see the glow.'

'Thanks, Mister Davis.' The lieutenant exaggerated the 'mister' slightly; it wasn't meant as an insult, simply an acknowledgement of Davis's promotion. Davis watched him go, collecting his crew from beside their tank. It was good to see faces you recognized.

Davis walked slowly back to his tank and shook the sleeping gunner. 'Inkester...and you too, DeeJay...Spink. Up you get...come on, show a leg...come on lads, rouse yourselves.' It was like trying to waken the dead, thought Davis. Left alone, they'd sleep here in the open for a full twenty-four hours. 'On your feet!'

Spink groaned and then said, sleepily, 'Go and get us a cup of tea, Dad.'

'I'm not your bloody father, lad...up you get.'

'Oh, God...' DeeJay was stretching himself, a lean figure unfolding from his sleeping bag, rubbing his face with his

240

fists like a child.

Am I their bloody father, wondered Davis? Sometimes it seemed he was. 'Come on, lads.' He spoke more gently. 'You've got ten minutes to get yourselves washed up, then I want the tank cleaned.'

'Christ!'

'Properly cleaned, Inkester...bright, sparkling and Bristol-fashion, understand? Positively glowing. I'm not having any of us doing our fighting in a mobile shit-house, am I Spink?'

'No, sir.'

'Jump to it then, lad.'

'I thought they were resting us, sir.' Inkester was awake now, his voice resentful.

'Sorry lad, they're running thin on charity.'

DeeJay was already climbing on to the hull, a dark shadow silhouetted against the heavy sky. He steadied himself against the barrel of the gun. 'Y'know something, sir? If we 'ad a bloody trade union, they'd 'ave us all out on strike by now.'

'What did you think about Eric copping it?' Inkester was trying to remove burnt explosive from the breech of the gun where it had become plated on to the metal by heat.

'He didn't really cop it,' answered DeeJay. 'Not like a real wound, anyway. He wasn't shot or nothing. He just hurt himself.'

'It'll count as a wound, you bloody see. If we dished out Purple Hearts he'd get one for that. He'll be allowed to wear a wound stripe. He got it in battle, in wartime.' Fatigue had drained Inkester's face and he was white in the lights of the fighting compartment. 'Wonder what they'll be like?'

'What what'll be like?'

'Our medals!'

'What fuckin' medals? You aren't half a git, Inky!'

'War service medals. We'll all get them. 1985 to

241

whatever...victory medals...defence medals...just like the last war. They'll look good alongside the GSM I've got.'

'Bloody gongs...you're pathetic. I'll tell you what, I'd trade every one I'm ever likely to get for Eric's Blighty. He's a lucky sod!'

Spink was wiping oil from the faces of the Clansman's instrument dials; it was surprising how dirty the inside of a tank could become, he had even found a potato crisp packet...must have been the delivery crew's.

Inkester asked: 'Were you scared, DeeJay?'

'That's a fucking daft question!'

'Well, were you?'

'Course I was bleedin' scared. You'd be an idiot if you wasn't.'

'Stink was scared, weren't you Stink?' The loader didn't answer. 'Well, so was I,' admitted Inkester. 'You two thought how many of us there are left?'

'Shut up, Inky...I don't want to know.'

'Well, 'ave you seen *anyone*?'

'It's bleedin' dark out there...what d'you think I am, a bloody owl? They'll be around.' DeeJay didn't want to think, didn't want to start weighing up the odds of his future survival. He hadn't lied when he had admitted being scared; there had been times when he had wanted to throw open the hatch, hurl himself out into the open, and run like hell as far away from the battlefields as he could get. The only thing that had stopped him was the realization his survival was less likely outside the hull of the Chieftain. And when there were lulls in the fighting it wasn't too bad again, just so long as he didn't think about it.

' 'Ere! Aren't you getting married today?'

'Oh, Christ, Inkester. Why don't you belt up?' The realization it was Saturday wrapped itself around DeeJay's brain like a damp suffocating blanket. Saturday. He should have been in England...probably suffering from a Tetley's hangover...no, he would be sleeping it off now, in his Mum's house, his own bed; the bed he had slept in as a kid.

242

Saturday. What was Cathy doing? She'd be asleep, too; her wedding dress hung in the stripped-pine wardrobe they had bought on his last leave. What the hell did she want with a stripped-pine wardrobe? They would be getting army furniture...quarters. Well, they'd have got them pretty soon, anyway. She'd been collecting things for ages, though; sets of pans from sales, bedding, a place setting of a knife, fork and spoon each week from her wages. Every time he went home on leave she would take him up to her room and show him the things she'd added to her collection. As he thought of it, he realized he could actually smell her room, feminine, talcum powder. She used the perfume he had bought her in the Münster NAAFI, expensive, French, and it scented the bedroom, clinging to her sheets and pillows. They used the bed when her family were out. Old Daphne, her Mum, wasn't a bad old stick, she damn well knew they slept together...she even sort of helped them, though she wouldn't have liked it to be too obvious. 'Come on Steve, leave 'em alone a bit, they haven't seen each other for three months...you'll be wanting to have a little chat with each other, won't you? Your Dad and I will go down the pub. We'll meet you there, about ten o'clock in the lounge...come on then, Steve...see you two both later then.'

'Do you love me, Dave?' The top of her head barely reached his mid-chest height, and she would be staring up at him with her wide blue eyes, trying to read the answer in his face. She would hold him extraordinarily tightly, pulling him against her until he could feel her breasts flattening against his body.

' 'Course I do. That's why we're gettin' married.'

'Tell me then...you never tell me in your letters. And you didn't even write for the last three weeks...only the telegram.'

'We had manoeuvres...I was out in the field. There's no time for writing letters, then. Being in the army's just like work you know, but it isn't nine-until-five every day.'

'You still haven't told me.'

243

'I'll tell you tomorrow.'

'Don't be daft.' Her eyes were soft, filling slightly with hurt.

'All right, I love you.'

'You could say it a bit nicer; kiss me, then tell me.'

Her first kisses were always gentle, testing. He could taste her lipstick. 'I love you, Cathy.'

'Mmmm. That's better...ooh, don't bite. Don't they feed you in Germany?'

'Let's go upstairs.'

'That's all you think of.'

'I can't kiss you properly standing up.' He had his hands under the back of her sweater, his fingertips beneath the taut strap of her bra. Her skin was warm and smooth. He could feel an erection beneath his trousers, pressing hard against her stomach.

· 'What are you thinking about, DeeJay?' Inkester's voice echoing inside the Chieftain.

'Fuck all!' Why the hell did Inkester have to drag him back? Christ, they were the best thoughts he'd had in days...he was home...he had been home for just a while...not long enough.

'I was thinking about Davis. Y'know, if we weren't Davis's crew we'd be bloody dead, DeeJay. I reckon we owe him. Straight up.'

'Cobblers!'

'It's not cobblers. I've been thinking about it; noticed yesterday and today. He's bloody careful is our WO.'

'Like how?' Play Inkester's game; if he wants to chat for a while, why not? Maybe Inkester never daydreams.

'Well, like when we went down the hill to the road after Lieutenant Sidworth bought his; remember, us an' Sealey. Davis put us in exactly the right place...best protection, good position. It bloody looked dangerous but we were safer there than up on the hill in the open. And later, in fact every time we moved position, he was careful, every time bloody careful; not just drive up and think we'd got hull-down, but exact...just right...and good cam...natural cam...cover...everything. I tell you, it wasn't all luck DeeJay, it was sort of genius. Maybe he's got an instinct. You know. I've read about things like this, tankies who got themselves right through the last big war, and Korea and places, without a bleedin' scratch...there's always got to be someone who gets all the way through. Well, this time, it's going to be us.'

'You stupid bastard!' This time DeeJay was angry. If he could have reached Inkester through the narrow gap between the back of his driving seat and the gun, he would have grabbed him and smashed his stupid face.

'What's wrong with you?' Inkester knew the driver's anger was genuine, and was startled.

'You'll fucking jinx it, you daft bugger! I don't want you, nor any other nig-nog talking about luck, skill or anything to do with why we're alive and the others aren't. I don't give a fart about surviving yesterday, or today...even tomorrow. I'm alive now, and that's all that matters.'

Spink interrupted in an attempt to distract the two men; there was nowhere to go inside a tank if someone started throwing punches. 'I think our WO is a bloody lunatic.'

Spink's remark was a mistake. Inkester grabbed him by the collars of his coveralls and dragged him forward until their faces were only a few inches apart. 'You think what, Stink?'

'I don't mean he's mad or anything, honest...just I thought that he was going to murder me.' To his relief Inkester pushed him away.

'I'd have bloody murdered you, too,' DeeJay said fiercely.

'Davis is a fuckin' good commander, Stink.' Inkester reached down beside his seat and brought out a bar of chocolate. He broke it into three equal parts and to Spink's surprise gave a piece to each of them. 'We're all mates in this tank, we fight together. But remember, Davis is ace, Stink, genuine essence!'

TWENTY

Another new troop. New men. They weren't even from his own regiment...unless you counted some of the reserves who had reached the division in the past few hours. Strangers, all of them. Maybe it was better like that. If he thought about them too much Davis knew he would go crazy as they got themselves killed off. They were really only replacement equipment, not men with faces and names; limited-life equipment, lacking durability, intended to be used and discarded. When they had reported to him, he had tried not to look at them too closely. Their names were on his list, but he had not even attempted to remember them.

'If you ask me what's going on once more, Inkester, I'll crown you. You've heard the orders, and you've got eyes like the rest of us.' He was getting snappy...testy. No damn wonder. 'Spink, what are you up to?'

'Reading, sir.'

Reading. God, twenty-four hours ago the lad was a breathing disaster area, and now he was cool enough to read a book while they waited for an enemy attack. He realized he knew nothing at all about Spink; not even his age...nothing about his background. Did he even have a christian name? Inkester and Hewett, he knew them; everything about them, faults, weaknesses, good points, what made them both tick. But Spink? 'Spink, how long have you been in the army?'

'Eight months, sir.' There was the sound of his book, some paperback, closing.

'Where are you from?' A few minutes ago he hadn't wanted to know the new men, and here he was questioning Spink. It was different though with your own loader, he told himself. If Spink was going to buy it, then the odds were that he would too. And it was necessary to work close to your crew, understand them.

'Winchester, sir. Hampshire.'

'I thought that was the home of the Green Jackets. Why didn't you join them?'

'Don't like walking, sir.' There was a touch of humour in the lad's voice.

'What were you doing before you signed on?'

'Insurance, sir; clerk. It was dead boring.'

Insurance clerk. 'O-levels, Spink?' You would need reasonable educational qualifications in an insurance company.

'Yes, sir, six.'

'Six O-levels and you want to be a loader.' Six O-levels were enough for a commission!

'No, sir. I want to be a troop leader.'

Saucy young bugger. Davis smiled to himself; Spink might do it. Perhaps quicker than he anticipated if the war lasted, and if he stayed alive.

Another dawn; the third of the war. There was the familiar smell of diesel fuel, oil, stale explosives and the crew, inside the Chieftain. They were sited facing southeast, fine rain making it difficult for Davis to see through the episcope as the breeze caught the mist and swirled it against the hull. It was barely wetting the surface of the ground yet; he wanted full torrential rain, the kind of downpour the dark night clouds had promised earlier.

The gusty breeze was moving the brown leaves of a tall beech to the Chieftain's left, billowing the soggy camouflage netting that broke the outline of the hull. To their rear a thousand meters away was the River Oker, running northwest towards the Hahnen Moor. They were hull-down behind the low railway embankment that led from

Braunschweig to a nearby cement works; there would be no more trains for a long while, the track was destroyed in a hundred places, the lines twisted and curled, distorted, the embankment blasted flat. Davis's visibility was less than two thousand meters.

He had been eavesdropping on the different radio wavelengths, hoping to obtain some reasonable idea of what was happening along the front. Many of the conversations meant nothing, but he could follow the battles taking place somewhere in the mist and low cloud; seven kilometers ahead. The sounds were there when he opened the hatch, the noises of war dampened by the low cloud, but closer, woolly. The rain wouldn't slow them much...bloody Scotch mist! Still, with luck, it might cut down the air activity.

'Charlie Bravo Nine this is Zulu, over.'

'Charlie Bravo Nine, over.'

'Everything okay?'

'Yes, sir.' What was the new captain's name? DeYong! Probably Dutch; he had an accent that was difficult to identify.

Davis had sited the Chieftain carefully during the night; optimistically hoping for heavy rain. He could remember a time a few years ago on exercise when a troop of the regiment, sent to defend positions near a river, had remained stationary for almost twenty hours in a downpour. When the time came to move, they couldn't. Every one had sunk in the soft earth and had to be towed out by recovery vehicles with kinetic ropes. You didn't make errors like that in this situation; not if you wanted to live.

Was the rain getting heavier? Rain. It would turn the broken ground, churned by the shell and rocket fire ahead of the advancing Russian armour, into a swamp. It would restrict air activity, and enable the NATO reinforcements more time to be brought up to the front. Every road in the abandoned territory which might have been useful to the Russians had been destroyed, but many behind the NATO lines were still in reasonable condition. Rain favoured the defenders.

Visibility? It seemed less. A thin line of poplars he had been able to see clearly only minutes ago, was hidden. Was it increasing mist, or was the drifting smog of the battlefield already closer?

He saw four simultaneous explosions, the flames brilliant white, the smoke and debris hurtling upwards before merging into the low cloud and the grey background a thousand meters ahead. Armour was moving close to a narrow roadway, skirting a plantation of young larches; NATO armour pulling back. He recognized a squadron of West German Leopards with their distinctive wedge-shaped hulls and low profile, black crosses on the sides of their turrets; tanks of the Heer covering the movement of several of their Marder personnel carriers. The sound of NATO artillery was increasing, the shells shrieking overhead, deep banshee howls of the rocketry, explosions now felt and heard, but mostly unseen.

DeYong's voice was guttural with anticipation on the squadron net: 'All stations standby, fire as targets show, out.'

'Wilco. Out.'

Nothing visible in the mist. The air was shaking, concussions thumped against the hull like waves battering a ship in a storm.

'I'm blind down here,' DeeJay complained loudly.

Inkester was making co-ax traverses of the gun, scanning the open ground through his sights; Spink's hand already rested on the next live shell in the racks.

Were there gunships above the cloud? Davis thought he caught a glimpse of a line of dark shapes moving eastwards. Lynx? He was guessing. If they were NATO helicopters it was dangerous work for them, operating at low level in almost zero visibility. They would be picking their targets by the infra-red emissions from the engines of the Soviet ground vehicles. To Davis it meant that all NATO armour was already safely back out of the way.

'Gas, gas, gas...November, gas, gas, gas!' Unnecessary warning, for the tanks had been closed-down since standby at battle stations. So much for the Geneva Convention, Davis thought.

'Masks on, lads,' he ordered.

'It's ours...must be our gas...' Inkester's voice was surprised. 'Wind's drifting the smoke back towards the bloody Ruskies...can't be their own gas...wind's the wrong way for them!'

Ours. Retaliatory, they had always promised. Why not? The Russians had been using it for the last couple of days. What kind? Nerve, blood agent, corrosive? It didn't really matter...they said mustard gas was the nastiest, the most painful, blistering deep into your skin, burning out your lungs...one way or another they all killed. The Geneva Convention ruled you couldn't destroy a man with gas — what difference was there between death from that, or the smashing, pulping, tearing of a high-powered bullet or white-hot shrapnel in your stomach, the seconds of screaming agony within the hell-fire of napalm? Were the latter more humane, he wondered? Christ, animals chosen to die in a slaughterhouse were given more consideration.

A huge ball of flaming material roared down through the low cloud and exploded three hundred meters ahead of Davis's Chieftain.

'Christ!' Inkester gave a startled exclamation as his vision was obscured by billowing smoke.

'Aircraft!' said Davis. Whose aircraft? There was no way of telling. Men and equipment dying together; he could imagine the terror of the last terrible moments, as the plane went out of control too close to the ground for survival...Survival, that was what war was all about. Survive a battle, anticipate the next...no, try not to anticipate...just survive every minute; count only the ones behind you, not those still in front waiting to be survived.

So many of the dead he had seen in the past days

250

appeared to be smiling, grinning at him; an illusion, ragged lips surging from teeth, flesh shrinking on the bones. Why would they smile? Was there humour for them in death?

'Why are we waiting...' Inkester began singing, but with a nervous tremor to his voice: bravado.

'Zulu this is Alpha, we are engaging.'

'Roger Alpha.'

Alpha! Alpha Troop somewhere to Davis's left, beyond his sight. Engaging!

'Zulu, this is Alpha.' Voices urgent; responses immediate. 'Soviet BRDM-2s...we see four...recce patrol...'

Davis tried to pick out their guns against the tumult of sound and the deep throb of the Chieftain's engine. It was impossible.

'Zulu, this is Alpha...we've taken them out...' The voice jubilant. 'All four!'

'Good work, Alpha...any casualties?'

'No casualties.'

Four taken out. Made them sound like sitting ducks. BRDMs...wheeled recce vehicles. Maybe the Russians were having trouble with the softening ground; Alpha had been well-sited, undetected until it was too late. A trap well-sprung.

'All stations, this is Zulu, expect contact.'

What was happening to the rain he had prayed for? It was lighter; had stopped. Davis could see the line of poplars again, some now broken, one tilted and resting on its neighbour.

Rocket explosions drew lines of deep craters across the open ground closer to the troop position, the field became an instant forest of black smoke columns, alive, growing, spreading.

'Charlie prepare for action...' Davis used the troop net.

The shells were exploding closer, some just behind the Chieftain; heavy stuff plunging deep into the ground before it detonated, each hurling several tons of earth skywards.

'Charlie Nine, this is Zulu, do you have contact?'

'No contact yet.'

The sound of the combined NATO and Soviet bombardment was now so great that Davis found it necessary to concentrate to prevent the dislocation of his thoughts. It was a monstrous duel, with the divisional armour at its centre. A shell landed five meters away, making the Chieftain shudder, splattering the hull with clay and thin mud. The woods to the left were being systematically demolished by a creeping barrage climbing the steep hillside, turning ancient trees to chaos.

Davis saw blue sky through the smoke as more heavy artillery shells landed nearby, rocking the tank violently.

'Hullo Charlie Nine this is Black Dog...target, over...' An infantry request to Davis for support.

He replied, 'Charlie Nine, send, over.'

'Black Dog...missile launcher moving into position...your gun barrel two o'clock northern edge of poplars. Will fire burst for your reference, watch for tracer. Over.'

'Charlie Nine, wilco. Out.'

'Got your eyes on the position, Inkester?' Davis watched the left end of the poplars. A few seconds later he saw a line of tracer bullets pass between the first and second of the distant trees, towards the ruins of a small farm building. 'Okay, let's get on it.' Inkester brought the gun round and Davis saw the building in the sights. Inkester's first round exploded, but even with the ten times magnification Davis was unable to see the result.

'Hullo Charlie Nine, this is Black Dog. Left twenty reduce fifty, over.'

'Charlie Nine, wilco. Out.' The miss had been due to the difficulty in calculating the exact target of the tracers fired from cover away to the Chieftain's left. Davis made the necessary corrections. He enjoyed working with the infantry, it was like playing to an audience. The Chieftain lurched as Inkester fired again, and this time the explosion of the shell was more spectacular.

'Hullo Charlie Nine...this is Black Dog...you are on

target, out.'

On target. One more kill, thought Davis, coolly reported as if it were a dummy on a range.

'Tank,' shouted Inkester.

Davis had seen it simultaneously. 'Zulu, this is Charlie Nine...T-62 eleven o'clock, am engaging, out.'

'Zulu, roger. Out.'

The smoke ahead was denser now, but Davis could still see the outline of the first tank as Inkester lined it up and fired.

The attack, fiercer and more determined than Davis had experienced in the past days, lasted almost four hours before dying away. But, for the first time, all the NATO tanks had remained in position and there was no withdrawal. Squadron after squadron of Soviet armour and mechanized infantry had hurled themselves against the NATO line and been repulsed. Ahead of Davis the smoke fog was drifting away towards the north-east, unrolling the devastated landscape of the battlefield in front of him, uncovering the obscene carcasses of wrecked vehicles, the corpses of men.

Inkester shouted a wild, jubilant cheer.

'We've beaten them off, sir...' There was enough of Spink's face visible through the eye-pieces of his mask for Davis to know the loader was grinning.

Davis just nodded. He had learnt too much in the past days to be anything but cautious in his hopes. He was feeling satisfied that the line had held, but knew it must have been as costly for the NATO forces as for their enemies.

He checked his troop on the network. There were no casualties, and the feeling of relief warmed him further. There might well be losses amongst the squadron, but at least he had managed to keep his own team intact. Team. With dismay he realized his original intention to avoid establishing close ties with his replacement crews was already falling apart. He knew it was a weakness he might well regret.

The sky had brightened and the cloud was now broken so that patches of sunlight drifted across the open ground, chasing the columns of dark smoke spiralling from the battle debris. He could see only one living being amongst it all; four hundred meters away a solitary Russian infantryman, still wearing his mask and protective clothing, wandered aimlessly in the open. Others must have seen him, but none fired. After a few minutes the soldier turned and stumbled slowly away until he was lost in the distance, a lonely bewildered man, perhaps demented, insane. The medical officers called it battle-fatigue.

'What are the Russians up to, sir?'

'Inkester, you must have been a bloody aggravating kid!' Davis leant back in his seat. To his right, through his episcope, he could see the sector at the rear of the NATO defence lines, sparsely wooded country that was little more than a long sweeping plain until it met the outskirts of Hannover some forty kilometers away. He deliberately allowed his thoughts to drift, encouraging them away from the jaggedness of war, using memories to soften reality. He was with Hedda and the boys at Hamburg Zoological Gardens. The afternoon was warm, the children sticky-handed and the animals lethargic. The children were more interested in a playground than the animals; he and Hedda sat in the shade while the children exhausted themselves, shrieking and laughing. He couldn't remember how many Cokes he had bought, it seemed like a dozen, plus an equal number of ice-creams. When they had returned home the exhausted children were pleased to get to bed, and Hedda had brought him a beer on the apartment balcony. It had been a happy day, a family day, and the evening was good, too. It was satisfying just sitting there, drinking the beer and hearing Hedda prepare supper, knowing the kids were asleep in their room. It was the best part of being a father, a husband. Hedda had been in a loving mood; it had been a good day, all round. There were others like it to think about.

His eyes were half-closed and he was almost asleep. There was a sudden bright glow of light which penetrated his eyelids like the burst of a photographic lightbulb; he could feel intense heat on his cheeks. The light did not die away but increased rapidly until pain forced him to react. He ducked. The interior of the Chieftain was lit by sharp-edged beams flooding through the vision blocks in the turret.

The twenty kiloton nuclear warhead of a Soviet SS-1 Scud missile exploded close behind the NATO front line, its skyburst destroying all unprotected living things beneath it for an area of two and a half square miles.

Davis's mind had grasped and interpreted the brief warning. He attempted to shout but no sounds would come from his throat. For the first time in his life terror completely overcame him. He tried to scream to dispel the agonizing fear which twisted at his intestines, but his years gagged him.

The silence broke with the sudden roar of the pressure wave which lifted the stern of the Chieftain's fifty-two ton hull three meters from the ground, tilting the bow against the embankment until the tank was near vertical, the muzzle of the gun driving deep into the earth as the crew were hurled forward on to the instruments and controls.

The flame-blackened debris of uprooted trees, shrubs and buildings blasted past. The Chieftain's hull dropped, the suspension units shearing from their mountings as it bounced crazily.

A second vast concussion, the implosion, spun the tank sideways as though it were weightless, shaking it like a dog with a rag before discarding it, the thunderous roar dying only slowly.

The terror remained with Davis; it was night outside the Chieftain, swirling dust clouds thicker than the densest battle-smoke. The ground beneath the tank was no longer solid, quivering, rippling as it transmitted the shock of more distant nuclear explosions.

Spink, supporting himself against the breech, managed to switch on the fighting compartment lights; fine dust and fuel droplets haloed them in miniature rainbows until the wiring shorted and the tank was in darkness again.

He had seen Morgan Davis briefly; reaching forward to pull Inkester back into his seat. The gunner's head, his respirator torn away by impact with the sharp edges of the Chieftain's equipment, was cut and bleeding; his eyes were wide, staring like those of a hare cornered by a dog.

'Hewett...Spink?' Morgan Davis shouted the men's names, his voice urgent. There was a burst of red flame near the ammunition locker. Spink tried desperately to open the hatch above him, but the hatch lever was jammed. He heard Davis again: 'Hang on, lads...it's over...it's all bloody over!'

The flames were growing, spreading along the floor beside the charge bins, scorching Spink's legs. He turned quickly towards Davis's cupola, the only escape route left. The warrant officer was sitting motionless, blocking his way. The bright reflection of the fire made a halo around him. Like a painting on an icon.

Electronic edition produced by
ePubNow!

www.epubnow.com
www.digitalmediainitiatives.com

Made in the USA
Coppell, TX
19 June 2020

28840414R00144